MW01504290

"So you have green floor and indicated that

Once settled, Xanth said, "Funny thing about vulcans. No one in Galactic Central has ever heard of them. Or any species that looks like that. They must be from some planet we haven't contacted yet."

Al grinned. "You do have a lot to learn. Vulcans are just actors made up with fake ears."

"But actors are people who perform in Movies."

"Right."

"Human blood in Movies is always red."

"Yes, we humans have red blood."

"So 'actors' aren't human?"

"What? Of course they are. They just pretend to be aliens."

"How can they pretend to have green blood? If you cut them doesn't red blood come out?"

"They use fake blood."

"So they have fake ears and fake blood."

"Yeah."

"And they willingly replace all their red blood with artificial green blood so they can perform their parts."

"No, no. The fake blood is just used for a scene where they're bleeding. It doesn't actually come out of the actors."

"Where does it come from?"

"The person doing the makeup."

"Do makeup persons have green blood?"

Al grimaced. "No! They just make the fake blood for the scene!"

"They make the blood."

"Yes. It's not really blood. Just some syrup and food coloring."

"That wouldn't work. Artificial blood has to mimic the action of real blood in carrying oxygen to the cells..."

"It just has to LOOK like blood!" Al exploded and waved his hands in the air.

Xanthan Gumm

Robin Reed

Copyright © 2006 Robin Reed

10-Digit ISBN 1-59113-899-X
13-Digit ISBN 978-1-59113-899-0

All rights reserved. No part of this publication may be reproduced, stored in a retrieval system, or transmitted in any form or by any means, electronic, mechanical, recording or otherwise, without the prior written permission of the author.

Printed in the United States of America.

The characters and events in this book are fictitious. Any similarity to real persons, living or dead, is coincidental and not intended by the author.

Cover art © 2006 Richard Carbajal

Barstow Productions
http://www.barstowproductions.com
2006

To my mother, who has always supported my desire to be a writer.
To Leah, my close long-distance friend.

Acknowledgments

Thanks to my copy editor for her expert editing. Any remaining mistakes are my own. Hey, I've seen that in the beginning of lots of books and thought I would never have a book of my own to put it in.
Thanks to Richard Carbajal for the great cover.

Chapter One

On the fringes of the galaxy, nearly 8,000 parsecs from Galactic Center, a single-engine, single-occupant spacecraft could be seen approaching a small blue and white planet. The spacecraft was a Glexo Nebula with an overhead fusion injection engine, 53,000 light years on the meter and a pair of fuzzy dice hanging from the rearview monitor. The planet was a small, oxygen-nitrogen atmosphere, not terribly impressive bit of space debris that had cooled, congealed, and spawned a dominant intelligent life form that liked to get down and get funky.

The driver of the little spaceship was breaking every galactic law on the books concerning this particular small blue planet. It was absolutely forbidden to visit this planet or even its solar system. The only way to get at all close to it was to take a cruise ship that skimmed the planet's solar system, giving the cruise takers a vicarious thrill and allowing them to go home and tell their grandchildren that they had been within less than a light year of the forbidden planet called Earth.

That was exactly how Xanthan Gumm had arrived in the Earth system. He (though the pronoun "he" wasn't entirely accurate, as there were three distinct genders in his species) was a fairly ordinary resident of a small housing station near the middle of Galactic Center. He was a humanoid just under one devito tall with mustard-yellow skin and all the usual features of his species, which had evolved long ago as an amphibious species on some watery planet that no one remembered the name of. He was wearing sneakers, shorts, and a t-shirt from the resort planet Qaaxle. He had taken a vacation from his job as a framadort converter, and booked a trip on the cruise ship "Kathie Lee." When the ship arrived in the Earth system, and all the other passengers were gawking out the view window, Xanth was down in the hold revving up his Glexo Nebula, and preparing to break the law.

Here he was, about to orbit that forbidding and forbidden planet, Earth. A little help from a friend who worked on the cruise ship opened the doors of the hold, a long burn of the Glexo's engine brought him within sight of the third planet, and a short burst of his maneuvering jets put him into orbit. He was here! The legendary planet where the natives had invented something that no one else, in all of the civilized planets, had dreamed of, something called The Movies.

Xanth had seen every Earth Movie he possibly could, given that he couldn't watch them all the time. He did have to go to work and convert framadorts. But when he was home he was watching Movies on his wall screen. Earth was an amazing planet. An entire species, called human beings, devoted their lives to nothing but creating Movies. All the humans were like busy little bees making the best form of entertainment ever invented. What those humans didn't know was that their efforts were viewed and appreciated on all the planets and in all the habitations of Galactic Civilization.

It was known that everything that happened in Movies was fiction, the creations of this story-obsessed culture. The things that Earth people could imagine were astounding. The Godfather and his family, the Creature from the Black Lagoon, the shootout at the OK Corral, World War II... All fiction!

When the streams of images from Earth first started arriving, it was thought that this new planet was the most violent place in the universe. These "human beings" shot each other, stabbed each other, blew up each other, and tried to smother each other by pressing their mouths together. Soon, however, galactic scholars determined that the images were just stories, incredibly imaginative fictions. Watching these "Movies" became the most popular pastime in the galaxy.

But if The Movies were just stories, then the actual culture that humans lived in was a mystery. Galactic scholars could only guess that Earth was a peaceful, happy place, with all of its people cooperating in the making of Movies.

The only thing that was known for sure was the name of the king of the planet: Steven Spielberg.

Xanth was close enough now to see some detail on the planet's surface. He decided to look at this new world more closely. He was quite nervous about landing. No one knew what really went on down there, except that it involved a lot of worry about body odor. So Xanth pushed a button on the dashboard of his Nebula, which made the little ship's viewscope extend into viewing position. In a moment, the main video display cleared and began to show the creatures of Earth going about their lives.

The resolution wasn't all that great. The viewscope wasn't meant to see that much detail from that much distance, and the focus was fuzzy. What it showed was largely what Xanth expected. He fixed the viewscope on one small community of the Earth natives and saw them working hard for the common good, and being rewarded with rich, full, happy lives.

Then he noticed that there was something wrong. He tried to adjust the viewscope. That was the problem: it was focused in much too closely on the planet surface. Xanth laughed to himself. What a dumb mistake! He hadn't been looking at humans at all, but at an "ant hill", the home of a much lower order of Earth life.

Xanth stowed the viewscope and prepared to enter the atmosphere of the mysterious planet. He was incredibly nervous and excited. He had dreamed of this day all his life.

Even while he converted framadorts, he had known that his destiny was to go to Earth and appear in The Movies. It was not unknown. Others had done it before him. Once in a while, someone from Galactic Center or elsewhere in the civilized planets disappeared and the next time anyone saw them was in an Earth Movie.

However, they had usually changed their names. Xanth had put a lot of thought into what name he should use on Earth. Xanthan Gumm was just too ordinary. How could he be a star of The Movies with a name like that? No, he would have to think of something else. Like the Altairan who was called "Chewbacca" in several Movies, or the Alpha Centauran who gained fame on Earth simply as "E.T." Or the sand dweller from Deneb IV who was known on Earth as "Barry Manilow"

Chapter Two

Far below, not on but under the surface of the planet called Earth, dug into a mountain, was the main tracking station of NORAD, which was entrusted with the vital mission of detecting anything coming in from space that might constitute a threat to the United States of America. NORAD was created to detect, as early as possible, any nuclear missiles, launched from anywhere in the world and aimed at the United States. Deep in the heart of the mountain was the most sophisticated radar tracking technology that humanity could create. Billion dollar supercomputers used all of their high-speed processing power to notice even the tiniest object that might be a threat. When something was detected, a signal was instantly relayed to a screen where two highly trained NORAD personnel sat alertly watching for the first blip that would mean the start of a global thermonuclear war.

"Gin!" Lt. McCollum said, and slammed his hand down on the console. Lt. Robert McCollum had had an illustrious career as a special forces operative, and had been decorated many times over for his actions in Afghanistan, Iraq, and Malibu.

"Damn!" Sgt. Conroy muttered and gathered up the cards to shuffle them and deal the next hand. Sgt. William Conroy had been appointed to this position in the first line of defense of his country by none other than the Chairman of the Joint Chiefs of Staff, General David Eastlesswater. The general called Sgt. Conroy "The finest soldier I have ever had the honor of working with." Sgt. Conroy called the general "Uncle Dave."

These two ever-vigilant soldiers were at their station when the radar detected Xanthan Gumm's little spaceship approaching Earth. Radar signals bounced off the ship and raced back to receiving dishes on the ground. Electronic signals zipped through supercomputers. A blip appeared on the screen, along with the message, "Unidentified object. Possible missile. Emergency Situation." The siren that was supposed to go off didn't. The last person who had dusted the console had accidentally turned down the volume by bumping the knob.

"All right," Sgt. Conroy said, "this time I win for sure." He dealt the next hand. Things had gotten just a little bit relaxed at NORAD in the last few years. No one really expected any missiles to come any more. This was lucky for Xanth, because that meant no one would be launching America's secret orbital antimissile system that could easily have turned his Glexo Nebula into space dust. Instead, when he hit the button for "Atmospheric entry mode," all the windows of the ship were covered by heat shields and the Glexo began to make a controlled fall into the gravity well of the forbidden planet, with no humans yet aware that they were about to have a visitor.

After the ship had descended far enough, according to the instruments, Xanth pressed the button marked "Atmospheric Flight". The heat shields retracted and the agrav systems took over from the main engine, controlling flight in the gravitational pull of the planet. As the heat shields pulled back, Xanth saw the surface of the Earth for the first time with his own eyes. It was beautiful. Green dotted with the shimmering blue of lakes and the rich earthy brown of strip mines. Xanth was happier than he'd ever been in his life, for this was his dream. This planet created the entertainment for a galaxy and didn't even know it. Soon, he would be a part of it, known throughout the galaxy for his roles in Earth Movies, maybe as a kindly, gentle soul, like *E.T.*, maybe as a vicious eater of humans, like the ones simply called *Aliens*. It didn't matter. He, Xanthan Gumm, would be a Movie Star.

All he had to do was show up in the Earth city called Hollywood, which was the center of all Movie-making, find Steven Spielberg's office, and soon he would be in The Movies. Now, this part of his plan had been necessarily a little vague. No one knew much about the geography of this forbidden world. Sure, maps were often part of the electronic flood of information that was sent out daily from the planet, but like everything else they were assumed to be fictitious. So Xanth wasn't really sure where Hollywood was. Still, he figured that since the creation of entertainment was the main focus of all human activities, he could just stop and ask for directions if he got lost.

"Hollywood!" Xanth was so excited he exclaimed the wonderful name out loud. "Here I come!" Now he was getting low enough that he could actually read some of the road signs. He saw one that said CHICAGO–10 Miles. That was encouraging. Miles were an Earth unit of measurement, and CHICAGO was a place where everyone sang and danced, according to one Movie. Xanth was almost in Hollywood!

Back in the underground NORAD complex, Sgt. Conroy started to say, "Uh, Bob, you know..." then thought better of it, and stopped.

"What?" asked Lt. McCollum. He was concentrating on his cards. He had just drawn a four of hearts, but he needed a three of diamonds.

"Oh, nothing."

"No, really, what?"

"It's just that..." Sgt. Conroy paused and cleared his throat. Then he discarded a card.

"Go ahead, Bill, just say it." Bob snatched up Bill's discard. Damn! Not a three of diamonds!

The blip that had been on their screens, trying to tell them that something unknown was coming in from space, was now gone, as Xanth's ship was too low to be seen on radar. The screen showed nothing.

"Uh, well, what does NORAD stand for?"

"WHAT?" Bob looked up from his cards. Sgt. Conroy looked embarrassed, but determined. "I've been stationed here for six months, and everyone talks about NORAD this, and NORAD that, but I never can find out what the letters stand for."

"Are you serious? Everyone knows that."

"Well? Then what does it stand for?"

"North American Radar Air Defense, of course."

"No, sorry, Bob, that's NARAD."

"Oh." Lt. McCollum had to stop and think. He had been sure that it was North American Radar Air Defense. "Well, how about Northern Organization for Radar Early Detection?"

"Nope. That's NORED."

"This is ridiculous. We work here– we should know what it stands for. Northern Organization for Radar Anti-Detection?"

"That fits, but it doesn't make any sense." Sgt. Conroy shook his head.

"You're right. Hmmm. We could call your Uncle Dave. He would know."

"He told me never to call him at work." Just then, a door opened in the cavernous room where all the computers and radar screens and other equipment clicked and hummed and Lt. McCollum and Sgt. Conroy sat at their station, and when they saw who it was they scrambled to snatch up their cards and hide them. Bob slid the deck into a pocket just as the tall, imposing figure approached.

"We could ask him," Bob whispered.

"What does he know?" Bill whispered back. "He's a ground pounder."

General Les. S. Moore walked up to their station, leading with a chin the size of a Tomahawk cruise missile.

"That's General Ground Pounder to you, airman," he said

Chapter Three

Xanth flew over territory that was steadily becoming uglier and uglier. What had happened to the beautiful green and blue planet he had seen at first? Now, the predominant colors were black and gray. There were tall cylindrical structures everywhere, all billowing out clouds of noxious gases. An instrument on the dashboard that measured whether an atmosphere was breathable suddenly lit up and beeped fiercely, the needle escalating into the danger zone. Xanth hit the accelerator, hoping to leave this area of poisoned air behind as quickly as possible. The atmosphere-measuring instrument calmed down and the needle settled back into the safe zone just as Xanth passed, but never noticed, a sign that said, "Gary, Indiana".

Things were soon better and then there was -- an ocean! A huge, glittering body of water, bigger than any Xanth had seen before. Xanth had very little experience with planet surfaces, having lived in Galactic Central all his life. Once his parents had taken him on vacation to Qaaxle, which had small lakes, but that had been nothing like this, with water stretching from horizon to horizon.

Then, on one of those horizons, a city appeared. It had to be Hollywood! All along one shoreline, in a dizzying array of heights, widths, and styles, were buildings, buildings, and more buildings, as far as the eye could see! Xanth steered his ship towards this magnificent city. The Movies were waiting!

He decided to fly really low, and try and spot some real, honest-to-goodness humans. There weren't many on the streets. It was very early in the day, so maybe they weren't up and around yet. There was one! Xanth flew even lower to take a look at it. From all his experience with Movies, he easily identified this variety of human as little-old-lady. She was holding a leash that led to another Earth creature, a dog. Xanth flew over them, blasting past them just ten feet or so above their heads. Looking back, Xanth was horrified to see that he had blown the poor old lady's head clean off! His first encounter with a human and he had killed it! No, no, the little-old-lady was still moving. Shaking a fist at him and shouting something, in fact. Oh, the part that had blown off was called a hat, Xanth remembered with relief.

Xanth took his ship up for another look at the human city stretching off into forever. He'd spotted his first human! "I bet that little-old-lady will tell everyone that she saw a genuine UFO!" Xanth laughed to himself. UFOs were big in Earth entertainments, though the laws about going to Earth were so strict that there couldn't possibly be as many ships visiting the place as The Movies showed.

After the horrible rocket roared overhead, and then lifted higher into the sky, the old lady knew exactly what to do. She picked up MacArthur, her poodle, who was still trembling, and set off for home. It was finally happening. She had been warning everyone for years. They said it wouldn't happen, but now it was, and she knew exactly what to do.

Once in her apartment, she put down MacArthur and picked up the phone. She had the number right next to the phone. A woman answered.

"NORAD," she said, "how may we help you?"

"I want to report that I just saw a genuine Russian Nuclear Missile. It's time to launch the counter-strike!"

"General, this may seem silly, but, we're trying to remember what NORAD stands for."

Gen Les S. Moore loomed over the two soldiers at their radar station. He was six foot four, and his height plus his immaculate uniform gave him an air of total authority. Not to mention his chin, which jutted out so far that soldiers joked that his chin could be in one room while the general was in another.

"What?" the general asked.

"Um, it's just that, uh, we don't know exactly what the letters NORAD stand for." Sgt. Conroy stuttered. "Do you, er, happen to know?"

9

Gen Moore stared at the two. "Two soldiers under this command," he said, "entrusted with the first line of defense of this country," he continued, "don't know what the acronym NORAD stands for. Is that right?"

"Uh, Yes, sir."

"YOU IDIOTS! IT'S NORTH AMERICAN RADAR AIR DEFENSE!"

"Begging your pardon, sir, we already thought of that. That would be NARAD."

The general paused. "Then it's...it stands for...um..." He stopped and thought, rubbing his massive chin with his right hand. Then he clearly came to a decision.

"Soldier! Get me the Pentagon on the phone immediately!"

"I saw a genuine Russian nuclear missile!"

Corporal Anne Kleegle groaned inwardly. Another crank call. She was on duty answering the phone in the NORAD complex. "Excuse me, ma'am?" was all she could think to say in response to the old lady's announcement.

"The Russians are attacking! I saw one of their missiles!"

"Ma'am, I really doubt you saw a Russian missile." But the old lady was adamant. "You know it was a Russian missile," Cpl. Kleegle repeated into the phone, "because it was driven by a short, ugly, beady-eyed, yellow-skinned creature, and you read once in *The National Babbler* that that's what Russians look like when they're not disguised as Americans."

"That's right," the old lady said, "and besides, it scared my little dog MacArthur so much he's still shaking. Only a Russian would be that rude."

Corporal Kleegle rolled her eyes. "Ma'am, even though we still keep an eye out for nuclear missiles, we really don't expect them to come from Russia anymore. Not since the breakup of the Soviet Union."

"Breakup? What do you mean?"

"Uh, you know, when the whole Soviet Union fell apart? There is no Soviet Union anymore. It was in all the papers. And on TV too."

"I don't believe any of the pabulum-puking liberal-bias media. If they say that there's no more Soviet Union, then it's just Commie disinformation."

Cpl. Kleegle tried to remember all the stuff that was in the headlines when she was nine years old. It all seemed like ancient history to her. "Well, Ma'am, the Soviet Union had a leader named Gorbachev, and he reformed their system. The whole thing collapsed, and now Russia is just a small country. The president now is named Putin."

"Gorb what? Poot who?" the old lady stammered. "What happened to Kruschev?"

Chapter Four

The phone rang several times, and then clicked. "Thank you for calling the Pentagon," an official-sounding voice stated. "If you are calling to report an invasion by a hostile foreign army, or a planned terrorist action, press one. If you are an American citizen who wants to enlist in the armed services, press two. If you are a member of a hostile foreign army or a terrorist who wants to defect, press three. If you are a current member of the armed services who wants to ask a question, press four. If you are a defense contractor, press the number that corresponds to the amount, in billions of dollars, your latest contract is worth. To speak to an operator, press zero."

Sgt. Conroy pressed four. The voice returned, saying, "Thank you for calling the Pentagon internal information line. To report a matter of national security, press one. To report a lost or stolen ship, aircraft, or toilet seat valued at three million dollars or more, press two..."

"This is going to take a while, sir." Sgt. Conroy told General Moore. "Voice mail."

The general shuddered. "Never mind, soldier," he said. "At this time of the morning they're all down at Phil's getting breakfast, anyway."

"All right, Ma'am, all right. I'll put you through to my superior." Cpl. Kleegle told the old lady. Hmmm...Who could she pawn this call off on? Cpl. Kleegle decided to send the call to that Army general that no one liked.

She paged him over the complex-wide intercom. "General Moore," came his curt reply through her speaker. She also heard another voice in the background saying, "Northern Organization for Radar American Defense?" What the hell were they doing down there? Oh, well, it was none of her business.

"General, I have a woman on the phone who insists on speaking to a superior officer. She has some wild story about seeing a Russian missile. I think she's completely nuts."

"I'll take it, Corporal. Put it through to my office." With a curt "As you were" to McCollum and Conroy, the general left them and threaded his way through a maze of corridors, then through several rooms where top secret computers ran top secret programs, then through another room where an ultra-top-secret computer ran an ultra-top-secret program that the first set of top-secret computers didn't even know existed. Finally in his office, General Moore secured the door and pressed a button on his desk. In moments, a flashing message appeared on the computer screen on his desk: "OFFICE SECURE. NO LISTENING DEVICES DETECTED."

General Moore sat at his desk, swiveled his chair, and picked up his phone. He pressed the flashing button labeled "Line 1".

"Yes, Mother," he said. "What is it this time?"

Xanth took his ship up to get a better look at the city. It was big enough to be Hollywood, and it was on an ocean, but something didn't seem right. There were no palm trees, for one thing. Also no blonde females driving convertible automobiles or muscular males riding small boards on the waves of the ocean. In fact, there weren't any waves to speak of.

Then some activity came into view. Time for the viewscope again. Xanth focused the instrument. He saw a group of humans he recognized as "police". They were having a discussion with a man who lay on the hood of the policemen's "squad car." The discussion involved hitting the man over and over again. The man being hit was of the group of humans inaccurately called "black." All of the policemen were of the group just as inaccurately called "white." This was promising. Xanth had seen images of just such events in the broadcasts from Earth. They were always recorded by a bystander with a-- Xanth looked carefully. Then he scanned the area. He found no one except the policemen and their interviewee.

Damn, Xanth thought. No one was nearby recording the beating with a video camera. This couldn't be Hollywood!

"Yes, Mother," General Moore said. "Yes, Mother," he said again. He listened for a while. While he was listening his mind wandered to his dislike of this Air Force installation. He yearned for a good honest battlefield where tanks and soldiers could stay on the ground where God meant them to be. Since he had been assigned to The Committee, he had been ordered to experience life in each branch of the service. He had already spent six hot, miserable months at Parris Island, and now was entombed in this mountain. He did not look forward to six months at sea.

Then his mother's voice cut through General Moore's musings. "But--" he tried. Then, "Yes, Mother. All right, I'll check." He put his hand over the phone and muttered a few choice words that he hoped his mother couldn't hear. He keyed the intercom, to talk to Lt. McCollum and Sgt. Conroy.

"This is General Moore. Are you two absolutely sure that there are no Russian missiles on the screen?"

"Yes, sir."

"Thank you." General Moore picked up the phone again. "I just checked again, Mother. There are no Russian missiles. Are you satisfied?"

The intercom channel was still open. "There is the UFO, sir," said Conroy.

"The WHAT?" General Moore. Moore tossed the phone aside.

"The UFO, sir. Over Lake Michigan. It's being tracked by our system and by the tower at O'Hare."

"I'll be right there!" The general bolted out of his office. His mother's voice came faintly through the phone receiver as it lay on the floor. "Are you there, sonny? Are you there? How dare you ignore me! You wouldn't treat me this way if your father was still alive!"

Xanth had gone up just a little too high when he did his survey of the city. Now his radio was full of voices demanding to know who he was and what runway he wanted to land on. Then a highly authoritative human voice cut through all the others. "This is General Les S. Moore, United States Army. I demand that you identify yourself!"

14

This was the moment that Xanth had been waiting for: first contact with the humans. His first chance to deal directly with the inhabitants of the forbidden planet, his first opportunity to establish a dialogue with the inscrutable humans, his first chance to ask directions to the intersection of Hollywood and Vine. "My name is Xanthan Gumm. I am a resident of Galactic Center. I have come to Earth to be a Movie Star. Can you tell me how to find Steven Spielberg?"

The atmosphere was tense in NORAD headquarters. General Moore manned the radio, exerting every ounce of command presence that he possessed. He stood once again at the main console, fiercely eying the blip on the screen that represented this unknown threat to the United States of America. Lt. McCollum and Sgt. Conroy stood to the side, ready to spring into action at the general's slightest order.

"Listen, whoever you are, I have read all the manuals that cover the eventuality of contact with extraterrestrials. I know what to expect. And no alien being is going to appear on Earth immediately speaking perfect English. That is just ridiculous. So you might as well admit that this is a hoax."

Xanth just said, "English is the common language of all Galactic Civilization. Everyone in the galaxy speaks English." What was the matter with *him*? Xanth thought to himself. Hasn't he ever seen "Star Trek"?

"Scramble everything we have in the area," the general told Lt. McCollum. "I want a visual on this thing. And if it looks threatening, shoot it down."

"Yes, sir."

"Once again, I am asking you to identify yourself." The authoritative voice came through Xanth's radio. "If you do not, you will be assumed to be hostile." Hostile? Xanth thought. Why would they think I'm hostile? Well, the best way to break the ice when meeting new people was to tell a joke. If he could only think of one.

"The UFO does not conform to any known aircraft, sir." Sgt. Conroy reported.

"What weapons does it have?" General Moore asked. "Rockets? Lasers? Particle Beams?"

Xanth thought of a great one. "I just flew in from Canis Majoris," he said into his radio, "and I am Dog tired. But, Siriusly, folks..." He started laughing to himself.

Sgt. Conroy looked up with an expression of pure panic. He managed to get out one word. "Puns!"

General Moore hit the alarm, then keyed the base-wide intercom. "FULL ALERT!" he screamed into it, "FULL ALERT!" Throughout the base all personnel scrambled to meet the oncoming invasion.

Chapter Five

With every available fighter jet in the Great Lakes region screaming towards Xanth at speeds measured in Machs, and the highest levels of the military on alert, there seemed little doubt that the one-time framadort converter and would-be Movie Star was about to be blasted into a fine powder that would settle on the citizens of Chicago and make at least those of them who were allergic to powdered space alien experience a day of mild sinus congestion.

Fortunately for those people, who would never learn that they had an allergy to space-alien dust, which is a rare allergy indeed, fate stepped in, in the form of the left front votulator flange on Xanth's Glexo Nebula.

A mechanic at the Glexo dealer had told Xanth to get the left front votulator flange replaced, but Xanth was late for work so he had figured he could do it later. Then he had completely forgotten about it.

The left front votulator flange sprang a leak and lost all of its votulator fluid. This caused a chain reaction in the little spaceship's systems that resulted in the catastrophic failure of the entire agrav array. So Xanth owed his life to the left front votulator flange, because just as the entire available fleet of America's finest airborne weaponry came blasting over the horizon and prepared to lock onto the invader, his ship started to plunge earthward like a Skwazalian pea bird (which is actually not a bird, but a fish, having been misnamed by a scientist with a horrible hangover and blurry eyesight) dropped out of an airship at 10,000 feet.

"The object has completely disappeared from the 'scopes, Sir." Lt. McCollum reported to General Moore. The general leaned over and glared at the radar screen as if it had disobeyed a direct order. "What are all those blips?" he asked.

Robin Reed

"Our planes. They're trying to get a visual on the object." Just then, two of the blips came together, merged into one big blip, and then faded out. "Oh my god," Lt. McCollum said.

Xanth, from the cockpit of his tumbling ship, saw the Earth aircraft approaching the spot where he had been a moment before. They were just like the ones in "Top Gun"! Was someone making a Movie here? Was he going to meet Tom Cruise? Everything on Earth was so exciting!

Just moments before, ace pilot Eric Schneckman had craned his neck, looking up in the sky for whatever it was he had been sent to shoot down. Its radar signal had vanished, so probably the object had, just like all the UFO's he'd read about, sped off at speeds inconceivable to human science. All he saw above him was a serene blue sky with high, thin clouds. Yup, he thought, the aliens were gone for sure. Probably to their secret base on the dark side of the moon.

Ace Pilot Fred Smeg didn't believe in aliens at all. He had approached the coordinates he'd been given prepared to blast a terrorist missile out of the sky, or maybe a filthy drug smuggler with tons of cocaine in a small plane. As long as he got to blast something out of the sky, he would be happy. When the unknown craft disappeared from radar, Smeg figured, more accurately than his colleague Schneckman, that it must be falling, or was flying low to avoid the approaching fighter jets. Smeg craned his neck down, but all he saw was Lake Michigan, scattering the light of the sun and making it difficult to see anything.

The net result of these two opposing viewpoints was that neither pilot saw each other, and at the speeds they were traveling, proximity alarms that went off in their respective cockpits were too late to prevent the two planes from colliding and their blips from vanishing on the radar screen that General Moore was staring at so intently.

Xanth saw in astonishment the fireball that erupted above him, but he also saw, when his ship tumbled to give him a downwards view, how fast the unknown city was coming up to greet him. He suddenly remembered the mechanic telling him to get the left front votulator

18

flange replaced, and the reason he hadn't thought it was important at the time.

"You can go without it for a while if you stay in space," the mechanic had said, pointing a tentacle at the offending flange, "but you'll be sorry if you try and fly in an atmosphere without getting this baby fixed."

Of course Xanth had forgotten about the whole thing. He lived in Galactic Central, a vast collection of artificial habitats, carved-out asteroids, and free-floating condo developments. He had been in a planetary atmosphere exactly two times in his life, once on the vacation to Qaaxle he had taken with his parents, and once when he had had a horrible mining job that he had quit after a week. The visit to the mechanic was months before he had decided to go to Earth, so the whole thing had slipped his mind.

Now, it was the foremost thing on his mind. For even if the failure of the left front votulator flange had saved him from death at the hands, or rather the heat-seeking missiles, of the United States Air Force, it was swiftly delivering him into the grasp of that single-minded force, gravity. In just a few seconds his Glexo Nebula would meet the pavement of the city below and his trip to the forbidden planet would be over.

Below, walking along the shore of Lake Michigan, Robert Bledsoe was mulling over the depressing string of short-lived jobs, failed marriages, and never-realized dreams that constituted his life. There was no question about it, he was a failure, through and through, and would never accomplish anything. He was born in 1957, just before the Russians launched Sputnik and the entire space age. Robert's childhood had been filled with images of brave men and women going out to conquer the universe. In reality there were Armstrong, Aldrin, and...that other guy, who stayed in orbit when the others landed on the moon. In books there were the Lensmen, the Foundation, the Stone family, all kinds of people exploring all kinds of planets. He had discovered the works of Robert A. Heinlein in a school library at a young age, and read and reread every one of them a dozen times. Science fiction became his reality and reality just a

dreary interim he had to get through until he could get his nose into
another book.

Now he was forty-eight, and it was clear he would never see
anything beyond the gravity well of the planet where he was born, or
meet any travelers from elsewhere. He still consumed hundreds of
science fiction books a year, but the drab dust of reality had settled
into his soul and he no longer had any belief that his life would add
up to anything interesting.

Then he noticed a lot of noise overhead. He looked up. The sky
was full of UFO's! He had never dared believe they could be real.
And they moved so fast, just like in all the reports! And made
booming noises, and...oh, they were jets, military planes. Nothing
extraterrestrial after all.

Still, it was odd. It was like the annual air show held over the lake,
where the finest fliers the Air Force could provide looped and twirled
and sonic-boomed to the delight of many thousands of spectators
below. But that had been held a month earlier, and today there were
no spectators. Two of the jets hurtled towards each other at
tremendous speeds, and if it were an air show, they would have
veered off and barely missed each other, causing the crowds to oooh
and aaah. Instead, they crashed, causing a vast ball of flame to erupt.

"Oh my god!" Robert exclaimed, calling on a being he didn't
believe in, realizing that this was something real, something bad. Two
men had piloted those airplanes, and there was no sign of the bloom
of parachutes, no comforting realization that the pilots were all right.

Xanth worked frantically at the controls of his ship. There must be
some way to pull up, to not splat himself onto the hard surface of the
Earth city. He pulled every lever and knob on the control panel, and
entered commands furiously into the computer. The radio went on
and off and changed stations randomly. The viewscope popped in and
out of its housing, the navigation system gave him coordinates for
every planet in galactic civilization. None of it helped much.

Then Robert Bledsoe saw it. A craft, a...something, that was no
kind of military plane he had ever seen or heard of, was tumbling

wildly towards the ground. It had a pointy front end, and massive engines in the back. It had wings of a sort, and someone else might have thought the craft was an airplane, but Robert was sure it wasn't. It was hard to take it in because it was tumbling, but Robert would have bet his life that it was something that was not manufactured on the planet of his birth. Finally, his inner life had met up with his reality and he was getting a glimpse of something from beyond.

"Son of a bitch," General Moore breathed, still looking at the empty spot on the radar screen where two good men, two of the finest pilots the U.S. Air Force had, had died in a fiery crash. They had been killed defending the United States from a scum-sucking alien, an abomination from outer space, and a new purpose was born in the General, a vow to personally hunt down and destroy the invader.

Xanth yanked desperately on the votulator modulator control. If he could balance the votulator fluid flow, he might be able to get the agrav array to slow the ship down at least a little. Then it came to him - of course! - he had a bottle of votulator fluid in the ship. Somewhere. Where the hell was it? The ship rolled over and something hit Xanth hard on the head and tumbled away. It was the votulator fluid! Xanth couldn't believe it. He reached out and fumbled under the seat, but the bottle slid away before he could grasp it.

It was going to land nearby! Crash land was more like it, but a whole scenario flashed through Robert Bledsoe's mind, a science fiction novel that was going to happen to him; it would be real. He would rescue the alien from the crashed craft. At first he and the alien wouldn't be able to communicate, but the alien would learn English, and they would become friends. They would have many adventures on Earth until the alien managed to build a ship, or contact its mother ship, whatever. Then, just before leaving, the alien would offer Robert a chance to go with him, to see for himself the marvels of the galaxy. Of course Robert would go! He wouldn't hesitate for an instant! Earth could eat his dust!

Xanth grabbed the bottle. Yes! It was hard to get the cap off while the ship was tumbling so much, but he did it. It was even harder to get the panel open that allowed access to various fluid ports and the fuse box, but he did that too. He slammed the votulator fluid bottle into the votulator fluid port, and the liquid drained into its proper tank. Almost instantly he felt the agrav array strengthen and the ship began to feel a little more under control.

Yanking on the steering wheel as hard as he could, Xanth managed to orient the ship so that his personal up and down were the same as the planet's. He was almost on the ground, and didn't have much time before he would hit.

Robert ran, harder than he had ever run in his life before. The alien ship was heading inland, and seemed to be more under control than it had earlier. It was going to come down in the park, and Robert just had to be there to be the first to greet the visitor from another world.

With a screech and a bang and continuing series of metallic groans, Xanth's ship met the earth of Earth and slid, digging a trench as it went, for about a quarter-mile before coming to a halt. Xanth was pressed against his seat belt and then, when it was finally over, jerked back against the seat.

Robert Bledsoe ran up to the alien craft, which still gave off billows of smoke and/or steam. He knew what he was going to say. He had rehearsed it in his mind while he was running. When he caught his breath, he started to say it.

"Welcome to Earth. I am Robert Bledsoe, and I hope that we can be friends." That was as far as he got before he heard a strange whistling sound behind him. He turned to look, and something was falling--

The tail section of ace pilot Fred Smeg's fighter jet landed squarely on Robert Bledsoe and snuffed him out instantly.

After a struggle, Xanth got the canopy of the Glexo open and for the first time breathed the air of the forbidden planet. There were no humans around, but a piece of one of the airplanes that had exploded earlier lay nearby. Xanth smiled. He had broken galactic law, he had sacrificed a lot, but it was all worth it. He was on Earth!

Chapter Six

The first human to arrive was awfully small, and was carrying some kind of agrav flotation device. Xanthan was surprised. The Movies only showed agrav devices when they were about space travel, and since humans had only very primitive, localized space capabilities, these Movies were clearly imaginary.

Xanth waved from the open hatch of his ship. He had thought long and hard about what to say to his first human, and had come up with this speech: "I am Xanthan Gumm from Galactic Central. I have come to Earth be a Movie Star!" Before he could utter a word of it, though, the little human opened its mouth and shouted, "Graaaaaaannmaaaaaaa!"

This explained a lot, Xanth thought as he slid down the side of the Glexo and planted his feet for the first time on the soil of the planet. This was a child, of course. Though why the humans trusted a child with the brightly colored, ovoid agrav device that bobbed up and down in the wind and was held down only by a thin length of string clenched in one small hand, Xanth had no idea.

"Hi." he said to the child, "are there any adult humans around? I need to announce my arrival and ask for an audience with your leader, Steven Spielberg."

The child, which Xanth could now see was of the "Black" variety of human, though his skin was actually a pleasant brown, looked at Xanth with big eyes, took one step backwards and screamed, "Graaaaaaaaaannnnnmaaaaaaaaaaaaa!" in a voice pitched so high it hurt Xanth's ears.

"Don't worry. I'm friendly. I just came to Earth to be in The Movies. Like *E.T.* You know *E.T.*?" The child just stared at him. "*E.T.* phone home." Xanth did his best impression. "Or how about..." he racked his brain for another friendly Movie alien. "Alf! Yes! Hi, I just want to eat a cat! I..." Right at that moment, he was hit from behind and knocked flat on the ground.

"You get away from him!" a high voice shouted. Xanth was stunned but he managed to crawl away a bit and turn over to try and see his attacker. It was another brown human, but very much larger, both vertically and horizontally.

It was a woman bearing a large black weapon with straps on it. Female humans carried these things. What were they called? The woman whacked him with it again. "You don't go near my baby boy," she yelled. "You don't do nothing to my baby, you hear?"

"I'm sorry, woman, uh, ma'am, I meant no harm to the child, I..."

"Walking around the park in some Halloween mask, talking to children, I know what you are. You just stay away from my baby."

"Ok, ok, please, I just wanted to meet my first human." The woman didn't acknowledge this statement, just took the child by the hand and yanked him away. This sudden jolt to one hand caused the little boy to open the other, and the string attached to his agrav device slipped out of it. The device began to float upwards. The child made a grab at the string but it was already too far up for him to reach.

The weapon was a purse, and the child was holding a balloon. Xanth had seen these things in the Movies. It was just surprising to see them with his own eyes. And since everything in the Movies was fictional, he didn't know if anything he saw on Earth would be the same as he saw on his wallscreen at home.

Seeing a chance to do the humans a favor and perhaps gain their confidence, Xanth sprang up and made a grab for the balloon. He was a little wobbly from being hit over the head a couple of times, not to mention crashing his ship, but he managed to close his hands on the bright red device and land back on Earth with it firmly in his grasp.

The balloon exploded, leaving Xanth grasping nothing, as shreds of bright red material fell to the ground. The sound of the explosion hurt Xanth's ears again, but that was nothing compared to the shriek that immediately issued from the mouth of the smaller human.

"HE B'OKE MY B'OON!!!" The little one screamed in a register that would normally be issued only by malfunctioning ore-grinding equipment. Xanth was still staring at the child in disbelief and holding his ears when he was knocked over again by the woman's massive purse.

"What you doing? You break my baby's balloon? I'll show you how to break things!"

Xanth managed to get away before the wild woman could hit him again, but she pursued him, dragging the screaming child in one hand and waving her purse in the other, until they were far away from the landing site of the ship. Xanth managed to crawl under a bush and hide, almost holding his breath, until he couldn't hear the violent woman or the wailing child anymore.

Then he waited some more. He believed in the Earth saying, "You can never be too careful."

While Xanth waited, a crowd was gathering around his ship. People had been arriving at work in the downtown area when the commotion in the sky had begun, and many of them had decided to investigate, hoping to find something cool to talk to their coworkers about at lunchtime. They were hoping mainly for dead bodies or parts of them. Nothing spices up lunch table conversation like a severed head or two.

What these corporate denizens found on arriving at the crash was part of a fighter jet, and all of a small alien spacecraft. However, since the spacecraft wasn't shaped like a saucer, a cigar, or any other shape that is traditionally associated with alien spaceships, they assumed it was just another airplane of some sort. The whole thing was kind of disappointing, actually. They would have been happier if they'd known about the squashed remains of Robert Bledsoe under the fighter jet fuselage, but they didn't, so they just stood and stared, using the whole thing as an excuse to not go to work yet.

Finally a woman ventured to say something out loud. "Shouldn't we call somebody?"

"I guess we could call the police." a man in a dark suit with a red and black tie said. He looked around to see who might take up his suggestion. Despite the fact that almost everyone in the crowd was carrying a cell phone, no one did.

Another woman, nicely dressed in a fetching skirt and blouse outfit with just the most adorable shoes she had spent too much on the day before, said, "We could call the fire department." Again there were no takers.

Various other suggestions were made. "Call the National Guard." "Call the FAA." "Call the FCC." The man in the black and red tie decided he was going to take charge. "We have to call the ultimate authority in matters like this." Everyone knew what he meant. "Call the TV stations!" a number of them shouted at once, and suddenly every cell phone in the crowd was active.

The ever-vigilant news media, however, was already on the case. Various traffic-reporting helicopters were heading towards the crash site and other news crews in vans were hurrying that way, the cameramen checking their equipment and the on-air reporters checking their makeup. When the helicopters landed and the news vans screeched to a halt, the crowd of onlooking office workers moved back to make way for them. As soon as the news vehicles, whether they arrived by air or ground, disgorged their camera-toting crews the onlookers found themselves being gang interviewed.

The reporters were relentless. They pursued anyone who might have seen anything, or who would at least look interesting on camera. They shouted questions to anyone and anything that moved.

"Did you see the crash?"

"Did you see anyone jump out the airplanes?"

"Do you know if anyone was hurt or killed?"

"How do you think this will affect the stock market?"

At some point one camera crew latched onto the find of the day. The little boy Xanth had met earlier and his Granma came by on their way home. Once the crews realized there was someone there who actually *had* seen something, they swarmed around the boy and the Granma like IRS agents around a particularly juicy audit report.

Then, with thirty-six cameras pointed at them, Granma told the tale of the weirdo in the Halloween mask who had bothered the little boy. Thinking fast, Regina Rogers of CBS asked the all-important question that was in all the reporters' minds. Poking her microphone in the boy's face she said, "How did you *feel* when your balloon popped?"

Newspaper reporters were there also, conspicuous by their lack of cameramen. No one paid much attention to them, and it was harder for them to get interviews. When the television cameramen turned on their lights and shined them on someone, that person would instantly put on what they hoped was their best TV face. People being approached for print interviews were less willing to talk, though it helped if there was a photographer who could at least take still pictures.

Two print reporters, though, didn't have much trouble finding someone to interview. "Bill Freeman, 'Press Review'," one of them said to the other. "How is your paper going to cover this event?" He poised to take notes in a notebook.

Instead of answering, the other reporter pointed the built-in microphone of his microcassette recorder at Freeman. "Sid Simon, 'Inside the Press' column," he said. "What is your magazine's view of the press coverage of this event?"

Just then, voices from the sky commanded everyone to leave and about a dozen military helicopters landed near the news choppers. Soldiers were suddenly everywhere telling everyone to get out so they could secure the area. The reporters, after failing to get any interviews with any of the soldiers or officers, but getting some nice footage of the helicopters landing, decided it was time to get their important information and videotape back to their respective offices. The original crowd of onlookers was pushed away, and the military was completely in charge of a small piece of Grant Park in Chicago.

Xanth, when he finally crept out from under his bush, had trouble finding the way back to his ship. He figured out that the tall buildings were further inland, and that the open sky in the opposite direction must be over the ocean. After walking that way for a while he saw the commotion of military helicopters landing, news choppers taking off, and office workers heading back to their cubicles. He stood on a small rise overlooking the site where his Glexo Nebula had crashed. It was now covered with men dressed in khaki. Xanth was at a complete loss as to what to do next. His plan had gone completely wrong. He had imagined that he would stand on top of his Glexo and proclaim his arrival to a gathered multitude of humans, and then be immediately whisked to Hollywood to star in The Movies.

He took a step to go down to talk to the uniformed men.

"I wouldn't go down there if were you," a voice said. Xanth turned and looked. A man lounged on a nearby park bench. "What? Why not?" Xanth asked him. "You don't want to make first contact with the military. They love doing alien autopsies. And if the aliens aren't quite dead when they meet them, somehow they end up that way pretty quickly." The man looked tall, even though he was sitting, and had a thick mustache under a large nose and sharp gaze.

Xanth rubbed his head, remembering Granma's purse. "I think I made first contact already. Maybe you can help me. How can I get to Hollywood?"

"You want to be in the movies."

"Yes. How did you know?"

"They all do." The man stuck out his hand. "Ted Granger. I'm a reporter with *The National Babbler*."

Reporter. Yes, Xanth flashed on images of reporters in The Movies. They talked to people and then printed or broadcast any information they found out. This was perfect. This man could help. "I hereby announce," Xanth said, "the arrival of the latest alien Movie sensation, Xanthan Gumm, soon to be bigger than *E.T.*, Alf, and Yoda combined!"

Granger just shook his head. "Sorry. Aliens are pretty much a yawn around my office. We don't even print their stories anymore unless there's some new twist to it."

"But I'm from Galactic Central, a representative of the teeming civilizations that inhabit the galaxy. I'm proof that there is life beyond the bounds of this planet."

Granger emphasized his earlier comment by yawning widely. "You're too humanoid looking. People will think you're just a small human in a mask. Give it up. Go home." Then he glanced down at the soldiers swarming around Xanth's ship. "Sorry. Guess you won't be going home in that. Tell you what. I'll see if I can peddle you to my paper." He took out a small pocket camera and quickly snapped Xanth's picture. "It would help if you could come up some new angle, something I could really sell to my editor."

29

"I-- I don't know." Xanth was feeling confused, uncertain. Had coming to Earth been a huge mistake? Should he be back in Galactic Central converting framadorts? He sat on the bench next to Granger. "This is so different than I had imagined."

"Here's my card." Granger offered a small rectangle of stiff paper. "If you come up with anything call me, and maybe I can get you some money from the paper." Xanth took the card and stuffed it in the pocket of his shorts. "Gotta go." Granger said, standing up.

"Hey - where do I get food on this planet?" Xanth asked Granger's departing back. "I haven't eaten since I was on the cruise ship. I feel like I've lost ten pounds in all the excitement."

Granger came back. "That's it!" he said, with a big smile on his face. "You're a genius! Be sure to call my office in a couple of days and I'll definitely set you up with some cash. Gotta rush. Deadline's looming." Then he left, almost running, and disappeared in the direction of the tall buildings.

Xanth watched him go, completely baffled. What was the man talking about?

He would not figure it out until three days later, when he would pass an outdoor booth that was selling various printed paper items. There he was - a picture of him, Xanth, in the upper right corner of the cover of *The National Babbler*, along with the headline:

SPACE ALIEN TELLS DIET SECRETS!
YOU CAN BECOME WEIGHTLESS IN THIRTY DAYS!

Chapter Seven

"Yes, sir!" someone shouted in response to General Moore's order, and rushed off to obey it. The general had issued the order as he stepped off the helicopter at the crash site. He didn't even remember, a moment later, what he had ordered. His mind was full of rage at the alien invader who had killed two fine pilots, and when he was angry issuing an order, any order, made him feel in charge of his unruly emotions as well as the lower-ranking soldiers around him. What he saw at the crash site was a beehive of military activity surrounding two downed aircraft. Or rather, a part of one aircraft and the evil-looking spaceship of the alien. He had been told that the TV reports of the crash had so far not mentioned the words "alien" or "spaceship". The civilians and reporters who had been the first on the scene had not realized that one of the craft was not of this earth. That was fine. He meant to keep it that way. There were people in the Pentagon already creating a secret aircraft project, backdated several years, that produced a plane looking exactly like the little spaceship, just in case reporters ever did try to find its origins. Of course, the project was highly classified and no one would ever find the plans, but the several billion dollars retrospectively allocated for it would no doubt be put to good use.

"Find me the man in charge here." General Moore growled at a passing lieutenant.

"Yes, sir!"

Shortly one Colonel Dobson walked up to the general and saluted. "Report, Colonel," General Moore barked.

"Yes, sir. As you can see, we have secured the site and will soon be removing the debris. We're waiting for a crane to arrive. My orders were to remove everything as quickly as possible. If I may say so, sir, this will make it very difficult for an investigation to determine the cause of the crash. Usually we investigate a crash onsite as thoroughly as possible before moving anything."

"Usually, Colonel, the site is remote, not in one of the biggest goddamn cities in the country, in the shadow of some of the tallest goddamn skyscrapers in the country."

Col. Dobson looked flustered. "Uh, yes, sir. But if I may, sir, we aren't in any shadow at the moment sir. It's morning, and we are east of all those buildings. This area won't be in the shadow of the buildings until late afternoon, and we should be gone by then, sir."

General Moore just stared at the colonel. His rage flared, this time aimed at the idiotic Colonel Dobson. "It was a metaphor. I just meant that we're near the buildings! Thousands of people could be watching us from those windows! Didn't they teach you about metaphors in college?"

"Yes, sir!" Col. Dobson snapped a salute. "Uh, well, actually, no sir. I was a phys-ed major."

General Moore seethed inside. He longed for the days when a commanding officer could hang one of his men for any reason, no questions asked.

"As for people watching us, those buildings are too far away for anyone to see anything clearly. That's not a problem" the Colonel said.

Ted Granger, staff reporter with *The National Babbler*, stood at a forty-fourth floor window of a Michigan Avenue high rise and smiled. He raised his camera with its massive long lens and focused. It was the same lens he had used to get photos of Madonna breast-feeding her baby, of Brad Pitt walking on a nude beach, and of Madonna breast-feeding Brad Pitt. He could see the pimples on the chin of the general who was talking to a colonel. And what an amazing chin it was. Granger pulled back and began to snap off shots of everything that the military was doing down there.

Then he noticed a flatbed tow truck bumping through the park towards the landing site. Some soldiers tried to stop it, but after a brief talk with the driver, they let the truck through.

"Well, well," Granger said. "Right on schedule."

"What the hell?" General Moore said. A tow truck had entered the perimeter. Why didn't his troops keep it out? He stormed towards the offending vehicle, which came to a stop as he approached. Before he could shout at it to leave, two civilians got out. A man and a woman, both wearing brown suits. The suits were almost identical, except the woman had a skirt and one of those flight attendant girl ties.

"I don't know how you got in here," General Moore told the pair, "but you are getting right back in that contraption and leaving this instant."

The man was carrying a camera or device of some kind. It was obviously heavy and he held it with both hands. The woman produced a badge and flashed it so briefly that General Moore couldn't read it.

"Federal agent," she said. "Group 19."

Before the general could object that he had never heard of any such agency, the man in the brown suit pressed a button on his device and a whining sound could be heard coming from the thing.

With his job done there at the landing site, and all the troops beginning to ship out, General Moore began to realize he couldn't put it off any longer. He had to do it. The damnable extraterrestrial had not only invaded the earth and killed two pilots, it had brought him, General Les S. Moore, to the city where his ninety-two-year-old mother lived. For that alone, the alien must suffer.

If he didn't go see her while he was here, General Moore would be the one to suffer. He sighed. "Get me a car," he ordered. "Yes, sir!" snapped a lesser officer and went to obey. General Moore's mother was the reason he had left Chicago at the age of eighteen, and the reason that kept bringing him back. He sighed again as a Humvee pulled up, driven by a corporal.

"Take me to Hyde Park."

"Yes, sir!" the corporal responded. "Um, sir, where is that?"

"You're not from Chicago, are you, soldier?"

"No, sir."

"Lucky you. Just drive. I'll direct you."

"Yes, sir!"

Going south on Lake Shore Drive, the General became gloomier and gloomier. The young corporal almost missed the turnoff because General Moore was thinking about other things and forgot to tell him where to go. As they wound their way through the narrow streets of this old part of the city, and finally arrived at Kimbark Avenue, the General was sunk into his thoughts so much that he didn't notice when they stopped.

"Sir."

"Hmmm?"

"Sir, this is the address you gave me. Sir."

"Oh, yes. Wait for me."

"Yes, sir!"

"And do something useful while you're waiting. Polish the vehicle or something."

"Yes, sir!"

"And..."

"Sir?"

The General couldn't think of any more orders to give. "Nothing."

"Yes, sir!"

There was nothing left to do but to approach the three-flat building in front of him, the building he had spent his childhood in, the building where his mother still lived. As he stepped onto the porch, MacArthur started barking. He rang the bell for the first-floor apartment.

There was a wait. Then the door opened and the general's mother gave him a glare that he could never have equaled, even at his most commanding. "Wipe your feet!" she barked.

General Moore drew himself up his full height and saluted. "Yes, ma'am!"

Chapter Eight

As Xanth walked into the city he was feeling more and more unhappy about his situation. He had been on Earth for almost two hours and he still hadn't met Steven Spielberg! Not only that, he was hungry and had no idea where he might get food.

He saw more and more humans, but most of them just rushed by him without looking at him. He supposed the reporter from *The National Babbler* was right. He was too human-looking. He was shorter than most of the humans but not enough to be considered too strange. He had yellow skin with a scaly texture, large pointed ears and a hairless head. Frankly, stopping and looking at himself in the window of a building, Xanth thought he looked a little like a small Creature from the Black Lagoon, or maybe a large Yoda. Or a bald Dr. Ruth.

Maybe the reason that the humans didn't think he was an alien was because he was wearing clothing. It was a noted oddity, a matter of much discussion in the Human Psychology class he had taken at Galactic University (actually the course was officially titled Abnormal Psychology, but it amounted to the same thing) that humans, as shown in their Movies, believed aliens never wore clothing. With the exception of *E.T.* briefly wearing a costume for a human holiday called Halloween, and some others in which the aliens are posing as human, invariably aliens didn't wear clothing in The Movies.

This was ridiculous, of course. Even before Earth culture got Galactic civilization so firmly in its grip, most of the races of the galaxy wore some kind of clothing. There were the Pt!ng, who only wore their skin on formal occasions, but they were unusual. And they were never invited to anything casual. After the fascination with Earth became so big, many Earth fashions raged and died out, only to be replaced by another fad. The most outrageous one that Xanth could remember was a fad for the very strange costume called a Zoot Suit.

You haven't really lived, Xanth had always thought, until you've seen an eight-limbed, two-headed yarigor in a Zoot Suit.

He managed to get across a couple of streets, moving with the crowds of humans, who followed the commands of the colored lights. This at least was something that he had expected; these lights were in many Movies, though they were not always obeyed. He was glad these particular humans were obeying them. He did not want to be hit by a car.

This city resembled many scenes from The Movies. He recognized the look of an Earth city, with all the people walking on the sidewalks. The train that rumbled overhead on an ancient-looking steel support platform was familiar too. Now that he thought of it, this place called Chicago had been mentioned in many Movies.

There was of course the one where everybody sang and danced, but there were others. In one, Kevin Costner was an incorruptible lawman fighting the evil of Al Capone. The cars in that Movie looked different than the ones he was seeing, and the people wore different kinds of clothing. Galactic scholars were divided on why some Movies showed distinctly different types of clothing, and cars, and some had people riding horses with no cars in sight. Also most Movies were in full color but many only in shades of gray. Xanth figured it was just a matter of each Movie coming from the imagination of a different human. It was all fantasy of one kind or another.

Since the scene he was walking through did resemble some of the Movies he had seen, Xanth was more confident that he was somewhere in Hollywood. "Chicago" was part of the "back lot" in a studio. It made sense.

The buildings in this part of the "back lot" were quite tall, and all the extras streaming in and out of the doors were staying in character, hurrying through their imaginary lives. Xanth wondered where the cameras were.

He stopped at the corner of one of the buildings and stood there, with no idea in this or any other world what to do next. He was hungry, hungrier than he had ever been. Wasn't there any food on this planet?

A voice rose above the ambient sound of the city. It was a voice of power, and authority, a voice that spoke with absolute clarity and assurance. Xanth was drawn to the voice. Here was a human who could help him, he was sure.

"God is Justice!" the human shouted as Xanth walked up to him. He was a tall, thin man, with a sharp nose and chin. He was dressed in ragged blue pants and a shirt and light jacket not in much better shape. He clutched a black book in his hands, hugged it as if holding onto it for his very life. He was not entirely shaven, as if he ran a razor over alternate parts of his face each day. "God is salvation!" His voice rang out over the hurrying crowds that completely ignored him. His appearance did not inspire much confidence, but the absolute surety of what he was saying made Xanth think that he was a man who knew what was what.

"Excuse me, sir..." Xanth began, but the tall human didn't turn to look at him at all.

"You will get your just desserts in the house of the lord!" the man shrieked above the hum and clatter of the city. This definitely confirmed Xanth's opinion that this was the right man to talk to. Dessert! It was the first mention of food he had heard on Earth.

Xanth raised his voice to try and pierce the man's self-absorption. "Excuse me sir! I'm very hungry! Is the House of the Lord a restaurant? Where is it?"

Finally the man heard Xanth and looked around. He was looking at normal human height, though, and didn't see who had addressed him. Xanth had to say, "I'm down here. Sir. I just need to know where your restaurant is."

The man lowered his gaze and with one look at Xanth he backed up and sucked in his breath. "A demon! Come to test me!" he said, considerably less loudly than his earlier tone.

"I really need help, if you could, sir. I'm from outer space, what you would call an alien. I came here to be in the Movies, but nothing has gone right and I just need to find some food, so if you could direct me to this House of the Lord place, I'd..."

"Back!" the man shouted, producing a piece of wood from under his shirt, or rather, two pieces, crossed in an X shape. "Get behind me, Satan!" The man was clearly frightened.

"My name is Xanthan Gumm," Xanth said, not seeing any need to follow the man's instructions. He couldn't talk to the man from behind him. "I need help to find the House of the Lord." The tall man paused and some of the fear faded from his face. "Is it possible?" he asked himself. "Have I been given the mission of bringing this lowly Satan-spawn back to God?"

Not knowing if he was supposed to say anything, Xanth didn't. The man leaned forward, toward him, still keeping the wooden X-thing between them. "If you are sent by the Prince of Lies to deceive me, beware the wrath of God. If you are truly repentant and wish it so, I will instruct you." Finally, he seemed to be agreeing to tell Xanth how to get to his restaurant.

"Uh, yes, please do instruct me." Xanth's stomach growled. He smiled at the human, anticipating a nice big meal. "I heard what you said about just desserts." He told the man. "I would rather start with a main course, but if dessert is all you have, that's fine."

The man frowned and looked uncertain. "I don't know what your babblings mean, devil spawn. Speak plainly and tell me you repent before the lord."

Xanth would tell this man whatever he wanted to get some food. "Sure. I repent. Whatever that is. Who is the Lord? Is he the chef?"

"YOU SPEAK IN RIDDLES! YOU ARE SATAN HIMSELF! GET THEE AWAY FROM ME!" The tall man shouted. Xanth was so shocked he turned and ran around the corner. He leaned against the wall of the building and tried to think straight. Of all the strange human behavior he had witnessed this was the strangest. He couldn't believe what had happened to him since coming to Earth. He was lost on a planet of insane people! After a while he managed to calm down enough to poke his head around the corner and see if the tall man was still there. He was. He had gone back to shouting at the people scurrying by him, clutching his book and lost in his pronouncements.

Xanth edged out past the corner, intending to cross the street and get as far away from the tall maniac as he could. He could still hear the man's voice as he stood at the curb waiting to cross. "Christ said eat this bread, for it is my flesh, drink this wine, for it is my blood," the man shouted at no one and everyone. Xanth stood rooted on he curb, not crossing even though the light had changed. He was suddenly angry. All he had asked for was directions to the House of the Lord restaurant. The tall man must be trying to get customers for it, or why else was he standing on the street shouting? Then why wouldn't he tell Xanth where it was? He turned and marched on the imposing figure.

"All I wanted was directions to your restaurant!" Xanth shouted. "I'm a visitor to your planet and I don't think I deserve to be yelled at! You chase me away but you're still shouting about bread! I'm really hungry and I want to know where to find the House of the Lord!"

The tall human turned a furious gaze on Xanth. "I told you to flee before the wrath of God, devil! Do not babble to me about a restaurant! I am not talking about a restaurant! I am talking about our Lord Jesus Christ!"

Xanth paused. Was it possible he had made a mistake? Was the man really not advertising a restaurant? If not, why was he shouting about food? "Look," he said, "just tell me plainly if you are advertising a restaurant or not. If you are, tell me where it is, and if you aren't, then I'll go away. All right?"

"For the last time, demon! I am not saying anything about any restaurant!" the man shouted so loudly that several passersby glanced at him before hurrying on. "I am saving the souls of these wretches, telling them the one true word of God!"

"Fine." Xanth said. "That's all you had to tell me. You don't have a restaurant, that's not what you're talking about, that's all I needed to know. Okay. I'll leave now." Xanth turned his back on the crazy human and marched away. If the man wasn't talking about a restaurant, Xanth couldn't make any sense of what he was talking about, but that was not Xanth's problem. He would leave the man alone and find a sane human to talk to. If there was one.

Once again back at the corner where he had paused earlier, Xanth didn't know what to do. He heard the voice of the tall man behind

him, resuming his shouting. Xanth tried to ignore it. He still heard,
"Our Lord performed many miracles..." but he only looked away. He
heard, "The miracle of walking on water..." but he didn't pay any
attention at all. He was trying to think. What was he going to do next?
He had to find some food. He was starving.
Then the tall crazy human shouted. "The miracle of the loaves and
the fishes..." Xanth couldn't ignore that. The man was doing it again!
Shouting about food, as if he was purposely taunting Xanth and his
growling stomach! He wheeled back to the crazy man and ran
towards him. "Why didn't you tell me you have fish sandwiches? I
love fish sandwiches! Please give me one! Please! I am so hungry!"
The tall man just raised one foot and kicked Xanth in the chest,
sending him reeling back and crashing against a signpost. Xanth
gasped, trying to catch his breath. So the man wasn't going to give
him a fish sandwich, he wasn't going to tell him where a restaurant
was, and had resorted to physical force to repel him! All humans were
violent lunatics!

Stumbling down the street, still gasping for breath, Xanth regretted
more than ever his trip to this horrible planet. The humans sharing the
sidewalk with him gave him a wide berth. He walked, crossing
streets, walking up and down the city blocks, not knowing or caring
where he was going. As his lungs became more able to gather air and
the pain of the kick began to fade, Xanth had a thought. Was it
possible that the tall crazy man was talking about religion? Religion
wasn't completely unknown in galactic civilization. Many planets had
some variety of it. It was hard for anyone to remain a fanatic about it
if they lived in Galactic Central, where they were exposed to the
belief systems of many thousands of other cultures.

Come to think of it, Xanth had once seen a humanoid person
standing at the entrance of Galactic Park, doing pretty much what the
tall man had been doing, shouting nonsense phrases with complete
certainty. That person had been shouting things like "We are the
People of the Egg! We are the Children of Time!", instead of "God is
salvation!", but the basic idea was the same. Thinking about it further,
Xanth realized he had seen references to these God and Jesus Christ
characters in The Movies.

444444444

What an idiot he had been! He had mistaken a religion for a restaurant! No wonder the man was so angry! Xanth walked along the street, stomach still growling, mentally punishing himself for his stupidity. He would never succeed on Earth if he made such dumb mistakes.

A smell stopped Xanth dead in his tracks. It was a delicious smell. Some kind of meat was cooking, and there were other smells too that made his stomach growl even louder. Xanth looked around. Where could the smell be coming from? There were humans walking by him, vehicles driving down the street, and buildings all around.

Then he thought he knew. A short distance ahead of him was a sign that said WILLY WALDO'S. The W's in the name were two stylized loops. As Xanth watched, a man bustled out of the door of the place carrying a paper bag with W printed on it.

This was it! He had found a restaurant! He ran to the door of WILLY WALDO'S and pulled on one of the handles. The door opened! The wonderful smells came out and engulfed him. His stomach was ready to get some food, glorious food! Xanth ran into the building. There were people sitting at little tables all around him, and they were eating! Xanth ran to a man who was standing in the middle of the restaurant, wearing bright clothing with the stylized W all over it. "Please sir!" he said to the man. "How do I get some food!"

The human said nothing. "Please, I can smell it all around me, there has to be food here!" Xanth almost shouted at him. The man just smiled a broad smile and held a hand up jauntily, neither moving nor speaking. Xanth was mad at first, but it didn't take him long to figure something out. This wasn't a real human at all. It was a statue, made of plastic. It couldn't move or talk. Xanth reached out and tapped on the man's leg to be sure. Yes. Plastic.

This was odd, but then everything he had encountered on Earth was odd. The man the statue portrayed was even odder. He was up on a pedestal, something Xanth should have noticed before. The clothing he was wearing, or rather, that was shaped in plastic to form his outer shell, was in extremely bright colors, red, yellow, and blue. Xanth hadn't seen anyone outside wearing anything that bright. Even stranger, his face was dead white except where bright red surrounded his mouth, and his nose was bright red and as round as a ball.

Of all the things that he had seen in The Movies, all the inexplicable weirdness of human culture, Xanth was sure he'd never seen anything like this. The idea of a statue up on a pedestal stirred some memories, though. What kind of human was so revered that statues of them were built and placed in public buildings?

Then everything fell together. His earlier encounter with the religious fanatic, and some things he had seen in various Movies, made him realize. This statue was meant to portray a religious leader. He had wandered into some strange kind of church, and almost made the same mistake he had made before, of mistaking a religion for a restaurant. How stupid he would have felt if he had done that again!

However, the wonderful smells of food still surrounded him. This church must practice food preparation as part of its rituals. How could he get them to give him some? The obvious answer was to make them think he was a member of their religion.

Looking again at the statue, Xanth noticed that WILLY WALDO was written on the pedestal. So this strange religious figure was Willy Waldo. All right, he would just combine that name with some of the things that the tall crazy man had said, and he would be eating in a few moments. He could hardly wait. He marched up to the altar of the church. Two young women stood behind it. One of them gave a plate of food to a man who took it and moved away towards the tables. The other one glanced at him then looked surprised.

Not giving her time to speak, Xanth spread his arms in his best fanatical religious type gesture and said as loud as he could, "Willy Waldo is Salvation!"

Chapter Nine

"TEN HUT!"

General Moore stood at attention. Eyes front, chest out. He barely dared to breath.

"You sniveling maggot. You putrid, wretched excuse for a soldier. How dare you appear before me in this condition."

General Les S. Moore, with three stars on his collar, commander of thousands of troops, a man who struck fear in the hearts of his men, stood as rigidly as he could possibly manage. His drill instructor looked him up and down with a gaze that radiated contempt.

"You are a foul stench, a stain, a stinking fungus on the fine military traditions of this country. I only have one thing to say to a useless pus hole like you..."

General Moore waited for it. The pauses were the worst part.

A shrill whistle came from the next room. "...sit down and have some tea." Mrs. Moore said.

The general wiped his forehead with his handkerchief and sat down. While his mother went into the kitchen for the teapot he buttoned the offending left breast pocket that had set her off. How could he have forgotten to check everything before entering into his mother's presence? Another thing to blame on the damned alien. He never would have been so sloppy if he hadn't had the alien on his mind.

Mrs. Moore came back in the living room bearing the steaming teapot. She poured into two tiny, flowery teacups. General Moore picked his up and inhaled steam. His mother settled herself on the sofa. She was a small woman bent over with a dowager's hump, with sharp black eyes, hair pulled back into a bun, and a chin that was a scale model of her son's.

"So the commies finally lobbed one at us, eh? Did you give 'em what for?"

"It wasn't the commies, mother."

43

Robin Reed

Mrs. Moore put her teacup down on the doily-covered coffee table. "Don't be so naive, son. Even if it came from Mexico or Angola or one of them God forsaken places you know the commies were behind it."

Les Moore just sighed and gazed into his tea. Maybe he would see his future in there, like how the hell he was going to get out of his mother's house.

"I get it," Mrs. Moore said, "you're wanting to tell me about how the commies gave up, that there's no Soviet Union anymore, that we won the Cold War. Is that it?"

"It's true, damnit." Les couldn't help but say. "It's all true. I don't know what I can say to make you believe it."

"Watch your language in this house. It's disinformation. They're just waiting for us to drop our guard, and then, wham!"

"I'd like to wham you." Les muttered into his teacup.

"What was that?"

"Nothing, Mother. Look, the thing you saw today was not a Russian missile. It was a ship. A UFO. From outer space."

Mrs. Moore narrowed her eyes. "You mean the Russkies are sending spaceships after us now? I knew that Sputnik thing was a plot to drop poison on us. I wrote a letter to Ike about it, too. He never answered, so he must have known about it all along."

He was two minutes into this conversation with his mother, exactly at the point he usually gave up and went along with whatever she said. So that's exactly what he did. "Yes, Mother," he said. "The Russians must have sent it."

"I told you so. So when are you going to run for President?"

At two and a half minutes, the conversation always turned to when he was going to run for President.

"I'm still, uh, making contacts, um, building support."

"Make it soon, son. I want to live to see my boy in the White House."

She was ninety-two and showed no signs of fading. General Moore was sure she would live to see the colonization of Mars.

"You know, Mother, military candidates haven't done all that well recently. Powell won't run and Clark lasted about two minutes."

44

Mrs. Moore squinted, trying to remember those names. When she failed, she came back with her usual answer. "There was Ike," she said.

"Things have changed a lot since Ike."

"What never changes is that we need a strong President." Mrs. Moore declared. "That Kennedy boy is weak. And Catholic. Never thought I'd see the day."

So she was up to Kennedy today. Sometimes she went up as far as Nixon, and the only thing she didn't like about him was that he was never in the military.

"The problem is," Les tried to explain, "that we don't have any countries to fight. These days it's just terrorists. You can't hold a proper war with those people. We keep trying, but they just sneak around and won't follow the rules."

"And the Russkies."

"Er, right. The Russkies. But they're lying low these days. Most people believe the, uh, disinformation, so they *think* that the Russians were defeated. I don't have much chance running for President when the war on terror is the best war we can come up with."

Mrs. Moore frowned. "But they lobbed that space thing at us. Isn't that bad enough?"

Les was about to shake his head when an inspiration hit him that would shape his life for years to come. The spaceship that had crashed in the park. Proof of alien life attacking Earth. Proof that the aliens meant to invade. There *was* an enemy worthy of him. An enemy that was as infinite as space itself. There were lots of people who already believed. If he could rally them, convince them that only he, General Les S. Moore, was preparing for the alien invasion that was sure to come, he would have millions of supporters.

He was so excited he stood and struck a heroic pose. "General Les S. Moore," he proclaimed. "Defender of the Earth!"

His mother looked up in surprise. "You mean defender of America." She said.

"Yes, right. America. Mother, I have to go. I have a lot of work to do."

"Willy Waldo Saves!" Xanth shouted, jumping around, doing his best religious fervor impression. "Willy Waldo is our lord and savior!" Using all the religious phrases he'd ever heard, either in Galactic Center or in Earth Movies, Xanth did his best to convince the acolytes in this church that he was one of them and that they should give him some of the food that they were preparing behind the altar. He bounced around, proclaiming at each of the tables, startling the people sitting there. He stood in front of the statue of Willy Waldo, the brightly colored religious icon with the orange hair and round red nose.

Two people in Willy Waldo's were paying particular attention to Xanth. One was four-year-old Martin Carter, who thought the little man who was running around and shouting was really funny. He laughed and pointed. His mother frowned. "Don't look, Marty." she said. "He's some kind of weirdo." Marty looked anyway. They were sitting at the table closet to the clown statue. Marty always wanted to sit next to Willy, because he saw him on TV and Willy did all kinds of magical things.

The other person really looking at Xanth, instead of looking away and pretending he wasn't there, as most people in a big city do when someone strange is causing a scene, was Alexander Warner. He was thirty-two, and had come into the Willy Waldo's to spend his last two dollars. He had no idea where he was going to get any more money, but he was spent in more ways than just financially. He was lost, unsure of anything, looking for something, anything, to make his life meaningful.

Alex had seen many religious proselytizers in his time. Just a few blocks away he had passed a tall man shouting out Bible phrases. None of it seemed to be the right thing for Alex. He knew if he found the right thing, the philosophy or religion that made sense to him, he would follow it absolutely.

Xanth wasn't having much luck getting some food. He approached the altar. The priests and priestesses, who were young humans in identical clothing and hats, stood back and looked a little scared. "Willy Waldo is our savior!" he said to them. Then, "Willy Waldo will grant us eternal life!" Nothing made them get some food for him.

One of the priestesses called out, "Tony!"
A moment later a large man in a suit and tie came out from the back of the church. He was large in all ways. Obviously he ate a lot of the food, and he seemed to be in charge. Surely he would give some food to Xanth.
"What's going on out here?" he growled. The young priestess pointed at Xanth.
"Willy Waldo saves!" Xanth said, sure that Tony would be impressed and help him.
"Get the hell out of here." Tony said.
"Willy Waldo is the key to heavenly rapture!" Xanth pulled that one out his memory from some Movie he had seen.
"I'll call the cops if you don't get out right now." Tony was really angry. "This is not the place for that crap."
"I have a personal relationship with Willy Waldo? Willy Waldo is my savior?" Xanth hesitated. Tony wasn't doing anything to get some food ready. The priests and priestesses just stared at him.
Alex Warner watched all this from the back. The little man with the pointy ears seemed so sure of himself. Still, declaring a fast food clown to be the savior was just about the silliest religious pitch Alex had ever heard.
Marty Carter decided on the spur of the moment that his cheeseburger looked icky and picked up a little paper tub of ketchup, He was sticking his tongue in it and licking up all the ketchup when his mother saw him. "Marty! That's disgusting!" She grabbed Marty's hand and tried to take the little tub of ketchup away from him. They fought over it for a second before the tub flew up into the air, amazingly far, and hit the plastic figure of Willy Waldo right in the left eye. The tub fell off, leaving a smear of ketchup dripping down from the statue's eye.
"Call the cops." Tony said. One of the young priests scurried towards the back to comply. "If you're not out of here by the time they come, you freak, you're going to jail." Tony folded his arms. "You're interfering with the legitimate business of this establishment."

Xanth was defeated. His best efforts to convince them he was a member of their religion had failed. He decided to just give up and beg for some food.

"Please. I'm so hungry. I just wanted some of that food you're cooking. It smells so good. I haven't eaten since I came to Earth. I thought Stephen Spielberg would meet me and sign me to a Movie contract. Nothing's gone right since I got here and I am so hungry and please please please give me some food!"

Alex couldn't hear what the little man was saying now, but he saw him kneel as he talked to the manager of the restaurant. Alex had to admire such conviction, such surety, even if it was about something crazy. A woman and her little boy headed out of the restaurant, blocking Alex's view for a second.

"Get the hell out of here." Tony said. "This is a restaurant, not a church."

Xanth groaned to himself. He had done it again. First he had mistaken a religion for a restaurant, then he had mistaken a restaurant for a religion. He had never imagined things would be so confusing on Earth. He wasn't going to get any food from these people, either. All those good smells coming from the back and they wouldn't give him any. His stomach growled.

"All right." Xanth said. "I'm sorry." He turned and walked slowly towards the door. He hated to walk away from those delicious smells, but he would have to find food elsewhere.

The short religious nut walked past Alex and out the door. Whatever had happened, he had given up his preaching. Probably the manager had called the cops on him. He was certainly an odd-looking fellow, with his yellowish skin and pointed ears. Saddled with those kinds of birth defects, Alex supposed he too would have to find something to believe in.

Alex wanted to believe in something, find a way to make a pointless life bearable, but he was a skeptic. He needed proof of some kind. He stood up and picked up his tray. The closest garbage can was over by the clown statue. Alex went over to it and dumped his trash off his tray, then placed the tray on top.

He was about to turn when he noticed something funny. There was something on the face of the clown. It wasn't there before, Alex was sure. Not that he'd looked closely, but he'd walked by the figure before and hadn't seen anything.

Walking right up to Willy Waldo, Alex saw the orange hair, the bright red mouth, the little hat with the flower coming out of it. He saw Willy's plastic smile. But he also saw something else. Something that belied the clown's happy expression.

Alex Warner fell to his knees. Here it was. Proof. Proof that the little man was right. Proof that there was something real to believe in.

The statue of Willy Waldo was crying blood.

Chapter Ten

"First day on the job, eh kid?" Sergeant Wilcox asked. He turned his head and spat out the window of the cruiser. "Boy, I remember my first day."

The rookie, Quentin Stokes, nodded. The shirt of his brand new uniform felt a little tight. Maybe he should have asked for a larger size. He was sweating and nervous.

"Yup, back then I sure was green." Sergeant Wilcox said. "I even thought that people are sometimes good. I thought I was gonna save the innocent citizens of the city from the bad guys. Can you believe that?"

Stokes believed that, for that was pretty much the reason he had joined the force.

"I didn't know what I know now. Everyone is some kind of scumsucker. No such thing as a good person. Just creeps who haven't been caught yet. You'll learn, the world is a barf bucket, you bet. Every single goddamn person on the face of the earth is just one form of bottom feeding suckhole or another. You want some gum?"

Stokes was beginning to feel ill. Sitting next to the massive Sergeant Wilcox and listening to his philosophy was getting to him. He declined the offered pack of Juicy Fruit. "Come on, Sarge, there's some good people."

Wilcox belched. Juicy Fruit smell filled the car. "You'll learn, kiddo, you'll learn. I used to think like you do. The first time I arrested a little old lady for prostitution I began to realize the truth."

Thinking for a while as they tooled down State Street, watching all the people hurry through their busy city lives, Stokes thought he had an example that would stop the sergeant's tirade. "What about your mother? Everyone loves his mother."

"The old whore was my mom." Wilcox replied. "She was shaking her booty down on Lower Wacker Drive. I found out that's how she supported me and my three brothers after Dad left. She was something, my mom. The bitch."

Officer Stokes began to knead his temples. He was coming down with quite a headache.

The radio crackled and a dispatcher's voice said, "All units in the vicinity of LaSalle and Washington report to Willy Waldo's restaurant. See the manager about a disturbance. He reports a robbery attempt by a boy in a mask."

"A boy?" Officer Stokes asked. "Why would a kid do something like that?"

The sergeant hit the accelerator and they sped towards the location of the disturbance. "Oh, sure," he said. "Kids commit murder, robbery, all the major crimes. I arrested an eight-year-old once who ran a car theft ring. I heard about a three-year-old in Ohio who killed his whole family with an ax. Kids are no better than the rest of the world's human scum."

The patrol car made the five-block drive in under a minute, flashing the motto "Protect and Serve" painted on its side at the citizens it nearly ran over. In that short time, Sergeant Wilcox told Officer Stokes four more horror stories about crimes committed by children. Stokes' headache pounded fiercely and his mind was full of images of sweet little children mugging, robbing, and murdering. Then he saw someone suspicious on the street.

"There he is!" shouted Officer Stokes. Wilcox hit the brakes and the car screeched to a halt. Stokes was out the door, weapon drawn. He ran up to the suspect, cocked his pistol and shouted, "Freeze!"

The suspect said, "Ga?"

Stokes looked around, his head clearing. He noticed he was pointing his pistol at a baby in a stroller. A woman standing next to the stroller turned around. "What is it, officer?" she asked.

"Um, nothing, Ma'am. Just a, er, training exercise." He hastily holstered his weapon. Coming up from behind him, Sergeant Wilcox put a hand on Stokes' shoulder.

"Calm down, son, we don't want to shoot any babies unless we have probable cause."

"I'm sorry, sir. I got carried away."

"Happens to every rookie. Don't worry about it."

Stokes looked back at the mother and the baby. How could he have believed that either one of them could be a criminal? He shook his head and followed Sergeant Wilcox into the Willy Waldo's.

Watching them go, Anna Schuyler breathed a sigh of relief. She had been sure for a second that the young cop was going to find the kilo of cocaine hidden under little Billy in the stroller. She smiled and pushed the stroller down the street.

Xanthan Gumm watched from an alley entrance across the street. He had left the restaurant in a complete state of confusion and despair. He was very hungry. He was thousands of parsecs from home. The planet Earth had not welcomed him with open arms and a Movie contract. He had no idea in all of the galaxy what to do next.

He watched as the police car pulled up and the two men in uniform went in to the Willy Waldo's. Sure, *they* could get food whenever they wanted it. Police were the good guys in many Movies, though the uniformed ones were usually backup support for the wise-cracking black detective from Detroit or the white and black team of detectives who managed to blow everything up. Maybe these two were working on a Movie right now. Xanth decided to go and talk to them, see if they could help him. Maybe they could give him some of their food, too.

Xanth stepped out of the alley determined to talk to the policemen. Then he tripped over a foot. His face hit the pavement and one elbow managed to get twisted under him. He lay there for a minute, just waiting for the universe to humiliate him some more.

Instead, a voice said, "Are you all right, kid?"

Managing to turn over and sit up, Xanth saw the owner of the foot he had tripped over looking anxiously at him. The man was shabbily dressed and unshaven, but looked otherwise disreputable. He was sitting on the sidewalk with his back against a brick wall.

"Whew," the man said. "Either I'm more drunk than I thought, or you are one ugly kid."

Xanth shook his head. "I'm not a kid. I'm an alien. From outer space. I came to Earth to be in the Movies."

"Right. Can you spare some change? I'm really hungry."

Xanth was normally quite a level-headed fellow. He could be counted on to keep his head when everyone else lost theirs. He had never gotten really screamingly angry in his life. Until this moment. "YOU'RE hungry? You think YOU'RE hungry?" Xanth shouted. "I haven't eaten since I was outside the orbit of Pluto! I'm so hungry I could eat a miniature flerm worm!"

The disheveled man interjected, "If you're that hungry, I'd think you could eat a GIANT flerm worm."

"Don't be an idiot, earthling! Miniature flerm worms are a mile long! Giant flerm worms are the size of a planet! How stupid could you be!" Xanth paused, breathing hard. "Where was I?"

"You're so hungry..."

"Right. I came to Earth to be a Movie star but instead I've been kicked, yelled at, chased, and even worse, ignored!" Xanth hopped up on the man's chest and grabbed him by the lapels. "You Earthlings are so dense! Not one of you can see that I'm an alien! I'm not from here! I came from outer space! I have yellow skin! Pointy ears! Webs between my fingers! I'm a semi-aquatic life form from a lost planet who works as a framadort converter in Galactic Central, where I saw many Earth Movies and decided to come here and become a Movie star! You got all that, Earth dimwit? Is it clear to you now? Do you understand me NOW!? Huh? Do you!?"

The man thought for a minute. "So if you're an alien," he said, "what are your powers?"

"Powers? I don't have any powers." Xanth stepped off of the man and let him sit up.

"Then I don't believe you're a real alien."

"What do powers have to do with being an alien?"

Getting on his feet, the man said, "All aliens have powers. *E.T.* could levitate stuff and heal things. Starman brought a dead deer back to life. The Cocoon aliens made old folks frisky again, Mork could do all kinds of things. The Species lady could kill with a French kiss."

53

Standing now, the shabbily dressed man tried to think of more examples.

Xanth couldn't fault his logic. In Movies aliens could do a lot of strange stuff. He'd never seen anyone in Galactic Central do any of those things, though. He tried to think of something that would make this man think he had powers.

"Oh, yeah, and Yoda was a great Jedi Knight, with lots of powers. So what are yours?"

All Xanth could come up with was something that had impressed his teachers in school. "I know the multiplication tables by heart up to twelve times twelve." he said.

Sergeant Wilcox and Officer Stokes had just stepped out of the fast food restaurant and were conferring about what to do. The sergeant said to forget it; the kid was long gone and hadn't done any real harm anyway. Stokes wanted to pursue the matter.

"We could put out an E.P.A.," he said.

"A what?" Wilcox asked. "Environmental Protection Agency?"

"No, an 'Every Person Alert.'"

"You're thinking of A.P.B."

"What's that stand for?"

"All People Bulletin."

"That still doesn't sound right..." Stokes said, but then the two policemen were interrupted by an old bum who erupted out of an alley across the street, looking wild-eyed and shouting, "Hey everybody! There's a real alien from outer space here! Over here! A real alien!"

Chapter Eleven

Xanth was alone. More alone than he had ever been before. He had never been very social. He didn't know what to do at parties. When occasionally the workers at the framadort plant had gone out after work and invited him along, he had sat in whatever bar or restaurant they ended up in and listened to them talk on and on about their relationships, or how the local team was doing in the basefootbasketball playoffs, and wished he was in his nice comfortable room watching Earth Movies.

They talked so much about love and sex and finding the right person. Xanth had nothing to contribute to these conversations. Except for his three parents, Xanth was the only member of his species that he knew. He didn't know if he'd ever find one other member of his species, much less two compatible mates.

Now, he was even more alone than he had been in Galactic Central. Now he was on a small, horrible planet where he couldn't find any food, everything was confusing, and they actually thought Bob Dylan could sing.

Plus, he had sat down in an alley, next to a huge metal container that smelled very bad, and found that the spot he chose to sit in was wet. And squishy. While he was worrying about that, he heard footsteps. Someone was coming his way.

Xanth pulled his feet up and tried to hide beside the metal container. He didn't want to talk to any more crazy humans. The footsteps got closer and closer. Maybe the human wouldn't notice him.

The man came past the container, looking back and forth. Then he turned and looked right at Xanth. "There you are," he said. It was the shabbily dressed human who had run away screaming that he saw a real alien.

"Go away," Xanth told him.

"My name's Al," the man said, sitting down next to Xanth. "Sorry I ran away like that. I was just so surprised to meet a real alien." "Did you bring those policemen to take me away?" "What? Oh, no, they didn't believe me. They thought I was just a crazy old drunk. Of course, they're right. So you really are an alien, huh? Boy, I've seen every movie with aliens in it." Al paused and took a paper bag out of his pocket. He raised it to his lips and took a swig.

"You like Movies?" Xanth couldn't believe he'd found an Earth person he could talk to.

Al smiled and took another drink. "You bet. Ever since I was a kid. I remember Errol Flynn up there on the screen, he was so great with a sword."

"Was he an alien?"

"No! Ha! What a thought. No, he was just a movie star."

"Yes! That's what I want to be! I came to Earth to be a Movie Star! Just like *E.T.*!"

"Well, you're a long way from Hollywood."

"I am?"

"Couple thousand miles."

"Oh." This information was so deflating that Xanth put his head down and began to cry.

"Hey, hey there," Al said. "It's all right. This place isn't so bad. Gets damn cold in the winter, but it's survivable."

Xanth sniffled, "I didn't come here to survive, I came to be in the M-M-Movies!" His misery overwhelmed him and he cried steadily for about a minute.

When Xanth was about cried out, Al said, "Don't you have a ship? A flying saucer or something? Couldn't you go anywhere on the planet you wanted?"

Xanth shook his head. "Some soldiers took it away."

"Oh, the military got it, eh? Probably taking it to Area 51. Well, don't worry, you can get to Hollywood. Just hitchhike, or bum a ride on a train. It's not that hard."

"Really?" Xanth's nose was stuffed up and he could feel snot dribbling down.

"Here." Al offered him a handkerchief. Or at least Xanth thought it was a handkerchief. It was filthy and obviously Al had blown his own nose in it for years without washing it. Still, Al was the first human to show him any kindness, and he wasn't in a position to be fussy. He found a somewhat clean spot in the old rag and blew into it.

"There you go. You feel better now?"

Xanth nodded. "Except I am really really hungry. Can we go to your house and get some food?"

Al laughed. "House! My house! Boy, you really are from another planet."

"You don't have a house?" Xanth asked.

"My boy, I haven't had a house for over thirty years."

Xanth thought about that. It didn't make sense. He had never lived on a planet, but he had talked to people who did. Planets were strange and unpredictable. "But doesn't water fall out of the sky on this planet? Doesn't the temperature change radically at different times of the solar cycle? You have to have shelter on a planet surface!"

"Some of us just don't have shelter." Al shrugged. "We survive. It's all right, I'm used to it."

"We?" Xanth asked. There are more humans who don't have houses?"

"There are thousands here in Chicago alone. Plenty more in the rest of the country."

"But your government should do something to help you."

"Don't make me laugh. Actually, the government did do one good thing for me."

"What was that?"

"Thirty years ago, I was just a bum. Then in the eighties, when Ronnie was president, they decided to call us 'The Homeless'. Sounds a lot better, doesn't it?"

"I guess so."

"So, you didn't tell me your name."

"I'm sorry. Xanthan Gumm."

"Hmmm. That's a mouthful. Do you have a nickname?"

"I guess you can call me Xanth."

"Pleased to meet you, Xanth." Al stuck out his hand. Xanth looked at it, then remembered the human greeting ritual he had seen in all the Movies. He raised his hand and placed it in Al's. Al gave it a good shake and let it go.

"Were you always homeless?" Xanth asked.

"Hell no. I was once the vice president of a good company, I had a house, a wife, and two kids."

"What happened?"

"Something horrible happened that destroyed my life. I abandoned my home and job and started living on the streets. All because...because..." Now it was Al's turn to start tearing up.

"Because...because..." he blubbered.

"What?" Xanth asked anxiously. "What could be so horrible that it would drive you to leave a comfortable life and live in misery the rest of your life?"

"My company...SOB!...installed MUZAK in the offices!" Al started crying as hard as Xanth had a few minutes before.

Not knowing what exactly Al was talking about, Xanth still tried to console him. He handed him back his handkerchief and Al blew his nose in it with a loud honk.

"I couldn't take it," Al said. "I still go crazy if I hear 'The Girl from Ipanema'." He honked in the handkerchief again.

"I'm still awfully hungry." Xanth said.

"I think I know where we can get something." Al stood up. He took his paper bag out of his pocket and took a long drink from it. "This way." He turned towards the far end of the alley.

Xanth stood up and followed. Al led him on a journey of several blocks, avoiding the populated streets and cutting through alleys as much as possible. Finally, he stopped in an alley very similar to the one they had left.

"There we go." Al pointed to another smelly metal container.

"There we go where?" Xanth asked.

"We're behind a restaurant. They put their garbage in that dumpster."

"So?"

58

"So one man's garbage is another man's feast. The food is great here. The service stinks, though."

Xanth waved his hand in front of his nose. "Everything about this place stinks."

"C'mon, help me get it out of there." Al said, putting his hands under Xanth's arms and lifting.

"Hey! Hey!" Xanth shouted.

"Just look in the dumpster and see what you can find." Al lifted Xanth up to the dumpster. Since he had no choice, Xanth put his feet on the edge of the opening, where one of the two metal lids was open. The stench coming from the inside was enormous.

"Damnit!" Al muttered. "Cops!" He let go of Xanth and crouched next to the dumpster. He could just see the police cruiser passing on the street. Xanth was left teetering on the edge of the dumpster opening. Then he lost his balance and fell into the garbage container with a WHUMP!

"This is just fine," Xanth thought. His face was pushed into something even squishier than whatever he had sat in earlier. His hands were wet. Goo was seeping into his clothing. "This is why I came to Earth. Oh yeah."

Then he heard Al's voice from above. "The cops are gone. Are you all right?"

"Sure. I'm just wonderful." Xanth said. He pushed himself up on his elbow and turned over. "I'm dandy. Marvelous. Perfect." He spit some slime of unknown origin out of his mouth.

"See any food in there?" All stood on tiptoe peering into the dumpster.

"Gee, Al, I'm not familiar with many Earth foods. Can you look at this and tell me what it is?"

Al pushed himself up further. "I can't see anything."

"Come closer."

Al pulled up and tried to look into the dark insides of the dumpster. His feet left the ground and he balanced himself on the lip of the opening. "I still don't see anything."

"How about now?!" Xanth shouted. He grabbed Al by his shirt and pulled as hard as he could. Al gave out a grunt and toppled into the dumpster on top of Xanth.

A moment passed while both human and alien caught their breaths. Then they managed to untangle themselves and sit with their backs to the back of the dumpster. The smell continued to be horrendous.

"So what was that for?" Al asked.

"Just wanted you to have the same joyful experience I'm having." Xanth said. "I'm sorry. I shouldn't get mad at you. It's just that Earth is so different than what I expected."

"Don't worry. We homeless people go through a lot of anger and frustration. And right now, you're about as homeless as you can get. Hey!" Al pointed at something in the dark end of the dumpster. "I think we're in luck!"

Reaching over to where Al pointed, Xanth put his hand on something hard.

"Yes, that's it. Bring it over here. Food, glorious food!" Al said.

Xanth brought the object into the light. It was a square, flat box. "On Earth a cardboard box is food?" he asked.

"There might be a pizza in that box. The restaurant throws them away when someone orders one but doesn't pick it up. Have you ever had pizza?"

All Xanth knew about pizza was that it was often featured in the shortest, most puzzling Movies of all. Galactic scholars had given up making sense of these thirty-second or minute-long Movies in which humans extolled the virtues of various objects. Most Movie fans went to the bathroom, or went to get a snack, while they came on during a regular Movie.

MiniMovies (as they had come to be called) had their fans, though. Fans who collected the short Movies and never watched the longer stories that the MiniMovies were embedded in. They showed MiniMovies over and over again. They claimed that the MiniMovies had a hypnotic power, that they made people who watched yearn for things they could never have. MiniMovie fans had been found wandering the public ways of Galactic Central, looking for some mythological place called "The Mall".

"No," Xanth said. "But if it's food, I'll try it."

"You're in for a treat, my boy. Open the box." Al said.

It took a minute to figure out how to open the box. Finally Xanth figured out that it opened along the thinner, flat sides, with the top acting as an access panel. Inside was an even flatter object, but round instead of square. It had an uneven edge, and a bumpy, yellowish surface studded with irregular rocks of some kind, like the surface of a small moon.

"Can you smell it?" Al asked. "It's cold, but I can still smell it."

Xanth raised the box to his nose. There was a smell. It had trouble getting past the general stench of their surroundings, but it was there, and it wasn't unpleasant.

"Are you sure this is edible?" Xanth asked.

"You betcha." Al replied.

"Ok," Xanth said. He tilted the box towards his mouth. The pizza was pretty big, and its circumference was a lot bigger than his mouth, so Xanth internally disconnected his lower jaw from his upper jaw, and inflated his neck with the special air bladders that his species used for just this purpose. His mouth opened wide, then wider, then a whole lot wider still. To get the fullest extension possible, Xanth then separated the two halves of his upper palate, which made his mouth just wide enough to start sliding the pizza in.

When the pizza stuck to the box, Xanth pushed his tongue out as far as it would go, about three feet, and raised the barbs attached to his tongue that would have been used by his aquatic ancestors to snag a fish and drag it back in. The barbs were blood red and sharp as knives. In this case, it was a pizza instead of a fish, but the purpose was the same. The pizza slid into his mouth in one piece, and the teeth at the back of Xanth's throat started tearing at it and reducing it to pieces that could slide down into his stomach.

Once the pizza was entirely inside him, Xanth started returning to normal. He retracted his tongue, put his upper palate back together, refolded all the skin and tissue that was usually hidden, and then finally reengaged his upper and lower jaws. The air bladders deflated and Xanth's head returned to its normal size.

Then Xanth noticed Al, who had scrambled as far away as he could get in the confines of the dumpster and who was staring in wild-eyed horror at the now-empty pizza box, and at Xanth.

"Oh, I'm sorry," Xanth said. "Did you want some?"

Chapter Twelve

"When you were trying to convince me that you're an alien, why didn't you just do *THAT?*" Al asked. He was leading Xanth down a dingy street away from the business district where they had been earlier.

"Do what?" Xanth was following Al because he was the only human who had been nice in Xanth's whole miserable experience on Earth so far. Al had found some food and Xanth felt much better now. But he wasn't at all sure about where Al was taking him. The street was empty and trash blew around in the wind.

"That thing where you made your head so big." Al said.

Xanth shrugged. "That wasn't anything special. Just a way to eat something big."

"It looked pretty impressive to me. And that tongue. I thought it was a monster in itself, like the baby alien in 'Alien', bursting out of the man's chest."

"Oh yeah! That was so funny!" Xanth said.

"What?"

"And the part where the kosserads eat people! Those are my favorite Earth comedies!"

"What? What are you talking about?"

"The Earth Movies called 'Alien' and 'Aliens' and some others. They were great comedies."

Al walked along for a moment before he spoke. "Uh, Xanth, those were made to be scary movies. The Aliens go around eating people and inserting larvae into them and stuff."

"But that's what's so funny!" Xanth said. "The Aliens are all played by kosserads, the mildest-mannered species in the galaxy. They eat flower nectar on their home planet. In Galactic Central they're all file clerks or florists. Where I come from, everyone laughs at those Movies."

"Huh." Al said. He kicked a soft drink can and it rattled down the street and disappeared under a parked car. "Learn something new every day."

"Sorry I didn't offer you some of the pizza." Xanth said.

"Don't worry. I found that shrimp cocktail."

"Are those shrimp things supposed to have gray fuzz on them and smell that bad?"

"Nah. But food is food. I've had worse."

The alien and the human walked in silence for a while. "Where are we going?" Xanth asked after a while.

"To where I've been sleeping the last few months. It's a big secret, Xanth, so I hope I can trust you. I told you I'm homeless, but these days I do have a roof to sleep under. I found a basement I can get into through a broken window. I have invited a few other people to sleep there too. But if word got out, too many people would want to get in there. And if the owner of the building found out, she'd fix the window and kick us all out."

"I promise not to tell." Xanth said.

"I'm sure you'll like it there." Al said. "Especially after you hear the best part."

"Yeah? What's that?"

Al grinned. "We get to watch movies."

Xanth shrugged. "This is Earth. All you humans do is make Movies or watch them."

Al shook his head. "You have a lot of things to learn about Earth," he said.

They walked quite a ways further before Al indicated that they were getting close. The sunlight was slanting sideways and casting very long shadows of the human and the alien. Xanth was yawning by the time Al turned into an alley. They walked along one side of the alley, where it was dark even though the other side was still brightly lit, then into a narrow space between two buildings. Then Al knelt down on the pavement.

"You have to crawl into this hole and then push the window open." Al instructed. "I'll go first." He slithered into a lower area and then started to disappear through a hole in the wall. When his head and arms vanished, a filthy window with wire worked through it crashed back into place. Xanth hesitated.

"Come on, it's all right." Al's voice came from behind the window. Xanth stepped down into the hole, a rectangular space that was partly filled with trash. He got down on all fours and pushed the window. It swung into the blackness of the basement, then fell back when Xanth let go.

"Are you sure about this?" Xanth asked.

"Sure. Come on in."

The window swung open again with another push. Xanth stuck his head inside. He couldn't see much, so he leaned forward and put out one hand. Actually he leaned too far forward, so that he fell into the basement and hit the cement floor hard.

"Beep Beep Beeeeeeeeeep!" Xanth exclaimed.

Al rushed over and helped Xanth to his feet. "Are you all right?" he asked.

Xanth held his hand to his head, where he had made contact with the floor.

"I guess so."

"Come over here. I'll take a look at your head." Al led Xanth to the other side of the room. He pulled on an overhead chain and a feeble light sprang into being. Al peered at Xanth's head where he had been rubbing it. "You're bleeding a little. Doesn't look too bad, unless alien blood doesn't clot."

"No, it should be all right. Hurts a lot, though." Xanth rubbed the spot some more.

"So you have green blood, just like vulcans, eh?" Al sat on the floor and indicated that Xanth could do the same.

Once settled, Xanth said, "Funny thing about vulcans. No one in Galactic Central has ever heard of them. Or any species that looks like that. They must be from some planet we haven't contacted yet."

Al grinned. "You do have a lot to learn. Vulcans are just actors made up with fake ears."

"But actors are people who perform in Movies."

"Right."

"Human blood in Movies is always red."

"Yes, we humans have red blood."

"So 'actors' aren't human?"

"What? Of course they are. They just pretend to be aliens."

"How can they pretend to have green blood? If you cut them doesn't red blood come out?"

"They use fake blood."

"So they have fake ears and fake blood."

"Yeah."

"And they willingly replace all their red blood with artificial green blood so they can perform their parts."

"No, no. The fake blood is just used for a scene where they're bleeding. It doesn't actually come out of the actors."

"Where does it come from?"

"The person doing the makeup."

"Do makeup persons have green blood?"

Al grimaced. "No! They just make the fake blood for the scene!"

"They make the blood."

"Yes. It's not really blood. Just some syrup and food coloring."

"That wouldn't work. Artificial blood has to mimic the action of real blood in carrying oxygen to the cells..."

"It just has to LOOK like blood!" Al exploded and waved his hands in the air.

Xanth paused. Thought. Then said. "I don't understand."

"Look," Al said, "actors are humans who pretend to be someone else. They play a part. When it looks like they are injured it is just makeup! Fake! It washes off at the end of the day and the actor goes home!"

"Actors...play at being vulcans. At the end of the day, they take off their makeup and go home."

"Right."

"And actors are humans."

"Yes."

"You humans can alter your appearance to pretend to be other species?"

"Sure. Until I met you, I thought all aliens in the movies were humans in makeup and costume."

"That's funny! Ha ha ha! What an idea!" Xanth laughed heartily. Xanth was certainly learning about his new home. Some aliens in Movies were really from Galactic Civilization and some were just humans play-acting. You couldn't take anything in a Movie at face value. He should have realized it, with kosserads being scary people-eaters in Movies and a highly vicious and fearsome vonadian, with its ears of death, pretending to be a cute Earth creature called a mouse.

"I'll never figure out Earth." Xanth finally said dispiritedly. "I should have stayed home and been a framadort converter the rest of my life."

"A what converter?" Al asked.

"A framadort converter. That was my job in Galactic Central. It wasn't so bad, really."

Al looked puzzled. "What's a framadort, and how do you convert it?" he asked.

"Well..." Xanth started, but just then another voice interrupted.

"Help!"

Xanth looked towards the window and saw a shiny metallic head snaking its way into the room. He jumped up. What kind of creature was it? He'd never seen anything like it before!

Al had also gotten to his feet, but he was rushing towards the creature. "Al!" Xanth shouted. "Watch out! It could be dangerous!"

Al just reached up and started helping the thing into the basement. After a moment Xanth could see that it was a human. An old human, somewhat similar to the one he had seen that morning, though that now seemed a very long time ago. A little old lady, dressed in a stained and ripped print dress. The reason that he had thought she was some metallic creature was that she had a thin layer of shiny metal on her head. Wild gray hair stuck out in all directions from under the metallic cap.

The old woman got her feet on the basement floor with Al's help. She straightened up as much as she could and brushed off her dress. She spied Xanth standing in the middle of the room. "What's this?" she asked.

Al introduced them. "Xanth, this is Ginny, one of the people I told you about who sleeps here. Ginny, this is my friend Xanthan Gumm, who I met today. You'll never believe it, but he's a real alien from outer space."

Ginny smiled a big smile that showed that she had once been beautiful. "Finally," she said. "They finally sent someone to help." She walked towards Xanth and looked like she was going to hug him. Xanth stepped back enough to avoid her embrace. Ginny fell to her knees.

"You'll tell them, won't you?" Ginny asked with great sincerity and sorrow. "Please tell them to stop."

"Um...tell who to stop what, ma'am?" Xanth asked.

"The Rigellians. They send it all the time. Over and over. My satellite-blocking hat doesn't work anymore." She touched the metal foil on her head. "Over and over. I hear it all the time. Day and night. The same thing. Over and over."

Xanth was curious. "What do they send? What do you hear?"

"'(Love is Like a) Heat Wave' by Martha and the Vandellas. I been hearing it all the time for years and years. Please tell them to stop...please..."

"I'm so sorry, ma'am," Xanth said. "I'm kind of stuck here. I don't have any way to contact the Rigellians." The old lady dropped her head and collapsed on the basement floor.

Al pulled Xanth over to one corner of the basement. "You have to forgive Ginny. She's been like this for a long time. I should have realized you being an alien and all would set her off. This idea of hers about the Rigellians pumping that song into her head all the time is completely crazy."

"I'll say," Xanth said. "The Rigellians are into the Beatles and the Stones right now, not Motown."

Chapter Thirteen

The Pentagon was closing down for the night. Streams of secretaries and temp workers poured out of the huge defense department headquarters and down the steps, leaving General Moore fighting the current as he tried to enter the building. The Pentagon was the site of General Moore's fondest childhood memories. Actually, it was at the center of all of his childhood memories, and most of them weren't that fond. His mother had never allowed him a toy, a game, an activity, or a thought that wasn't devoted to the defense of his country. She drilled him on the miniature parade ground in the backyard of the building where they lived, taught him to take apart, clean and reassemble an M16 rifle in thirty seconds flat, and trained him in bayonet techniques. Then when he turned three years old, she moved on to more advanced topics.

The young Les Moore learned military history, from Alexander the Great to Eisenhower. He learned tactics, weapons, artillery, land and air defense, and how to inflate the estimated cost of a defense contract five-fold.

Finally getting through the doors of the structure that billed itself as the world's largest office building, General Moore found himself in the hallowed halls where he had spent so much time as a child. His mother had brought him there to take the official tour every summer vacation. And every Christmas break, spring break, and occasionally when his school was closed for a teacher work day. It wasn't easy to get from Chicago to Washington and back, packing in a full tour of the Pentagon, in one day, but by God, Mrs. Moore was up to it.

In fact, there was a tour group, the last of the day, just finishing up as General Moore passed through the lobby. It was the usual group of school kids and retirees, looking a bit shell-shocked after the vast distances they had covered and all the lists of people who had won the Congressional Medal Of Honor they had seen. The tour was organized into the three branches of the service, four if you counted the Marines, who were officially part of the Navy but didn't like to admit it.

General Moore could close his eyes and give himself the tour from memory. There was the Eisenhower Corridor, which of course honored the great general and President. The Pentagon generally had a dim view of Presidents, considering them civilian wussies who should never have been put in charge of the military, but when a President was one of their own, they honored him the best they knew how. But the place he had spent so many hours as a kid was the MacArthur Corridor. General MacArthur was the ultimate hero in his family. He could recite the facts of MacArthur's life before he could read. Every Halloween, he had dressed up as MacArthur, complete with corn-cob pipe. In fact, the pipe was always filled with tobacco and lit. Mrs. Moore mother was a stickler for authenticity.

General Moore couldn't help glancing towards the west side of the building, where this beloved structure had been greviously wounded on September 11, 2001. That section was all repaired now, but the general would always carry the grief and rage he felt on that day.

He pressed through the throngs of departing tourists and civilian workers, and found his way to a discreet, unmarked door. He used his ID card to enter, descended a staircase, and brought his thoughts to bear on the confusing events of that very afternoon.

He had been supervising the removal of the alien craft and the tail section of one of the fighters which had crashed in midair. A squad of soldiers was assigned to comb the area for small pieces of debris. It had to be done thoroughly, but also quickly, before the media could get too many pictures of the operation. The lakefront in such a large city was hardly the ideal location for such a salvage operation. He really didn't see how it was going to be kept quiet.

Then a flatbed tow truck had pulled up and a man and a woman in brown suits got out of it. They showed Les a badge and something the man was carrying made a whining noise.

This was the confusing part. Les had gone off to visit his mother, leaving the crash site when the alien ship was still there. He had abandoned his mission before the job was done. That was just not like him. Could those mysterious agents, the man and woman in brown, have done something to him? A quick visit to the lakefront site had confirmed that all evidence of the crash was gone. General Les S. Moore was not a man to take something like this lightly. Someone had messed with his memory and taken the evidence of the alien invasion right out from under his nose. He meant to find out who.

On the flight to Washington, he had decided that his experience that afternoon lent credence to the plan he had begun to formulate at his mother's house. His mother was crazy, but she had given him the idea of his life. He knew he had to run with it. The strange agents dressed in brown might even be further evidence that his plan was worth pursuing.

He reached the bottom of the staircase and found two Marines on duty. They stood on either side of a massive metal door. They saluted, but neither one said a word. They knew that he should know what to do. They also were well-armed and knew what to do if he failed.

General Moore pressed his thumb on a glass plate mounted next to the door. A light scanned it. There was a moment's pause. A click sounded, then the huge steel door swung smoothly open. General Moore passed through and the door quietly closed behind him.

He walked down a hall lined with doors. Here was where the secret business of the Pentagon was conducted, far from the tourists above. He passed the secret bureaus that handled design of weapons that were so far ahead of their time that they would surely safeguard the Pentagon's budget for years to come.

He passed the suite of rooms where the highest-ranking members of the military, along with their most ardent supporters in Congress, could meet to party their guts out and never risk being discovered by angry wives or inquisitive reporters.

He passed the cell where they kept the real Fidel Castro, who had years ago decided to give up communism if the U.S. would just let his country get wired for cable. It had been the height of the Cold War, and Cuba needed to be maintained as a nearby reminder of the Red Peril. A lookalike had been substituted and the real Fidel was spending the rest of his life in his cell. He was happy, though, because he had full cable with all the premium channels. General Moore glanced through the bars on the cell's door, and saw the aging former communist happily watching the Mary Tyler Moore marathon on TV Land.

Then the general reached his destination. A sign next to one door read "Committee to Find a New Enemy".

The general opened the door and entered the room. In the center was a large conference table that was covered with maps and papers. Against the far wall was a bank of computers that were used to research all the trouble spots in the world. On the right wall was an oil portrait of Admiral Sanderson's poodle, Oopsy.

This small room was at the center of the Pentagon's future. If the greatest minds that all three services could muster could not find a new, permanent enemy for the United States to face, then the Pentagon and the mightiest military ever seen on the face of the Earth might be reduced by short-sighted politicians to merely a token defense force, a skeleton crew meant to keep the armed forces in existence in name only. This could not be allowed to happen.

General Moore thrust his mighty chin high and in his excitement exclaimed, "I have done it! I have discovered the ultimate enemy!"

"Good for you," a single voice replied.

The general glanced all about the room. In his enthusiasm he had failed to notice that there was only one person present. "Oh, I thought there would be a meeting in progress." he said.

"They all went home early. I'm just here finishing up some work."

"Ah, well, perhaps I should save my idea for tomorrow."

"No, no, I'd like to hear it. It sounds important."

General Moore swelled up with pride. "I believe it will save the Armed Forces of the United States for the foreseeable future." he said.

"Well then, shoot." the other person said.

"Right. As you know, this committee has been charged with replacing the now-defunct Soviet Union as the ultimate enemy of our country. In the heyday of the Cold War, we were given billions of dollars every year to prepare for a battle that never came."

"Go on."

"Even though we here in the Pentagon knew that the Russians were less of a threat than the general public was lead to believe, we felt the threat itself was good for the country. It created jobs at defense contractors and military bases all over the country. It was good for the economy. It also gave the people a focus, someone outside to train their hate on. Since the Soviet Union collapsed, not only have all those jobs disappeared, the people have started to turn their hatred inwards, upon each other. This has led to many tragic events."

"Good summation." the person being addressed stated.

"We need to find a new enemy, a new evil empire, someone to hate."

"We haven't done that badly, what with the War on Terror, Afghanistan and Iraq."

General Moore shook his head. "How long can that last? Thirty, forty years? Today I was involved in a salvage operation involving what I strongly believe to be a craft of extraterrestrial origin. Assuming that it is proof of alien life, I feel that we have found the next enemy. Aliens! Ugly, bloodsucking, tentacled, hideous aliens! If we prepared a massive campaign of readiness to meet the new threat, it would mean an endless Cold War! Imagine the benefits to the military and the society as a whole!"

"But what if there are no aliens?"

"After today I am sure that there are." General Moore was really getting into the meat of his argument. "But it doesn't matter. It might be better if there aren't. No one could ever prove that aliens DON'T exist. In the meantime we would have built planetary defense systems, military bases on the moon, nuclear missiles orbiting the Earth that could be launched at the enemy at a moment's notice! And if the enemy never comes, that means the defense contracts never end!"

"Brilliant!" General Moore's audience of one clapped with enthusiasm. "Magnificent!"

The general felt himself fill with determination and the desire to put the plan into motion immediately. He was sure that he alone had saved America, returned America to the glorious, paranoid, foreigner-hating nation that it was meant to be.

"You really have to present that to someone more important than a cleaning lady." Mrs. McGillicudy said, taking her mop out of its bucket and applying it to the floor. "But personally, I think it's a winner."

Chapter Fourteen

The little basement room was dark, with one pool of light under the bare light bulb. Al and Xanth had talked for hours. Xanth had told Al all about life in Galactic Central, and Al had told some of the story of his life before becoming homeless.

Several more of Al's friends came through the window to spend the night. Besides Ginny, who huddled in a corner and occasionally pulled her aluminum foil hat tighter on her head, there was an old man who said his name was Puddintame. Then he stated that if Xanth asked again, he would tell him the same. Asking someone's name once seemed quite sufficient, so Xanth just let the man wander off and lie down.

Then a portly man wearing a sweater came in. Al introduced him as Robert. "Robert is a critic," Al said.

"Really? Are you a Movie critic?" Xanth asked.

"No," Robert replied.

Xanth was only vaguely aware of the existence of critics. They seemed to be a type of human that told other humans what Movies to see. He didn't really understand this. If you want to see a Movie, you see it. What did someone else's opinion have to do with it?

If this Robert was not a Movie critic, however, Xanth was at a loss as to what he might be. What else was worth criticizing? Movies were what humans did, the most important product of their culture.

"Then what do you criticize?" Xanth asked.

Al laughed. "It's more like who he criticizes. Robert here is a critic critic."

"A who what?"

"Robert," Al said, "tell us what you think of Roger Ebert."

Robert's face lit up. This was obviously what he lived for. "Ebert is a populist, a common man's critic, the ultimate movie fan, but very knowledgeable because of the sheer number of films he has seen and the number of years he has been seeing them. His one failing might

75

be that he likes movies too much, that he has little critical detachment. Ebert has become the most well-known movie critic in the world due to his TV show, but he is not really the best critic, despite his notoriety. He lacks restraint in his praise and in his condemnation alike."

Xanth glanced at Al. It was all gibberish to him.

"How about Ebert's new partner?" Al asked.

Robert frowned. "Mr. Roeper jumped from columnist to film critic without any background in the field," he said. "He is enthusiastic but certainly not comparable to the late, lamented Gene Siskel."

Robert finished and looked like he was expecting commentary on his pronouncements. Xanth turned to Al. "What is he talking about?" he asked.

"Robert critiques critics. He has an opinion on every critic who ever lived."

"Um." Xanth tried to think of something to say. "Should I care?"

"Nope."

"Oh."

Al smiled and said, "Gene Shalit."

"If having a funny mustache was the only requirement for critical excellence," Robert launched into another speech, "then Gene Shalit would be very qualified indeed."

Al leaned over to Xanth and whispered, "While he's going on and on, let's actually *see* a movie. Whaddya think?"

"We can see Movies here?" Xanth asked.

"I told you before. This room is under a video store. And we have a TV and VCR that Mrs. Chang put down here because they're old. But they still work."

Xanth shook his head. "Now you're making as little sense as Robert."

"Just give me a minute. It will all make sense." Al stood up. He walked into the darkness and Xanth could barely see him start up some steps. He disappeared upwards.

Robert finished his critique of Gene Shalit. He looked at Xanth almost expectantly. Xanth finally said, "I don't know the names of any more critics."

76

"Rex Reed," Robert offered.

"Uh, okay, Rex Reed."

"Rex Reed is a total embarrassment to the critical profession. He should have quit and become a plumber after the Myra Breckenridge embarrassment." Robert continued on, back in his element.

Xanth felt safe in his belief that all humans were crazy.

Al returned and started to fuss with a box on a stand that sat in the corner near the stairs. Xanth got up and walked over to him. Al was holding a cord, which he kneeled down and plugged into a metal box on the wall. He picked up and plugged in another cord also. Then he turned a knob on the box.

"What's that?" Xanth asked.

Instead of answering, Al handed Xanth a small, flat, rectangular object. "You've only mentioned it about a hundred times since I met you. I thought you'd like to make it the first movie you see on Earth."

Xanth turned the item over and over is his hands. It was completely unimpressive. The black plastic was a housing, and coiled inside was some sort of tape. "Al, I have no idea what this is."

Suddenly the large box that Al had been working on lit up and sound blasted from it. Xanth jumped and dropped the black plastic thing. Al did something on the box and the sound lowered to a reasonable level. The front of the box lit up and the whole room was bathed in a blue glow.

Earth was providing more and more surprises every minute. "What is it?" Xanth asked.

"It's a TV." Al said.

"Oh yeah, I've seen them in Movies. Humans stare at them and eat snacks."

"If you don't have TV, how do you watch movies?"

"I call up the central computer and order one. Then it comes up on my wallscreen." As he said the word "wallscreen", Xanth understood.

"Oh, I see." Xanth said. "This is a wallscreen, sort of." Except that this TV thing was showing only random wavy lines and patternless groups of white dots.

Al thrust a hand towards Xanth and said, "Hand me the movie."

This request was incomprehensible. A Movie was a series of images with sound. It wasn't an object, something that anyone could hand to someone else. It couldn't be picked up, tossed, carried, or handled in any way. Its only physical existence was as data in the central computer. Al must have completely lost his mind in the last minute or two.

Since Xanth hadn't replied, Al turned and waved his hand emphatically, expecting something to be placed in it. "Where'd you put it?" he asked.

Put what? was all Xanth could think. Then he remembered the small black plastic item that Al had given him earlier. Was *that* what Al was asking for? He bent down and looked for it. It was on the floor nearby. Xanth picked the thing up and handed it to Al.

Al inserted the little plastic item into another box that was on a lower shelf of the stand. It made some clicking noises. Al stood up and said, "Make yourself comfortable." He reached up and turned off the light bulb so the TV created the only light in the room. Then he sat on the floor opposite the TV and leaned back against the wall.

"I still don't understand..." Xanth said, but the TV suddenly started playing music. Xanth went and sat next to Al, looking at the TV. The face of the TV started showing a clear image.

It wasn't long before Xanth realized what he was looking at. He had seen it many times before. It had been his inspiration for coming to Earth. He had never thought, all those times when he watched it on his wallscreen in his room, that he would see it again on Earth, sitting in a smelly basement with his first human friend.

"But what are all the strange symbols near the bottom of the screen?" Xanth asked.

"This is a Chinese video store. Those are Chinese subtitles." Al said.

Xanth filed that away to ask more about later. He didn't want to spoil watching his favorite Movie.

Despite the constantly changing symbols on the screen, the Movie was as wonderful as always. Xanth laughed and cried in all the right places, watching it as if for the first time. When Elliot and his little sister came to love the alien, who they had feared at first, Xanth smiled. When the flowers came back to life, Xanth sniffled. When the young male humans flew through the sky on their bicycles, Xanth cheered.

E.T. was still his hero.

The Movie ended and Xanth turned to Al. "That was great. Thanks so much, Al. It really reminded me of why I came to Earth."

Al didn't answer. He was fast asleep, his chin resting on his chest, and he was snoring. Xanth hadn't even heard that, he was so engrossed in the Movie. In his right hand, Al was holding a glass bottle that was nearly empty. The remaining liquid was brown and the bottle smelled really bad. Xanth picked it up and put it further away so it wouldn't spill if Al moved.

Not knowing how to turn the TV box off, Xanth just let its glow continue to fill up the room. It was once again showing nothing but random shapes and lines. He didn't mind; it was kind of soothing.

So it seemed to be time to sleep, for the first time on Planet Earth. So much had happened to him. Could it be that the last time he had slept, it had been in the narrow bunk bed in his small cabin on the cruise ship? He felt like an entirely different person than he had been then.

There were no sheets, blankets, or pillows in the basement, but that hadn't stopped Al or the others from slipping into slumber. Xanth could see the forms of all the homeless basement residents in the TV glow. The light played off of Ginny's foil hat, but none of the humans were bothered by it.

So, Xanth lay down and closed his eyes. He was really tired. This day had been so very different than he had expected. He sank into sleep.

Suddenly he was awake again. And he was back in his ship, his Glexo Nebula, approaching the blue promise of Planet Earth. He was going to Earth! He couldn't believe he was finally there. He was going to be a Movie Star!

The Glexo handled perfectly and came to a perfect landing where two streets crossed. Xanth jumped out of his ship and saw street signs that said HOLLYWOOD and VINE. Of course! That's where he had intended to land.

He had barely gotten a look around when a human walked right up to him and extended a hand in greeting. The man was sharply dressed and perfectly tanned and had the glint of gold on his wrist. That must be his Rolex watch, Xanth thought.

"Hi!" the man said. "Sid Viscous, Unlimited Talent Agency. I'll be your agent."

"Great!" Xanth enthusiastically replied. He shook hands with Sid. Then the agent reached under his jacket and produced a thick sheaf of papers.

"Just sign this and we'll get started!" Sid said.

Xanth had a pen in his hand, though he didn't know where it came from. It didn't matter. He held the pen in the air over the paper.

"Three, Two, One, Contract!" he shouted as he signed.

"Funny! Fun-ny! Now, let me show you to your car." Sid motioned with his hand, and Xanth followed with his eyes. An incredibly long, shiny car sat with its rear door open, beckoning him to enter.

"Hey," Xanth said, "I've seen this scene in lots of Movies!"

"What scene?" Sid asked.

"The limo-scene, of course!" Xanth shouted with glee.

"You're such a funny guy!" Sid said, grinning.

Inside the limo, they sat on the luxurious seat and Xanth was flooded with happiness. He was here! Earth! Hollywood! He was going to be in the Movies!

"Next, we put your footprints and your star on Hollywood Boulevard." Sid said. The limo screeched to a halt. Xanth bounded out and he was bathed in flashes from hundreds of cameras. All the reporters tried to ask him questions but he just ignored them. The fresh cement had been prepared and Xanth stepped on it with both feet. He also wrote his name with his finger. His footprints and name would be there forever!

"Hey Sid! I'm glad we're *cementing* our relationship!" he cried out.

"Is this a funny alien or what?" Sid asked the crowd of reporters.

Xanth turned and even more cameras were taking even more pictures as his star on the Walk of Fame was dedicated. The gold star with his name in it was permanently placed in the sidewalk. His fame would last forever!

"Anybody want to see an impression?" Xanth asked, then went on before they could answer. "This is Marlon Brando describing the sidewalk on Hollywood Boulevard. Ready?"

Xanth gathered himself together and then let out a bellow that was his best imitation of a t-shirted Stanley Kowalski standing under the window of his lady-love. "STELLAR!" he shouted.

"This kid is the funniest!" Sid proclaimed to everyone. Then to Xanth he said, "There's one more thing you need to be an official Movie Star."

"Let's go get it!"

They were suddenly sitting in an auditorium, surrounded by hundreds of good-looking humans, all dressed in their finest. There was a stage where a man in a tuxedo and a woman in a dress that barely clung to her were talking.

"And the award for the best alien of the year goes to...XANTHAN GUMM!!"

Xanth raced up onto the stage, filled with happiness. They liked him, they really liked him! When he got up there next to the presenters, he addressed the audience.

"Say, does anyone know if Gwyneth Paltrow ever won an Academy Award?"

The crowd shouted back, "No, we don't know if Gwyneth Paltrow ever won an Academy Award."

Xanth almost laughed too hard to shout out his punch line. "Well, she's sitting right over there...why don't you *Oscar*?"

The audience roared and applauded. The woman presenter handed Xanth that shiny gold statuette and he held it over his head in triumph.

The auditorium faded and Xanth found himself sitting on a soft comfy chair in a plush office. Sid was sitting behind a huge desk. "Now that the preliminaries are over, let's see about getting you a part in a Movie." he said. He picked up the phone and started talking to someone on the other end.

"Steve?" Sid said, "I got a new alien for ya. Yeah. Sure. Yes. You bet. Uh huh. Yup. " He went on like that for quite a while before he put the phone down.

Xanth said, "Does he always talk that much?"

"Usually, yes."

"Then I guess he really is from *Shpiel-Burg!*" Xanth laughed himself silly at his own joke.

"You're a corker with the puns," Sid said, " A real corker."

They met with Steve and the great man instantly said, "Yes! He'd be great for 'Close Encounters with *E.T.* and Indiana Jones in Jurassic Park!'"

The filming of the movie was like a whirlwind. It was released and was a smash hit. Xanth found he had a newspaper in his hands. He ran up to Sid and said, "Look at the headline in Variety!"

The headline read: *GUMM GOES GREAT GUNS*.

Sid had another newspaper. "That's great, kid, but take a look at the paper that really matters. He held it up and Xanth saw that the paper was *The National Babbler*. In large print the headline screamed: *I HAD XANTHAN GUMM'S TWO-HEADED LOVE CHILD!*

"Well," Sid said, the only thing left to do is to show you your palatial Movie Star home."

Instantly they were in front of an enormous house. "Like it?" Sid asked. "It's Ranch Neoclassical Spanish Medieval style, the latest thing. There's a pool, a sauna, tennis courts, and seven hot tubs, one for each day of the week."

"Are there any geisha girls on duty?" Xanth asked.

"Geisha girls? Why?"

"Just in *geisha* want one, of course!" Xanth said, smiling at his own joke.

"Yeah, uh, you know," Sid rubbed his hand on his forehead. "I would cool it with the puns. Puns haven't really been in since the Marx Brothers."

Xanth's smile vanished. "But you always said I was funny."

"That's when you were making me money." Sid said. "Well, so long, have a good life." He started to walk away.

Xanth rushed after his agent. "Hey, wait! What about my career? What about all those other Movies you're going to get me into?" Sid turned and stared at Xanth. "What, you don't know? Aliens are pretty much a one-shot in this town, kid. One Movie, a sequel if they get lucky, maybe a franchise if they're scary enough. But none of them last long. The public always wants to see newer, better aliens."

"But it can't be," Xanth said, close to tears. "I came all the way from Galactic Center. I didn't do that for one Movie."

"Happens to the best of them. Most of them run through the money pretty quick and end up with some menial job. See for yourself." Sid pointed and they saw a sidewalk where a wheeled cart sat. A large umbrella mounted above the cart had the words HOT DOGS repeated several times around its rim.

Xanth stared. A female human stood next to the cart, waiting for her order to be processed. The proprietor of the cart was short, so he was standing on a stool behind the steaming containers where the food was kept. He had trouble seeing into the hot dog bin, so he extended his neck, raising his large head to where Xanth could see who it was. In that familiar voice, he said, "You want mustard on that?"

"It can't be!" Xanth shouted. "Not him! Please tell me it's not him!"

"Yup," Sid said, "*E.T.* sells dogs."

Xanth fell to his knees. The world spun around him. How could his dreams have fallen apart so fast? How could everything have gone sour in a flash?

"We have a contract! You have to give me work!" Xanth looked up and pleaded with Sid.

"Take a look at the last paragraph of your contract." Sid pulled the document out from his jacket and thrust it in front of Xanth's eyes. Barely able to focus, the miserable alien read the sentence that stood out from rest. "Unlimited Talent Agency reserves the right to chew up the client and spit him out." he read.

"But there must be something I can do. Please, Sid, please! I'll do anything!"

Sid obviously took pity on his client. "There might be something for a has-been like you. If you're willing to completely debase yourself and lose all your dignity."

"Anything. Anything!" Xanth cried out.

"All right." Sid snapped his fingers and Xanth found himself in a new place. He was in a box of some sort, but it was open in front of him. Bright lights shone on him and he could sense a crowd beyond them. They were all staring at him. A deep voice started intoning, "Ladies and gentlemen, welcome to..."

Xanth couldn't believe it. It was too much. It was the worst thing possible! He hadn't come all those light years just to end up like this!

"Noooooooooooooooooooooooooo!" Xanth cried out in his agony.

"...HOLLYWOOD SQUARES!" the voice finished and the unseen audience went wild.

Chapter Fifteen

"No no no no no no..." Xanth mumbled in his sleep. Then he was being shaken, and the game show set collapsed on itself, trapping minor celebrities in their fallen squares. Xanth woke up to the reality of the cold basement floor under a Chinese video store in Chicago.

Al was shaking Xanth. "We have to get out of here before Mrs. Chang opens the store," he said.

Xanth sat up and put a hand to his head. "I dreamed I was a Movie star, and I won an Oscar, but then my career died and the only job I could get was on a game show."

"You have to get up, Ms. Goldberg."

"What?"

"Never mind." Al said. "We can't let Mrs. Chang see us around her store. She hates homeless people."

As Xanth stood up, Al went around the room and rousted the other sleepers. He helped Ginny up and out the broken window. The early morning sun glinted off Ginny's foil-wrapped head as she tottered down the alley.

It was hard to get Puddintame up, but with Xanth's help, the old man was evicted onto the street. He muttered something that Xanth couldn't understand and moved off.

Soon Al and Xanth were the only ones left in the basement. Al looked around to see if there was any evidence that they had slept there. "That's about it," he decided. "Mrs. Chang doesn't come down here much, but when she does we can't let her find out we sleep here."

Al gave Xanth a lift under the arms to help him climb out the window. Then he followed, but bent over and pressed his hands against his back when he got onto the alley pavement.

"Are you all right?" Xanth asked.

"Yeah, I just get stiffer every day." Al straightened up.

"So where are we going to go?" Xanth asked.

"I don't know about you, but I gotta pee." Al said. He walked further down the alley and faced a wall. He lowered his dirty trousers a little and Xanth heard liquid splashing.

At least humans were normal in one way. Galactic scholars had noted that humans rarely eliminated waste in Movies. If they ever entered a room designed for waste elimination, someone always attacked them, causing a fight with a lot of shooting and smashed mirrors. Xanth supposed that's why Al was doing his "peeing" in the alley, where it was safer.

Al returned, zipping up his pants. "You gotta go?" he said.

"No, in my species waste takes several days to build up. I'll inform you when elimination is pending."

"Something to look forward to. I'm getting hungry again. How about you?"

"I won't be hungry again until that pizza from last night is fully processed."

"Okay, well, I usually go downtown and do a little panhandling in the morning. You can come with me, or do whatever you want."

They started walking towards downtown, which seemed to be in the direction of all the tall buildings. All the structures surrounding them were no more than three stories tall, but the cluster of downtown buildings that reached higher than the clouds were clearly visible. Xanth hadn't realized how far away from the center of the city they had walked the night before.

"I want to go to Hollywood and become a Movie star." Xanth said.

"You're not going to do that today. Hollywood is a long way away, like I told you."

"Oh, yes. Well, maybe I can get an agent today."

"You have to go to Hollywood first for that." Al said.

"Then I'll find a way to go to Hollywood."

"Good luck. You'll need money."

"I know about money. You go to a place called a bank and point a gun at the people there, and they give you money."

"That's one way," Al muttered, "But the cops might not like you if you do that."

"Cops are people who run around a lot and banter with each other and everything explodes around them."

"You really do know Earth only from movies." Al commented.

"Well, of course. Movies are the center of Earth culture. They are the highest purpose of the human race, and all human effort is bent towards creating as many Movies as possible. Some say that humans worship Movies, others think humans are the storytellers of the galaxy, that you make them and beam them out into space as a message to us, to let us know that you are here."

Al just shook his head. "We have got to have a long talk. But for now, let's just get some money for a good meal."

As they walked, the tall buildings got closer. Thinking about everything that had happened since he landed on Earth, Xanth remembered a puzzle he had put aside the night before, the puzzle of the Chinese symbols on the Movie.

"What about those symbols on the bottom of the screen when you showed *E.T.* last night?" Xanth asked.

"Hmm? Oh, yeah, Chinese subtitles"

"What is Chinese?"

"The language they speak in China."

"What planet is that?"

"It's on this planet. Far away over the ocean."

"But everyone on Earth speaks English."

"Where did you get that idea?"

"In the Movies..."

"Everything is 'In the Movies' with you. And you say 'Movies' as if it's capitalized."

"Of course, Movies are the most important..."

"...product of Earth culture. Right. But movies are made all over the world, in many different languages."

"Someone who is from a different part of the Earth has an accent, but they still speak English. Though sometimes they speak something else and there are words in English at the bottom of the screen."

"That's American movies. The words are subtitles. But movies are made in Spanish and Chinese and Swahili and Urdu and every other language."

"Al, I've seen almost every Earth Movie there is. Even people who are both from someplace besides Hollywood, who are from the same place and could speak to each other in another language, speak English to each other."

"In <u>American</u> movies. America is just one country."

"The idea of different countries is one of Earth's best comedy ideas. Places like America, Fredonia, France, the Duchy of Grand Fenwick, Tibet--all those different governments on one planet. Comic genius!"

"I give up! Come on, walk faster, I'm hungry." Al strode ahead and Xanth couldn't keep up so he walked behind the shabby human. They walked for several blocks before Al stopped and sat down on a low wall outside of an apartment building. This building was taller than three stories, but not one of the cloud-reachers, so Xanth supposed they were about halfway to downtown.

When Xanth sat next to Al, the human said, "I'm not used to walking that fast."

They rested, but Xanth couldn't leave the silence between them unbroken. "I'm sorry if I'm bothering you, but there's just so much I don't know about this planet." he said.

"I'm not sure I'm the one to teach you, Xanth. I can try, but there's a lot that doesn't make sense to me either."

That didn't make Xanth feel any better. If a native-born human was confused, what chance did he have?

"Okay, but tell me more about the language thing."

"There are thousands of languages on Earth."

"You have to be joking. Galactic Civilization has standardized English as the common language, and Earth, where English comes from, has thousands of languages?"

"Well, English is used all over the world. A lot of people know English even if they're born in other countries."

"So why don't they just give up those other languages and speak English?"

"They don't want to."

There was no answer to that. They sat in silence for a moment.

Then Al turned and asked, "There's something that I've been meaning to ask you."

"Okay." Xanth said.

"Radio waves, that carry radio and TV signals, take thousands of years to get to other planets. Galactic Civilization might be picking up our earliest broadcasts and wondering what they are, but you know about all these recent movies. What gives?"

"That's easy. After we started getting the signals, we put a tap in one of your satellites that sends the signals to us through underspace. Much faster."

"Hmm. Why in just one satellite? There are lots of them."

"It was considered too dangerous for a crew to be so close to this planet for very long. It is forbidden to visit Earth and even crews on official business stay as short a time as possible."

"I would bet that the satellite you chose is American, so you get mostly American movies and TV." Al said. "A whole galaxy basing its culture on a warped view of one planet. Amazing."

"We are sure about some facts, though. All Movies are fictional. Everything in them comes from the vivid imaginations of humans. Wars, countries, presidential elections, operas. All of that is made up. It has to be. Earth couldn't REALLY be like that."

Al almost turned purple and let out a huge laugh. He had difficulty staying seated on the wall.

"That's not true?" Xanth asked after Al calmed down.

"That is *so* not true, as the now-disbanded *Friends* would say."

"I don't believe it. I mean, look around us." Xanth waved at the passing cars, the old newspapers blowing down the street, a filthy old woman pushing a shopping cart. This is all a Movie set, right? The cameras are hidden somewhere?"

Al just guffawed and clung precariously to his seat.

"Ok, but there is one thing that we are absolutely sure is true. We know the name of the king of your planet."

"Oh yeah? Who is he?"

"Steven Spielberg."

This time Al did fall off the wall.

Cuban cigar smoke filled the office of the Committee to Find a New Enemy. Admiral Lee "Fancy Pants" Sanderson leaned back in his chair, under the large portrait of Oopsy. He puffed on his stogie and smiled.

In other seats around the conference table were General Sam "Sammo" Burns of the Air Force, and General Max "Bull" Durham of the Marines. Les Moore represented the Army.

"It's not a bad plan, Les, very bold," he said. "A whole new Cold War with aliens, huh?"

"The best part is that half the population is ready to believe in aliens already, with all that Area 51 and Roswell UFO crash nonsense." Les Moore leaned forward in his own chair, hands on the gleaming conference table.

"Uh, yes," Admiral Sanderson took his cigar out of his mouth and studied it. "All that nonsense. Right."

"Sammo" Burns coughed and looked away.

"And if I can only find out who the civilians in the brown suits were who took my evidence, maybe I can get it back and have something to show the public to get the campaign started."

"I don't like it." Sammo put in. "We'll be crucified in the press if we start saying aliens are real. We'll be a laughing stock."

"All we have to do is say that we're coming clean," Les said. "That we're finally releasing all the evidence that we've been suppressing all these years. The press will eat it up. Of course, we'll have to manufacture some stuff that looks old like it comes from the forties, but we can do that."

"Yeah...manufacture some evidence." Lee "Fancy Pants" Sanderson said. He seemed unusually interested in learning every fold and wrinkle of his Havana Gold.

"What do you think, Bull?" Les appealed to the Marine general.

"If those aliens want a fight, by God the Marines will oblige them." General Durham rumbled.

Les realized wasn't going to get much help there. He looked back to Lee Sanderson. "The way I figure it," he said, "we show the ship that crashed yesterday as the first step. Then we release all the 'old' evidence from Roswell. Pretty soon we can build up a convincing scenario of an alien invasion."

"You're new to this committee, Moore. Sammo and I chose you after General Koevner died while cavorting with an Asian prostitute."

"I thought he died in a bombing run over Jakarta."

"Yes. Her name was Jakarta."

"Ah."

"Anyway, you know that this committee already decided on terrorists and all that as the next enemy." Lee said.

"This is even better," General Moore stated. "A war without any soldiers getting killed, just like the public wants."

"Tell you what, Les. You don't have much until you find that ship." Fancy Pants puffed a perfect smoke ring, which sailed majestically through the air until it broke apart on the rocklike projection that was Les Moore's chin. "Why don't you see what you can do about that? If you find it, then we can think about your plan."

"Well, where can I start? It could have been any of the federal agencies that took it. Can you at least give me a lead?"

"Well, I'll give you a name. Someone you can talk to. You didn't get it from me, remember." Admiral Sanderson scribbled something on a yellow Post-It® note and handed it to Les. "You'd better get going. The trail won't last for long."

"Right." General Les S. Moore was nearly glowing with enthusiasm for his new project. "I think we're about to enter a new golden era of cost overruns and black budgets." He stood and saluted.

"Go get 'em, tiger." Admiral Sanderson said.

Les Moore left the room. There was silence for a moment, broken only by Admiral Sanderson's puffing. Then Sammo spoke. "Did you tell him?" he asked.

"I was going to ask you the same thing," the admiral said.

"Then who told him?" General Burns asked.

"Maybe he just made it up, like he said."

"That would be a hell of a coincidence."

"He'll give up on the whole idea soon."

"I don't know, Les may too stupid to know when to give up."

Admiral Sanderson shrugged. "If he is, my man will take care of him."

"I'd hate to see it happen, but if we have to..." General Burns shook his head, then gave a start. He swung his head and looked into the eyes of General Durham.

"Oh, no." General Burns said. "Bull is still here."

"Damn." Admiral Sanderson said. "I keep forgetting him."

"Do we have to...you know? Right now?" General Burns started easing his sidearm out of its holster.

Admiral Sanderson stood up and walked behind the Marine General's chair. "Say, Bull," he said, "what do think about what we just said? About the aliens and all?"

General Durham growled, "If those aliens want a fight, by God the Marines will oblige them."

Lee Sanderson grinned and made a knocking motion over Bull's head as if it were pure granite.

Sam Burns relaxed and re-holstered his weapon. Bull made Les Moore look like a recipient of the Nobel Prize for physics.

Chapter Sixteen

Al called the street Michigan Avenue. It was very wide, and carried a lot of traffic. Al said that further north the street was called "The Magnificent Mile", because it was, well, pretty damn magnificent. Or at least expensive.

"That's not the best place to panhandle, though," Al said. "Rich people don't feel guilty. You want some good guilt, the middle-class office workers in the Loop are the best."

Xanth stared at everything around him, looking up at the tall buildings and the large park across the street. The most magnificent thing of all was the open sky. He had lived in enclosed habitats all his life, and looking up into the blue sky made him feel like he was going to fall upwards forever.

"Why don't you stand over there and watch?" Al said. "I'm going to get us some breakfast." Xanth stood in a doorway and watched Al do his thing.

"Spare some change?" Al asked a young woman in business attire who was striding briskly down the street. She didn't even look at Al as she went by.

Al was about to address an older black human who was walking slowly in the opposite direction. Before he could say anything, the man asked, "You got any change mister?"

After the black man left, Al looked at Xanth and shrugged. "It happens. I've even given some to others when I've had a good day."

The next person who came down the sidewalk was a middle-aged, pale-complexioned male human. "Got any change?" Al asked him.

"Oh, um, let's see," the man said. "Just a moment." He took a leather wallet out of the back pocket of his pants. Unfolding the wallet, he looked through many small pockets that contained rectangular cards with numbers on them. He opened a larger pocket and removed a bunch of green bills. The man looked through them carefully, taking his time. Al stared at all the bills, then frowned as the man carefully tucked them back into the wallet and put it back in his pocket.

"One more minute," the pale man said. He reached into each pocket of his pants, searching carefully. Then he felt in his coat pockets, inside and out, and his shirt pocket.

"Nope," the man cheerfully announced. "No change!" The man laughed as he walked off down the street. Al stared after him furiously. The man turned back one last time and waved.

Xanth walked up to Al and put a hand on the homeless man's arm. "I'm sorry, Al," he said.

"Ah, I've met worse. You just got to keep on trying. Getting mad doesn't put food in your belly."

They strolled a little further up Michigan Avenue, and Xanth asked, "What's that building?" He pointed at a low building on the park side of the street with columns in front, and even more impressive, two massive statues of some Earth creature that looked very fierce.

"That could be our meal ticket," Al said. Xanth realized that Al wasn't looking at the building but at a bus that had pulled up in front of it. "Come on." Al pulled Xanth across the busy street, barely waiting for the cars to stop at the light. They walked in front of the bus, then onto the sidewalk near the fierce creatures. They were lions, Earth monsters that ate other Earth creatures. Good thing they were just make-believe like everything else in The Movies. About two dozen humans disembarked from the bus and milled around in front of the lions. Several of them stood with their backs to one of the statues, and another took their picture with a small camera.

Al grinned. "This is perfect," he said.

"What's perfect?" Xanth asked.

"We now enter little old lady land, just about the best place to get some sympathy."

Xanth had noticed that the humans in the group were all older females. "They come to the Art Institute from the suburbs," Al continued. "They're ripe for the plucking, but we need a story. Asking directly doesn't work, but with a good story I can eat for a week."

"What kind of story?"

Al glanced at Xanth. Then he smiled. "I have a great idea," he said. "Here's what you say."

After explaining what he had in mind, Al took Xanth's hand and they walked towards the little old ladies. When they were close enough, Al gave Xanth's hand a squeeze.

"Will that doctor help me, Daddy?" Xanth asked.

"I'm sorry, son," Al said, looking close to tears. "There's nothing he can do, since I was laid off and my insurance was canceled."

"I want to go home."

"I'm sorry, we lost all our money in the robbery. We can't even get on a bus to go home."

The gaggle of suburbanites was beginning to notice them. Al sighed. "And we don't know a soul in this city who could help us."

One little old lady stepped forward. She wore a pink track suit and had a fanny pack on a nylon belt around her ample waist.

"I couldn't help but overhear..." she said.

Soon the whole group of ladies was cooing and clucking over poor "Chuckie", the boy with the scaly yellow skin and pointed ears.

"What does he have?" one of them asked.

"Yellow Cardinium Pigmentosa," Al told her, "aggravated by, uh, facial cranial malformation and, uh, Spockitis of the ears."

"Aaaaaw." the lady said.

Fanny packs were unzipped and purses opened. When the ladies waved goodbye and made their way past the columns and into the Art Institute, Al was chuckling and pocketing quite a wad of that green Earth money.

A few minutes later Xanth and Al were settled into a booth in a restaurant on Michigan Avenue. Al studied a menu as if he was cramming for mid-terms.

"That was fun," Xanth said. "Imagine me, playing a human. I've only been here a day, and I pulled it off. Maybe I can be an actor."

Al grunted.

"Why did you call me Chuckie?" Xanth asked.

"One of my favorite movie characters." Al said from behind the menu.

"You were great. You really fooled those little old ladies."

"It was child's play." Al put the menu down. "Where's that waitress?"

In a moment, the waitress appeared. Al ordered a big breakfast of pancakes, eggs, and sausage, with orange juice and milk. "You sure you don't want anything?" he asked Xanth.

"I am thirsty. What do they have to drink?"

The waitress listed a number of things that were available.

"Do you have sour milk?"

The waitress made a face. "Sour milk?" she asked.

"Yeah. Really smelly and lumpy."

"We usually throw it out if it's like that, but I'll check."

After she left, Al said, "You like milk like that?"

"It's a specialty at Tenctonese restaurants in Galactic Central. It's pretty good."

"If you say so."

Just then a ggnorphodor walked in the front door of the restaurant.

The underground garage in downtown Washington, D.C. was dark and none too clean. General Moore brushed at his uniform, sure that he would have to change to a clean one as soon as he got home. He glanced at the piece of paper in his hand for the forty-fifth time. He had written "Level 5, seventh column on the left" on it while talking to the mysterious source on the phone. He counted the columns as he walked along. When he was getting close to the seventh column, he called out, "Hello?"

"Stop right there." a voice whispered from behind the column.

Les stopped and waited. "Are you alone?" the voice asked.

"Yes."

"Completely alone?"

"Yes," he said.

"No one hiding behind you?"

"No."

"You sure?"

"Yes."

There was a pause. Then the voice said. "There's no one with you?"

"Yes!"

"Okay, okay. Just have to be sure. Now what do you want to know?"

"I'm trying to find a civilian agency that took a spaceship from me in Chicago. They wear brown suits. Any ideas?"

"No."

"What?"

"Not a clue. Sorry. Is that all?"

"But Admiral Sanderson said you would know something."

"Oh, old Fancy Pants sent you."

"I told you that on the phone."

"Oh yeah. Right. You're that one. Okay. So what did you need to know?"

"I need to find a civilian agency that took evidence of life in outer space from me. They wear brown suits."

"Doesn't ring a bell. Sorry."

General Moore waited a second. "That's it?" he asked.

"Is what it?" the voice whispered.

"Do you know anything about government agents that wear all brown?"

"I'll tell you what I told the last guy. I don't know anything."

Les grimaced. "What last guy?"

"The one who wanted to know the same thing."

"That was me!"

"You didn't leave?"

"No!"

"You're throwing my schedule off. Go away and tell the next guy to come up."

"I'm not leaving until you tell me something."

"Oh, all right."

Silence settled over the dingy garage.

"Well?" General Moore said.

"What did you want to know about again?"

"MYSTERIOUS AGENTS IN BROWN SUITS!"

"Not so loud." The whispery voice seemed to mumble something to itself for a moment. "Okay, here goes. The agents who took the spaceship from you are from a black ops agency. They always wear brown suits."

"Yeah."

"Stop right there. Are you alone?"

"Yes!"

"What do you want to know?"

"I told you five times already!"

"Oh, it's still you."

"Yes, damn it!"

"I gave you your information."

"No you didn't."

"Yes, I did."

"Did not."

"Did so."

"Nuh uh."

"Uh huh."

"All you did was repeat what I already knew!" General Moore fumed.

"You didn't know that they were black ops," The voice from behind the pillar said.

"I told you that they were a civilian agency and the agents wore brown suits."

"BROWN suits? What does that have to do with BLACK ops? Besides, black ops agents could wear Hawaiian shirts and Bermuda shorts."

"I don't care what they wear!"

"You're the one who brought it up."

"Are you going to give me some information, or do I have to report to Admiral Sanderson that you weren't helpful?"

"Do you think being a mysterious source is easy? What kind of work environment is an underground parking garage? The pay is lousy, and don't get me started on the benefits."

Someone tapped General Moore on the shoulder from behind. Surprised, the general whirled around and saw two men in rumpled sports coats carrying note pads.

"We have an appointment with the source," the taller one with red hair said. His shorter, darker-haired companion nodded.

Les turned back to pillar seven. "I'm going to hold up the line until you give me something definite," he said.

"Follow the money. No, sorry, that's for the next appointment."

"Follow the what?" the tall red haired man said.

"He's still talking to me." General Moore snarled.

"Trust no one," the mysterious source whispered. "No, damnit, that's for that FBI agent. Who am I talking to?"

"General Les S. Moore, United States Army. I was sent by Admiral Sanderson."

"Oh yeah. Go back to Chicago. There is still evidence at the crash site."

"That's it?"

"Stop right there. Are you alone?"

General Moore shrugged and walked away. Obviously he had gotten what little information was to be had here. He passed a whole line of people who were waiting to consult the mysterious source. As he approached the elevator, an old man wearing a ratty raincoat was standing near the end of the line. "Is she as good as I heard?" he asked.

"What? She who?"

"You know," the man looked sly. "Deep Throat."

"I don't know if he uses that name. I was just told he's a 'mysterious source'."

"I saw the movie. Oh, yeah, that Linda Lovelace is something."

The old man was confusing Deep Throat the mysterious source with the old porn movie that had inspired the name. A movie that Les had never seen, of course. Not since college anyway. And that time at Alexander Haig's birthday party.

"It's not that kind of Deep Throat. It's a mysterious source who gives you information," Les told the old man.

"She gives you information too?"

"It's a man. *He* gives you information."

"Oh." The man in the raincoat thought for a moment. "Okay, but just oral. I ain't doing nothing kinky."

Chapter Seventeen

Xanth ducked under the table. Maybe the ggnorphodor wouldn't see him. "Where'd you go?" he could hear Al ask.

Al's head appeared upside down in the dark space under the table. "There you are. What are you doing?"

"That's a ggnorphodor!" Xanth said.

"That's a whoziwhat?"

"A ggnorphodor!"

"You must be speaking alien. I don't understand a word you're saying."

"Ggnorphodors are a very unpleasant species. Everyone else avoids them at all costs."

"And you saw one here in this cafe?"

"Yes! It came in with a group of young humans."

Al's head rose up out of sight. After a moment, it came back. "That's a kid in a mask," Al said.

"I'm not coming up until the ggnorphodor leaves."

"He's a human in a rubber mask. Come up and I'll prove it to you."

"Are you sure?"

"Yes, I'm also sure I'm getting a crick in my neck. Come out of there so I can talk to you right side up."

Xanth reluctantly poked his head above the table. He scanned the area. The ggnorphodor was sitting at a table with the humans he had accompanied into the restaurant.

"You see him?" Al asked.

"Yeah."

Al raised his voice until the whole restaurant could hear. "Hey kid! Nice mask!" he shouted.

The ggnorphodor turned and looked at Al. Xanth lowered himself until his eyes were just above the table. The humans with the ggnorphodor stared at Al too. Then the ggnorphodor reached up a hand and tore his face off. Another face was underneath. Al had been right. It was another young human.

"That's a relief," Xanth said as he pulled himself up on the padded seat of the restaurant booth.

"These, uh, gunyanorfs...," Al asked, "are they mean? Do they have an evil galactic empire?"

"Ggnorphodor. It's pronounced the same way it's spelled. They aren't really mean, they're just annoying. And there haven't been any evil galactic empires since Mongo became a constitutional monarchy. They're just irritating. They play practical jokes on everyone. They have a nasal laugh that will drive you nuts after a while."

"They don't seem to have noses, why the nasal laugh?"

"Half of their big bulbous head is nasal cavities. Believe me, you don't want to tell a joke to a ggnorphodor."

The waitress arrived and placed a steaming plate of food in front of Al. "We had some milk that was going bad, but the manager wouldn't let me bring it out. He thought you were a health inspector trying to trap him," she said to Xanth. "You want anything else?"

"Water, please."

"Okay." Then she left.

Al dug into his food with gusto, and didn't talk again until he had put away a large portion of it. Xanth kept his eye on the group of humans in the other booth, just in case the young man would turn out to be a ggnorphodor after all.

"That's interesting," Al said, with scrambled egg leaking out of one corner of his mouth.

"What's interesting?"

"That aliens like that are a real species."

"Of course they are. I told you. They're ggnorphodors."

"Yeah, but here on Earth they're just generic aliens. That image, of the big-headed, big-eyed alien, is everywhere these days."

"That's ridiculous. How could anyone on Earth know about ggnorphodors?"

"They're supposedly based on descriptions from people who were abducted by UFO's."

"That's even more ridiculous. Contact with Earth is strictly forbidden."

"You came here."

"Sure, but I just had one small ship. If any species was kidnapping humans, they would have to have ships in orbit, and make regular trips to and from Earth. The Galactic authorities would notice that."

Al shrugged. "I just said it was interesting. I didn't say I could explain it."

"I wonder what they're talking about," Xanth said.

Al didn't even look back at the young people. "Why do you care?"

"They're planning something. The female has large pieces of paper with drawings all over them, and they're all reading nonsensical things from other pieces of paper."

This time Al did look back. "Looks like scripts. They're probably from that film school near here."

Xanth sat up straight. "Say that again?"

"Columbia College is right down the street. We passed it. There's a lot of film students there."

"Are you telling me," Xanth asked in a reverent whisper, "that they are making a Movie?"

Al tried to say, "Maybe" but Xanth was already walking towards the group of young people, so Al said, "Oh boy," instead.

Striding up to the booth full of humans, Xanth posed dramatically and announced, "The latest alien Movie sensation is here. I, Xanthan Gumm, will replace *E.T.* in the hearts of human and Galactic residents alike. I am a member of a semi-aquatic species, a framadort converter from Galactic Central, a yellow-skinned, pointy-eared real live alien who has traveled many light years to bless Earth Movies with his acting ability. When do we start making the Movie?"

Xanth expected a stunned silence. Or possibly applause. The very least he expected was that the young Movie-making humans would pull out a contract for him to sign and say that they would take him to Hollywood with them, because if they were making a Movie, then of course they would be going to Hollywood as soon as possible.

One of the male humans leaned over and whispered into the ear of the female, who seemed to be the leader of the group. She said, "Oh," and lifted her purse from the seat next to her and opened it up. "Come on, everybody, give the kid what you can. He has some disease that makes him look like that, and his dad got robbed. Frank saw them over at the Art Institute talking to some people."

The rest of the group nodded and rooted around in their pockets. They were obviously not a group that had much money to start with, but each one came up with a few coins.

The woman collected the money and held out her hand to Xanth. "Here, kid. I hope you and your dad get home all right."

Al had come up behind Xanth, and he reached to take the money, but Xanth shouted, "No!" He knocked Al's hand away. "I am an alien. I swear it's true. I came here from Galactic Central on a cruise ship. I've watched Earth Movies all my life and the only thing I want to do is to be in one. Please, you have to believe me. Ever since I came to this planet humans have refused to believe me. I want to go to Hollywood. Take me to Hollywood with you. Please. Please." Xanth sank to his knees, almost in tears.

Now he got his stunned silence. The humans glanced at each other. The female leaned over and whispered to Frank. "He does kind of look like an alien. And we need Jeremy on boom. Maybe he could be our alien."

"We don't know anything about him." Frank whispered back. "And look at the dad. He's filthy. Anything could happen if we get mixed up with these two."

"Sir," the female addressed Al, "Your son really has his heart set on being the alien in our film. I don't know if you plan to still be in town tomorrow, but if you are, meet us in front of Columbia College at nine a.m. and we'll see what we can do. We can't pay, but we'll give you both some lunch."

Before Al got a word out, Xanth jumped up and shouted, "Thank you! Thank you, thank you, thank you!" He leaped up on the table and beamed at each young human individually. Then he thrust his hand towards the female, an Earth gesture he had seen many times in The Movies.

"Thank you, especially. You won't regret it. We can make your Movie and then go to Hollywood and we'll all be famous and everyone in Galactic Central will see me in my first Movie! Thank you!"

The human took Xanth's hand and shook it. "Well, you certainly have enthusiasm. Try to save some of that energy for your performance. My name is Rita, by the way."

"Gumm," Xanth said. "Xanthan Gumm. And thank you, Rita." Rita introduced her fellow filmmakers. Frank, Jeremy, who was the one who had worn the ggnorphodor mask, and Tony. Each one in turn shook hands with Xanth.

"Hey!" someone said. It was the waitress. "You can't stand on the table!"

Xanth jumped down and hugged the waitress, who looked very surprised. "Thank you!" Xanth shouted. "I'm going to be in a Movie! I'm going to be in a Movie! The waitress moved off, looking a bit scared.

"We'd better go," Al said. "Come on, Xanth."

On the way out Al paused to pay for his food, and Xanth kept saying "Thank you!" in the direction of the film students. Al dragged him out of the door of the restaurant, and he got in one last "Thank you!" just before the door closed.

"That was interesting," Jeremy said. "Do you think they'll show up tomorrow?"

"If they do, we have a 'real live alien from Galactic Central'," Rita said, and if they don't, you get to wear that mask of yours and I get to hold the boom."

Jeremy put the mask back on. "I think I look pretty cool in this thing," he said.

The waitress stopped at their table to ask if they needed anything more. When they said no, she gave them each a separate check. Then she moved on to the only other occupied table in the restaurant. "Do you need anything?" she asked the two men there. If the yellow-skinned kid was a little strange, these two were bizarre. They both wore hooded outfits that hid their faces, and their heads seemed awfully big. "No," one of them said. The waitress went back towards the kitchen.

"Look," the first hooded man said, pointing at Jeremy. "Our likeness has become so common, the Earthers want to look like us." The other one didn't reply. "What are you doing?" the first one asked.

The second hooded man placed a menu on a full water glass, then turned the menu and glass upside down. He pulled the menu out from under the glass, and the water was held there. The first hooded man could see coins inside.

"See, if the waitress wants her tip, she'll have to spill water everywhere," the second hooded man said.

"That's very good," the first hooded man said. Soon the restaurant was filled with the sound of irritating nasal laughter.

Chapter Eighteen

Xanth danced down the street, in a daze of wonderment. He was going to be in a Movie! This place, this city called Chicago, might be far from Hollywood, but humans still made Movies here. Of course they did. Making Movies is what humans did.

Xanth jumped, and skipped, and sang, "I'm going to be in a Movie! I'm going to be in a Movie!" Occasionally he ran back to Al, who followed much too slowly, and said, "I'm going to be in a Movie!" The fourth time he did that, Al said, "I think you mentioned that." The fifth time, he just gave Xanth a hard stare.

Xanth didn't care. He was going to be in a Movie!

They walked several blocks, with Al setting the course. They moved away from the broad Michigan Avenue, and under the steel structure that covered the next street. A train ran along the top of the structure, making a loud squealing sound.

Xanth didn't pay attention to anything. He was so happy he could have hugged all the humans who were walking by, but they all took one look at him dancing around and did their best to avoid him. At a street corner, Xanth turned to tell Al that he was going to be in a Movie, and Al wasn't there.

After a moment, he saw the shabbily dressed human through the glass of a store. Xanth walked along the glass and found a door, and let himself in.

The store was full of bottles. From floor to ceiling, bottles of all shapes and sizes covered the walls and the many shelves. Xanth walked up to Al, who was talking to a bald human who stood behind a counter. Xanth saw Al tuck a paper bag with the neck of a bottle sticking out of it into the inside pocket of his coat.

"Hey kid," the bald man said. "We can't sell anything to you. Get out of here."

"He's with me," Al said.

"Your kid, huh?" the bald man looked Xanth up and down. "My cousin has a retard kid. It's too bad."

Before Xanth could ask what he meant, Al hustled him out of the store. They walked for a while, and Al took the bottle he had bought out of his pocket, twisted the cap off, and took a swig from it.

"What is that?" Xanth asked.

"Whiskey."

In the Movies where people rode horses they always asked for whiskey in the saloon. Galactic scholars were divided about what exactly whiskey was. Drinking it generally led to the humans in the Movie shooting at each other, but almost anything could make humans in Movies shoot at each other. One scholar had listed all the things that caused humans to shoot at each other, and the list included eating, looking, and breathing.

"Please don't shoot me," Xanth said.

Al took another swig and ignored the remark. "Come on, I want to sit down and enjoy this," he said. He led Xanth into an alley.

In his short time on Earth, Xanth had become very acquainted with alleys. He was not very happy about this. Alleys generally smelled bad, and had no comfortable seating. Despite this, Al settled down with his back to a brick wall and began to seriously work on draining the contents of his bottle. A tall stack of flattened cardboard boxes was nearby.

"Can I have some?" Xanth asked. "I never got my water at the restaurant. I'm still thirsty."

"You don't drink this because you're thirsty."

"You drink liquid when you're thirsty. You're talking in riddles, Al."

"How old are you?"

"In Earth years?" Xanth thought. "About eighty seven."

Al offered the bottle, then pulled it back again. "Is that young or old for your species?"

"That's not very old for any species. Except the Maiflievians, who live for about a week."

"So are you old enough to drink?"

"I...don't understand. Anyone can drink. That's how we get liquids into our bodies. Except the Spunjbobbians, who absorb it through their skin."

"Can you drink booze? Hooch?" Al waved his bottle around. "If it's liquid, and I pour it down my throat, then I believe I will have drunk it." Xanth looked very puzzled.

"Alcohol, dummy, are you old enough to drink alcohol?"

"Alcohol is shown in a lot of Movies, and when humans drink it they act funny, but of course that's more of that crazy human imagination."

"Believe me, booze is very real."

"Come on, if any sentient being knew that consuming a particular liquid would lead to the aberrant behavior that is shown in Movies, that being wouldn't drink it."

"So Galactic Civilization has no booze at all?"

"Of course not."

Al stared. "Then I'm glad I was born on this planet."

"How old are you, Al?"

"Fifty-two. I think. This stuff is starting to work on me, so I could be wrong."

Xanth was shocked. Al looked awfully old for fifty-two. At fifty-two, Xanth had just started high school.

"So that stuff is really alcohol," Xanth said.

"Really really. Still want some?"

"Not if it would lead to aberrant behavior."

"Too bad. Aberrant behavior can be fun." Al took a big swallow from his bottle. Xanth couldn't see how much was left, because the paper bag still covered it. "Now excuse me while I get drunk."

"Okay. Let me know when you're 'drunk'."

"You'll know. Have you ever seen 'Leaving Las Vegas'?"

"Is that a Movie?"

"Yup."

"Does it have any aliens in it?"

"No, though Nic Cage has a certain out of this world quality."

"I might have. If it doesn't have any aliens I might not remember it much."

"Hmmm...hey, I know. We saw '*E.T.*' last night. When *E.T.* drinks some stuff at the house and Elliott acts weird at school, what caused that?"

"I always assumed it was a reaction to Earth's atmosphere. Some species take a while to adjust to planetary conditions."

"Your naiveté is touching. Alcohol. A chemical caused by permenfation. Termination. Fer-men-ta-tion. It makes humans stupid."

"That's why humans are stupid?"

"Very funny."

"No, really, that would explain a lot of things we don't know about humans. Is this chemical in the atmosphere?"

"It's in here!" Al waved the bottle again. He was beginning to sound a little strange, like he couldn't properly form words any more.

"Are you all right?" Xanth asked.

"I am...yes. I'm pretty damn all right. How are you?"

Xanth was worried. "So this alcohol stuff. You drink it on purpose?"

"No. We drink it happily. Gladly. Pretty damn happygladly." Al burped, then upended the bottle and sucked on it.

Neither human nor alien spoke for a while. Al drank, and Xanth worried. Al was his only human friend, and he needed friends on this strange planet.

Finally Al mumbled, "A whole galasky, an' no one ever gets bombed?"

"No," Xanth said. "Though the Fawsterbrookians do talk like you're talking, and they get their words mixed up a lot. They're pretty funny. I had lunch with one once. They eat special fruit that smells rotten. They leave it out for several days before they eat it."

"That's nice..." Al snuggled down inside of his coat and fell asleep.

"Al?" Xanth stood over the human and tried to decide if he was okay. He could see that Al was breathing, but otherwise he was completely out of it. Xanth bent over further, then jumped back and ended up halfway across the width of the alley.

Al, and even more so the bottle in his hand, smelled like a fawsterbrookian's all-you-can-eat buffet. Xanth had a very sensitive nose. His parents had said it was normal for their species. They said their ancestors on their lost home planet could smell a fish from a mile away. The odor coming off of Al was enough to make Xanth run a mile away.

What was he going to do? He knew no one on the whole planet except the man lying passed out in this alley. Xanth couldn't just leave him here. He didn't know the way back to the basement sleeping room. He decided to wait and see if Al would wake up.

He waited quite a while. Every once in a while he tried to cheer himself up by thinking, "I'm going to be in a Movie!" but it didn't help much. He waited so long that the sun started to go down, and the heat of the day began to turn to evening cool.

When Al stirred, Xanth jumped up and said, "Al!"

Al lifted his head, but didn't say anything.

"Al!" Xanth said. "Don't you want to go the sleeping room? We could watch another Movie."

Al fell asleep again.

"We don't have to watch alien movies. There are some others I like. How about 'Beethoven'? Boy, that dog is funny. Al?"

No answer. Xanth moved closer to Al. He decided that the least he could do was to move the reeking bottle of alcohol away, so that if Al woke up he couldn't drink any more of it. He gently picked it up, wrinkling his nose with disgust. He put it down a couple of feet away, next to the stack of cardboard boxes.

A hand immediately shot out from under the boxes, grabbed the bottle, and disappeared. Xanth jumped with surprise. "Hey!" he shouted.

The boxes started to move. Xanth stepped back. What new Earth strangeness was this? A box monster? A cardboard demon?

Some of the boxes fell to the side and pretty soon Xanth could see a pale, skinny human sitting up. His face was streaked with dirt and his hair stuck out in all directions. He was drinking from Al's bottle.

"That's my friend's alcohol!" Xanth said.

"Not any more, kid." The dirty human turned the bottle upside down and showed that it was empty. He tossed it away and glass shattered. "Thanks, I needed that." the man said. "Now what else you got?"

"What do you mean?"

"You got any money?"

"Uh, no." He shifted his gaze to Al briefly, and the skinny man followed his eyes.

"So Pops has some. Okay, let's see." the man pushed the boxes away and stood up. He walked to Al and started going through Al's pockets.

"You can't do that!" Xanth said. The man didn't reply. He stood up and flashed the remaining money Al had received that morning, then stuck it into a pocket of his filthy-looking jeans.

"You got a place to sleep? A basement? That sounds good."

Xanth didn't know what to do. This human wasn't nearly as nice as Al. But he needed help from someone. "Can you help me get Al there? Then you can sleep there too."

"I guess. How far is it?"

"I don't really know for sure. But we walked there last night and came back in the morning."

The man grunted, then bent over Al and started slapping him. "Get up, Pops, we gotta go." Al woke up and after some struggle he was up on his feet.

"Hey, Xanth," Al said. "Guess what, I'm drunk now."

"I figured that out." Xanth said.

"Which way?" the skinny man asked.

"Which way what?" Al asked.

"Which way is the basement you sleep in?"

"South," Al said, pointing north.

The small group set out, and traveled towards the city's south side. After a few blocks, the skinny man remembered something and asked, "What was that about watching movies? You can watch movies in this place we're going to?"

"It's under a store that has Movies in little black boxes," Xanth said. "You can watch any Movie you want."

"You say Movie like it's capitalized, kid. So you can get into the store?"

"Sure, Al did it last night. What Movie do you want to see?"

"They got one called 'The Big Heist'?"

"I don't know."

"Well, if they don't, me and some friends will act it out for you."

"That sounds like fun," Xanth said, as they slowly made their way southward.

Chapter Nineteen

By the time they got to Chinatown, Al was walking mostly on his own, which was good, because the skinny man had done nothing but complain the whole time. Complaining and using words that were often translated into beep language in Earth Movies. Many Movies had people speaking entirely in English. But often they had certain words in beep language. By comparing the same Movie in two versions, one with beep language and one without, it was determined that the beeps stood for certain common English words. No Galactic language expert had been able to determine which beep sound meant which word, and it was a complete mystery why only a few words were translated into beeps.

Xanth would have been interested if the skinny man had spoken in beeps. Perhaps he could have learned what the beeps meant and been able to tell galactic civilization the truth about Earth beep language if he ever got back. However, though the skinny man repeated the words many times, he always used the plain English versions.

Al managed to direct them to the right alleyway eventually, though they went down several wrong ones before he was clear-headed enough to do so. As they approached the little window entrance to the basement sleeping room, Xanth saw Ginny clambering into the hole, her foil hat glinting in the light of a street lamp. It was completely dark by then, and Xanth was very tired.

It was hard to get Al into the basement in his drunken condition. He was on the verge of falling asleep again, having exhausted himself during part of the walk by singing about not being able to get any satisfaction and acting like he was playing a guitar.

They all managed to get down into the little room and Al immediately curled up in a corner and fell asleep. Xanth sat in a bit of a daze against a wall. He watched the skinny man pace round the room. After a short time a pair of legs appeared in the window and the skinny man jumped. When the owner of the legs fully entered the room, the skinny man said, "Who are you?"

"My name is Puddintame. Ask me again and I'll tell you the same."

The dirty skinny man seemed angered by this, but he turned away from the old man and walked over to Xanth.

"Hey, kid, they got any money in this store upstairs?"

Xanth shrugged. "I don't know," he said. "Earth people always seem to want money. Why is that?"

"You're kidding me," the skinny man said. "Gotta have money."

"Where I come from, we use money because it's in Earth Movies. Just for fun. But we don't quite know why it's so important on Earth."

"So you're not from Earth?"

"Oh, no. I'm from Galactic Central, and I came to Earth to be in the Movies, like my hero, *E.T.*"

The skinny man glanced at Al. "Poor bastard," he muttered. "It's hard enough living on the streets without a mutant idiot kid."

"What was that?"

"Nothing. So, they don't use money in fairyland or wherever you're from?"

"Galactic Central. Billions of space-based habitats that orbit the black hole at the center of the galaxy."

"Whatever. How do you buy things without money?"

"As I said, we use it just to be like the Movies. But when I don't have any with me I can still get what I need."

"So you don't have to work?"

This was a non sequitur if Xanth had ever heard one. "Of course we work. Everyone has an assigned job. I'm a framadort converter."

"Why do you work if you don't need money?"

"What does work have to do with money?"

"You are a stupid kid. You work and they give you money."

"Even for a human, you're not making much sense. I work because it's my assigned job. I get money, or food or whatever I need because I'm a citizen."

"That's stupid."

"It is not."

115

"Yeah it is. Here in America, you work for money and use the money to buy what you need. Or if you're like me, you take the money from the suckers who do work."

"What do you mean, take it? If someone has something you need, they're happy to share it with you."

"Is that what Daddy does?"

Xanth looked at his sleeping friend. "Al has been very nice to me. He let me eat a whole pizza we found, even though he was hungry himself."

"What a pussy."

"What?"

"Never mind. I'm tired of waiting." The skinny man leaned over and grabbed Xanth by the arm. "We're going upstairs to see what there is to see."

They found the steps that led up to the store, but they were completely in the dark, so they stumbled a few times as they went up. The skinny man dragged Xanth by the arm, and it began to hurt. The skinny man bumped into something and said some more non-beep words. Then Xanth heard a door opening, and a little bit of light filtered down.

The space above was dark, but some light came in from the street. The skinny man let go of Xanth's arm and looked around. The store was not very large, but there were many shelves that displayed little boxes with pictures on them. Xanth picked one up and held it to the light. This one was a thin box, that wasn't big enough to hold a tape like he had seen the night before. Xanth would have to ask Al about that. On the box, a man and a woman faced each other with odd expressions on their faces. There was lettering on the box, but it was all in that language that was in the subtitles the night before.

"Do you know how to read these letters called 'Chinese'?" Xanth asked.

"Do I look Chinese?" the skinny man said, which was not an answer to the question. Conversation with this man was considerably more difficult than it was with Al. In fact, this man was beginning to make Xanth feel very uncomfortable.

Xanth tried a different question. "Do you want to see a Movie?"

There was no answer, but in a moment, the skinny man started talking to someone. He had found a telephone behind the counter. "You gotta see this place," he said. "We can have ourselves a party." He talked some more and then hung up.

"I think I'll go downstairs and get some sleep," Xanth said. The skinny man grabbed Xanth by both arms. "You will do exactly what I say, kid. And that doesn't include running away to call the cops."

Xanth had not intended to call any cops. In the Movies cops crashed cars and shot people a lot, and neither of those activities were what Xanth wanted to happen right then. Even though it would be amusing to hear the cops sing that song that goes "Bad boys, Bad boys, What You Gonna Do?" he just wanted to get some sleep.

"We'll both go down and wait for my friends," the skinny man said.

In the basement, they found that Robert had arrived. When Robert saw Xanth he said, "Oh, I'm glad you're here. Would you like to hear my review of Leonard Maltin?" He waited expectantly.

"Do you know this moron?" the skinny man asked.

"He was here last night. He sleeps here too."

"Are we going to have the whole city in here?" Skinny muttered.

"Well?" Robert asked.

"I don't think this is the best time, Robert," Xanth said.

"I put a great deal of thought into my opinion of Mr. Maltin," Robert said.

"Shut the hell up," Skinny told him.

"Really, Robert, our new friend doesn't seem interested." In fact, Skinny looked more than a little angry, and Xanth had pretty much decided that he wasn't a nice man at all.

"When I put the weight of my professional knowledge and consideration into an opinion," Robert persisted, "I expect that others will want to hear it."

"All right," Xanth said. "What do you think of...whoever you said."

Robert beamed. "Well..." He broke off as the skinny man's fist met his face and he was knocked to the floor.

He soon met some more people who weren't nice. Skinny waited
outside for the friends he had called on the telephone, and three more
men arrived, one of them carrying a box of cans. They all climbed
down into the basement and started opening up the cans and drinking
from them. The man who carried the box said, "Bastard just watched
me carry this out. Didn't even try and stop me." This was
understandable. The man looked exactly like the scary people in the
Movies who ride motorcycles and do bad things to the main
characters. Xanth thought of asking this man if he'd ever been in a
Movie, but decided not to.

"Should have picked me up some Slim Jims too," Skinny said.

"You and your Slim Jims. Those things'll kill you. Did Geordie
get the cigs?"

Geordie must have been the third man, who was also carrying a
box, though it was smaller. He looked less like a motorcycle Movie
bad guy, and more like a Movie homicidal maniac. He ripped open
the box and passed out smaller packages to his friends. "The clerk at
my store was nice too. Let me come behind the counter and get
these." He grinned widely. "He might live to tell about it, too."

As the men talked, they also used the non-beep words. When did
humans speak in beeps? Xanth wondered. The English words were
nothing special, just relating to sexual relations and excrement. Why
do humans sometimes say "beep" instead? It didn't seem he would
solve the mystery, so he filed it away to figure out later.

The last member of Skinny's group came through the window but
had trouble getting all the way through. He was a very tall, very fat
man. He managed to push his way into the basement and set his
sneakered feet on the floor. He turned around to face the others.

The motorcycle man with all the tattoos looked dangerous, Skinny
and Geordie were clearly not nice, but this man was a walking threat.
He had a huge scar across his face, and it distorted every expression
into one of menace. Xanth backed away from him. This human
looked like the worst of the lot. He looked like he could break you in
two by just looking at you.

118

"Golly, fellas," the large man said in a voice that made him sound like a singing chipmunk, "That was pretty darn hard."

Chapter Twenty

Skinny laughed. "Don't get your fat ass stuck in there, Jerome, or we'll never get out of here."

Geordie said, "So what do we do for fun around here?"

"What else?" Skinny said. "Trash the place."

Skinny, Geordie, and motorcycle man started towards the stairs. Jerome began to follow, but Skinny turned back and said, "Stay down here and don't let these people leave."

"Gosh, don't I get to go to the party?" Jerome asked in his high voice.

Skinny handed Jerome a couple of the cans from the box and one of the small packages. "Have your own party," he said. Then skinny and the other two went up the stairs.

"Gee whiz," Jerome said to himself. Then he settled himself directly under the window, and pulled on the top of one of the cans. It made a little noise of escaping gas. Jerome tilted it upside down and poured whatever was inside into his mouth.

Xanth had no idea whatsoever what to do next. When he had dreamed of Earth while converting framadorts at the framadort factory, it had never occurred to him that he would wind up held hostage in a dirty basement while Earth bad guys had a party.

Jerome set the empty can down on the floor. It had the word "Duff" written on the side. Xanth didn't know what that meant, but his sensitive nose told him that it was alcohol. He just couldn't imagine why humans would purposely drink something that smelled like the substance that Kwikadian slime beetles regurgitate to feed their young. Xanth actually knew what the substance that Kwikadian slime beetles regurgitate to feed their young smells like, because he had once had to take an order of framadorts to the Kwikadian habitat in Galactic Central, and the female Kwikadian slime beetle that signed off on the order was feeding about fifteen little Kwikadian slime beetle larvae at the time. It wasn't the substance that Kwikadian

slime beetles regurgitate to feed their young itself that had Xanth
nearly doing some regurgitating himself, as nasty as that substance
smelled, so much as the fact that the substance that Kwikadian slime
beetles regurgitate to feed their young is made in the female's
stomach after she eats one of her young for every one that she feeds.
Xanth shuddered at the memory of his visit to the Kwikadian
habitat, but shortly Jerome did something that made the smell of the
alcohol in the can seem comparatively less like the substance that
Kwikadian slime beetles regurgitate to feed their young, and more
like the flower garden in Galactic Park. Jerome opened the small
packet that his friends had given him, which had the word "Laramie"
printed on it. Jerome then searched in his shirt pocket and came out
with a small device, flicked the device with his thumb, and produced
a flame.

As soon as Xanth saw the flame, he knew what Jerome was doing.
He might have been unclear on some Earth customs, but this one he
was utterly familiar with. He might have not paid much attention to
what Earth people were drinking in the Movies, but he sure knew
what they were smoking.

Jerome was about to light a cigarette. Xanth was sure of it before
he even saw it in Jerome's hand. Sure enough, the large human took a
small white tube out of the packet and put one end in his mouth. He
lifted the flame to the little tube and inhaled, causing it to burn.

Xanth leaned forward. This was fascinating. Smoking was in so
many Movies that it could not be ignored. Some Movies seemed to be
entirely about smoking. Blowing the smoke, smoke rings, letting the
smoke curl up in lazy whorls in the air, making any scene in a Movie
mysterious and, well, smoky. Like everything else in Earth Movies,
smoking had been adopted by Galactic culture. At least, for a while.

Galactic scientists had set forth with great diligence to figure out
what was actually in Earth cigarettes. They had gone through many
substances, dismissing one after another. The trouble was, taking
smoke into one's lungs, no matter what you were burning to create
the smoke, just wasn't healthy. Lungs are meant to process fresh air,
not the byproducts of combustion. Particulate matter from the smoke,

no matter how innocuous the substance being burned, was not good for delicate lung tissue.

After a while, the Galactic government had announced that smoking, no matter how cool it looked in Movies, could not be recommended. Humans must have some plant or some artificial substance that could be smoked safely and which couldn't be duplicated. As strange as humans are, everyone agreed, they wouldn't take smoke into their lungs if it would hurt them.

The smoking fad died out throughout Galactic Civilization. It hung on for a while among water breathers, who had never actually smoked anything, but had put white tubes in their mouths to look like they were. Before long even they realized that it looked pretty silly, so they stopped.

Methane breathers, though not the brightest creatures, had given up smoking even earlier, when a methane breather had tried to light a cigarette and his methane bladder exploded. One fatality was enough for them to know they should not mess with this strange Earth custom.

Now, Xanth was about to learn the secret of smoking! The enormous human in front of him was lighting an actual Earth cigarette, and would soon blow out actual Earth smoke.

When the white puff came out from between Jerome's bulging lips, it whirled and twirled in the air just like in a Movie. Xanth took in a deep breath, eager to learn what the amazing substance in Earth cigarettes smelled like. He took it deep into his lungs. Then he doubled over, hacking and coughing, trying to expel from every cell in his body the worst smell he had ever smelled in all of his eighty-six years.

The word "terrible" didn't describe the smell. The words "awful", "disgusting" and "horrible" hardly did it justice. The smell was so unbearable that Xanth had to be out of that room, out where he could get some fresh air, or risk coughing up his lungs in little pieces onto the cracked cement floor of the basement.

He leaped for the window, placing one foot on Jerome's head on the way. This was a mistake. Jerome grabbed Xanth's ankle with his left hand and pulled. For a second Xanth was grasping at the trash and dirt outside the window, trying and failing to find a hand hold and pull himself out, and a second later he was back in the basement, lying on his back and coughing from the cigarette smell that filled the little room.

"Gee, I'm sorry," Jerome said. "Lenny told me not to let you leave."

Xanth managed to raise himself to his hands and knees and crawl to the farthest corner of the room, away from Jerome and his cigarette. Maybe that would be far enough that the smell would be bearable, though Xanth doubted it. He ended up near the bottom of the stairs, where he could hear the other three men carrying out their plan to trash the video store.

"How can you possibly smoke that?" Xanth asked.

Jerome pulled the cigarette out of his mouth and looked at it. "Tastes good like a cigarette should," he said. Xanth recognized that as a Mini-Movie slogan that had helped fuel the smoking fad in Galactic Central.

"That's the whole reason you smoke? Because a slogan told you to?"

"What slogan?" Jerome asked.

"Tastes good like a cigarette should," Xanth said.

"Sure does," Jerome replied.

"That was the slogan."

"What was the slogan?"

"Tastes good like a cigarette should."

"That's what I said." Jerome inhaled a big lung full of smoke and let it out. Xanth's position across the room was not far enough to get away from the smell. He coughed.

"I mean, in the Mini-Movies. There's also the cowboy who smokes all the time, and when I was younger I thought the ones where the cigarette is too long were funny. They have to put a bubble in the windshield of the racecar, or a hole in the wall into the apartment next door. Then another type came out that was one silly millimeter longer than that."

Jerome just puffed and looked at Xanth. He obviously had no idea what Xanth was talking about.

"Please, you have to let me out of here. I can't take that smell."

"Lenny said I shouldn't let anyone leave."

Lenny must be the skinny man. Xanth tried to think, which was hard with his lungs burning.

"Your friends didn't want you at their party, huh?" Xanth asked. The party was in full swing, judging from the sounds of things being smashed and glass breaking that came from upstairs.

Jerome frowned. "Lenny gave me an important job," he said.

"He didn't give you much of that alcohol drink, did he?" Xanth asked. Jerome had emptied one can and the other one sat next to him, unopened. He picked it up and popped the top.

"That'll last a few seconds," Xanth said. "Then you'll have to sit down here without any, while they have whole box of those cans upstairs."

"They'll bring me some."

"I'm sure. I'm sure they never forget you, always remember to include you in whatever they do."

Jerome looked mad, but whether it was at Xanth or because of the way his friends treated him, Xanth wasn't sure. Jerome downed the second can of alcohol, then smoked some more. Xanth tried not to gag too loudly.

"I could get some for you," Xanth said.

"Lenny told me not to let anyone leave."

"I'm not talking about leaving. I'll just go upstairs and ask Lenny for some more cans."

Jerome tried to think of something wrong with this plan, but obviously couldn't, because he said, "Okay."

Xanth stood and started up the stairs. He went up into darkness and stopped behind the door that led into the store. The sounds of smashing were a little quieter now. Perhaps Lenny and his friends had smashed everything that could be smashed.

Slowly and carefully, Xanth pushed open the door. He stepped out from behind it. He was behind a counter, so he couldn't see the three men. He crept as quietly as he could and looked over the counter.

Lenny, Motorcycle Man, and Geordie had obviously not been satisfied with smashing all the video displays, and had graduated to smashing each other. The lights of the store were on, and Xanth could see the three men lying on the floor along with hundreds of video boxes and the overturned shelving. They didn't seem to be completely unconscious, but they were definitely in the state that Al had called "drunk". He didn't think he could risk trying to get past them to the front door of the store.

Xanth saw the telephone behind the counter. He didn't know anyone on Earth to call, but maybe the central computer could help him. He lifted the heavy black handset, as he had seen Lenny doing. The base unit was also black, and had a round dial that had numbers printed around it. This was just as he had seen in many Movies, but he wasn't sure what the dial had to do with anything. Other Movies had telephones with push buttons on them. Both types had to be purely decorative. Surely the central computer would answer when it sensed he had lifted the handset.

He waited quite a while, and all the central computer did was send him a monotonous tone. Xanth whispered, "Hello?" The tone just went on and on. Xanth said, "I need help." Nothing.

It was rare, but even in Galactic Central things sometimes went wrong, and the connection to the central computer in a particular area would be lost for a while. Earth technology was backward compared to what he was used to, so maybe their central computer worked less well also. Xanth hung up the telephone. He wasn't going to get any help that way.

Taking one more look at the three men on the floor, Xanth saw that they were moving a little. One of them had obviously smashed Motorcycle Man with a life-sized cardboard picture of a female human in a skin-tight costume. Motorcycle Man's head stuck through the cardboard where the female's head should be.

Xanth took a deep breath and pulled the door open fast, slamming it against the wall. He ran down the stairs and shouted, "Jerome! Something's wrong! Come look!"

The big human was still sitting under the basement window, smoking.

"Come on, come on!" Xanth shouted. "Your friends are in trouble!"

125

"I'm not that stupid," Jerome said.

"You have to go up and see what's going on up there!" Xanth said.

"You're just trying to trick me."

"They're in trouble!"

"Lenny told me to stay here, and I'm staying here."

"Lenny told me to come get you!"

"Well why didn't you say so?" Jerome asked, and started to get up.

Xanth followed the lumbering figure of Jerome up the stairs. His plan was to slam the door closed behind Jerome and lock it, then try to get Al and all the other homeless people out of the basement before the bad men could break the door open again. As plans go, it wasn't much, but it was all Xanth could think of.

Jerome pulled himself up to the top of the stairs and started into the store. Triumphantly Xanth slammed the door and turned the little mechanism that would lock it.

Before Xanth could even step down one step, a huge hand punched its way through the door, searched around a bit, found the lock and unlocked it. Then the door opened. Jerome reached out and grabbed the surprised Xanth and dragged him up the stairs.

Well, that was it. His plan had failed. He had traveled all this way to be killed by bad humans. All the Galactic warnings were right. Earth was a dangerous place and he had been a fool to come here. At least he would die in a Movie store, so he would die surrounded by the things that had drawn him to the forbidden planet.

Jerome shoved Xanth into the center of the room. He stumbled over all the little boxes on the floor. The other three men were getting up. They surrounded Xanth in a very threatening manner. Xanth closed his eyes. He didn't want to see his own death.

"Haiii-ya!" a voice shouted. Lenny and his gang turned. Between Lenny and Geordie, Xanth could see a small woman with gray hair. She was standing at a door that he hadn't noticed before. Stairs behind her led up to yet another level of the building. She was of the variety of humans that always fought with no weapons but could take on any number of bad guys with kicks, hand movements, and a lot of flips through the air. Xanth grinned. This should be good, he thought.

The woman was much smaller than any one of the men, and compared to Jerome she seemed very small indeed. Lenny gave her a contemptuous look and started to advance on her. The rest of the men followed.

"You not come closer," the woman said. "I am black belt in kung fu."

Xanth grinned some more. Kung Fu was so cool, the way he fought off all those cowboys, even though they had pistols, just by kicking them. If this woman could fight like that, this should be really good.

The group of men stopped for a moment. Then Lenny said, "Come on, she's bluffing."

While they hesitated, the old woman had managed to move closer to the counter area where the cash register was. The cash register was on its side, still closed despite obvious attempts to break it open.

"You not listen, you regret it," the woman said, still edging towards the counter. She stood with her arms raised in a threatening manner. She did not seem at all fearful of the hulking men.

Lenny didn't say anything; he just advanced on the old woman.

To Xanth, the next few moments seemed to be a blur. Lenny reached out to grab the woman, but she wasn't there. She moved behind the counter so fast that no one could have caught her. Despite his surprise, Lenny followed her, backed up by his three friends.

When they got behind the counter, Lenny said, "Where'd she go?" Xanth knew where she had gone; she was crawling around the counter on her knees, and carrying something in her hands. She got to front of the counter, jumped up, and pointed the thing she was carrying.

The men saw her but didn't have much time to react. From where the old woman now stood, Geordie was the closest to her. There was a tremendous flash and boom. Xanth's ears started to ring from the loud noise.

Geordie looked surprised as he was blown backwards, hit the bulk of Jerome behind him, then slid down to the floor.

"Next asshole move, get next demonstration in kung fu," the old woman said, pointing what Xanth now recognized as a shotgun at the remaining members of the gang.

Chapter Twenty-One

So humans really do shoot each other, Xanth thought. It wasn't all fictional. Galactic scholars had portrayed Earth as a place where people lived in peaceful artistic communities dreaming up all the violence that they showed in their stories.

Though it was possible Xanth was still in the middle of a Movie shoot and there were cameras hidden somewhere. He would definitely have to figure out the truth pretty soon.

If humans really did shoot each other all the time, that meant Xanth had come to the most violent planet in the galaxy. On purpose. They might even shoot an alien. Could he be in danger?

No, they must be making a Movie. Though the old woman was definitely mixing genres. She was the type of human who was supposed to fight without guns, like Jackie Chan or Bruce Lee. In fact, she should be able to take out hundreds of bad guys who had guns without using any herself.

"I thought humans like you didn't use guns," Xanth said, trying to clear up the mystery. Perhaps he should have thought things through a bit before speaking. He was standing in the center of the store, and the old woman with the shotgun had her back to him. She was concentrating on the bad guys, who were on the other side of the counter. When Xanth asked his question, it surprised the old woman, who probably had not known before that moment that he was there. She wheeled around and pointed the shotgun in Xanth's direction.

Seeing this, Lenny made a break for it. He moved quickly around the counter. Jerome and Motorcycle Man started around the counter the other way.

Xanth stood, rooted to the spot, watching everything as if it were a Movie. The business end of the shotgun got closer and closer. Xanth pointed behind the old woman. "Uh, the bad guys are..." He stepped forward, tripped over a pile of Movie boxes and fell to the floor.

The shotgun went off, and on the last display shelf that Lenny and his friends had not knocked over, a copy of "Titanic" exploded. Xanth crawled away from the direction the gun was pointing and struggled to his feet.

Now the old woman was in the middle of the store, and Lenny, Motorcycle Man, and Jerome were headed towards her. She seemed unsure where to aim next, waving the shotgun around as if trying to hit a bird in flight. Xanth walked up next to her.

"Can I help?" he asked. The shotgun moved in his direction.

"No, I'm a good guy. I'm on your side." He was proud that he was dealing with humans on their own terms. Everything else on Earth had proved to be confusing and disappointing, but he knew that a gunfight had clear rules. The bad guys lost, the good guys won, and certainly good guys never shot each other by mistake.

"You a burglar," the old woman said, trying to point the gun at Xanth. Up close Xanth could see that she couldn't see very well, and was pointing in the direction of his voice. When he moved she kept the shotgun aimed where he had been when he last time he said anything. This wasn't exactly in the rules of the gunfight. For one thing, old women usually played a smaller part in a Movie than the good guy. In fact, old people usually died in Movies.

Maybe I'm the main good guy in this story, Xanth thought. The old woman will get killed, and I'll snatch up her shotgun and avenge her death. He really didn't want her to get killed, but that's how it usually worked.

While Xanth was thinking all this, the three bad guys were getting closer. Thinking quickly, Xanth stepped behind the old woman, who was only an inch or two taller than he was, grabbed her by the shoulders, and turned her towards Lenny as he approached. Lenny was trying to avoid the front of the shotgun and sneak up next to the old woman so he could take the gun from her.

"Point straight forwards and I'll tell you when to shoot." Xanth told the old woman. He turned her back and forth, keeping Lenny in sight. Each time Lenny managed to get away from the muzzle of the gun, Xanth pointed it, and the old woman, at him again.

Pretty soon this dance had Xanth and the woman turned around, with their backs to the counter. Motorcycle man and Jerome had been hanging back, waiting to see if Lenny got killed before they did anything.

Xanth formulated the perfect plan. "Okay," he told the old woman, "do a back flip over the counter, and you'll end up with the counter between you and them. Even better, do it in slow motion. That would be really cool."

"What?"

"Do a back flip."

"I can't do no back flip. You crazy?"

"Come on. Jackie Chan would do it."

"Jackie Chan in movies. You think we in a movie?"

"Of course."

"You crazy burglar."

"*I'm* not a burglar, *they're* the burglars."

Burglars who were pretty close to catching hold of the waving shotgun and taking it away from the old woman. Xanth looked around. Even though he wasn't going to get his cool back flip, he thought retreating behind the counter was the best option. He pulled on the woman's shoulders and brought them both around near the overturned cash register.

"Okay, point straight out at them. I'll go see if my friend can help us."

"Where your friend?"

"In the basement."

"More burglars in basement?"

"No, just people who sleep there."

"People sleep in my basement?" The old woman let out a string of strange sounds, which must have been "Chinese." Then she reverted to English. "Dirty bums in my basement? Worse than burglars. I shoot them too."

"My friend Al is down there. Please don't shoot him. Maybe he can help us."

"You want to help, call police."

131

"I don't think a chorus of "Bad Boys" is going to make the bad guys give up."

"You are burglar if you don't want to call police."

"I am not a burglar. But if the police come, they'll just shoot everyone and sing that "Cops" song."

"Police shoot bad guys."

Xanth glanced at the bad guys. They were standing at the other side of the counter, watching the discussion.

"Ten bucks the kid escaped from a fruit farm," Lenny said.

"I'll take that," Motorcycle Man said. "I say he's a circus freak."

"Gosh, fellas," Jerome put in. "I think he's an alien."

Jerome's friends looked at him condescendingly. Lenny whispered to Motorcycle man, "Maybe Jerome's an alien."

"I heard that," Jerome said. "You know I'm from the south side."

"The south side of Mars," Lenny said. He and Motorcycle Man laughed.

Xanth rolled his eyes. "There's no life on Mars. Not since the Martians invaded Earth about a hundred years ago. One ship made it back to Mars, but they brought Earth viruses with them. The whole civilization was wiped out."

Everyone was staring at Xanth now. "I guess you wouldn't know that part," Xanth said. "It wasn't in the Movie."

"Great," the old Chinese woman said. "I caught between burglars and lunatic."

"Do you want me to help or not?" Xanth asked, wounded. "Would a lunatic stick around to help?"

"Then call police."

"All right, all right. I'll call the stupid police."

There was a pause. Everyone's eyes were on Xanth. "How do I call the police?" he asked.

"On the telephone!" Everyone else said.

"Okay! Sheesh!" Xanth picked up the hand set and listened to it. "Your central computer is still out. All I can hear is a tone."

"That is dial tone, you lunatic," the Chinese woman said.

"Watch out!" Xanth shouted. Motorcycle Man had been reaching towards the barrel of the shotgun. The old woman moved it away and shouted "No one move!" She backed up a little and pointed the gun squarely at Jerome.

"Why are you pointing it at me?" Jerome asked. "I'm not the one who tried to take it."

"Shut up," Lenny said.

"Well I wasn't." Jerome pouted.

"Now CALL POLICE!" the old woman shouted.

"I told you, the computer doesn't answer!" Xanth shouted back.

"Call 911!"

Oh, that explained it. There was a code that activated the central computer. Xanth lifted the handset and shouted into it, "Nine one one!" Nothing happened, so he tried again. "Nine one one!"

The droning tone continued.

"Dude, you have to dial 911," Lenny said.

"Dial?"

"Like, push the 911 buttons," Motorcycle Man said.

"No, " Lenny said, "I used it before, it's the old kind, with the dial."

"Whoa, I never used one of those."

"My grandma has one. It's freaky."

"What do I do?" Xanth asked. He looked at the phone. There was indeed a dial, as he had noted before. And a hole in the dial next to each number. He poked his finger into the hole next to the number nine.

"Nothing happens."

"Turn it, man," Lenny said.

Xanth moved his finger, and the dial moved. He discovered he could push the dial all the way until his finger hit a metal stop. He held the dial there.

"Now what?"

"Let it go," the Chinese woman said. Xanth pulled his finger away, and the dial rotated back to where it had started, making clicking noises as it went.

"So that's going to activate the central computer?"

"Central what?" Lenny asked.

"Is the central computer going to answer now?"

Robin Reed

"Someone at the police station should answer."

"You mean a human just sits there all day waiting to answer the phone? What's wrong with Earth's central computer?"

Lenny said, "My grandma has a computer."

"You're grandma has a computer but she still has a dial telephone?" Motorcycle Man asked.

"Yeah. Pentium Four, DVD, the works. It's really freaky."

"ONE ONE!" the Chinese lady shouted. The shotgun trembled in her hands.

"What?" Xanth had been following the conversation about the computer.

"You dial nine, you not dial one one!"

"Oh, right." Xanth placed his finger in the One hole and pulled the short distance to the metal stop, then repeated the motion. The monotonous tone stopped and he could hear some clicking.

"Emergency," a woman's voice said.

"Uh, hi. Is this a person?" Xanth asked.

"Yes, sir. What is your emergency?"

"I was really expecting the central computer. Earth really doesn't have a central computer?"

"Do you have an emergency sir?"

"That's amazing. Your job is just to answer the phone, huh?"

Lenny said, "This kid belongs in a home somewhere."

"I'm telling you, he's an alien," Jerome said.

"Why do you keep saying that, Jerome?" Motorcycle Man asked.

"Look at him," Jerome said.

"Man, my cousin is messed up worse than that. At least this kid has a nose," Motorcycle Man said.

"If you don't have an emergency, please hang up, sir," the woman on the phone said.

"Oh, yeah, right. Sorry," Xanth said. "There are these, um burglars, I guess, in this video store owned by an old lady who's kind of like Jackie Chan but she won't do a back flip."

"Where is the store?"

"In Chicago."

134

"Where in Chicago?" Xanth could hear the lady getting impatient. He didn't know why. He was answering all her questions.

"Where are we?" Xanth asked the old Chinese lady.

"I talk," she said. You hold this." She held out the shotgun. Xanth took it from her, surprised. He tried to keep it pointed at the bad guys, but he couldn't hold it still. It was heavy.

The old woman talked into the phone. Lenny looked at the shotgun, obviously trying to decide if he could snatch it away from Xanth. Xanth hoped he didn't try. He wanted to leave the shooting to the humans. They were good at it. Besides, he really didn't know how to activate the weapon.

Fortunately, the whole situation ended before Xanth had to shoot anyone. Flashing colored lights appeared outside the store window, and two policemen knocked on the front door. The Chinese woman opened the door for them, and Lenny and his friends went peacefully. Jerome cast one look back, as if to confirm that he had seen an alien.

While all this was going on, Xanth gratefully put the shotgun down. His hands were a bit cramped from holding it so tightly. All in all, things weren't bad. He had survived his first Earth shootout, and would have a story to tell for a long time to come. Maybe someone would make a Movie about it, or maybe they were making it already.

He had come through it all without a scratch. Just a few minutes before, he had been sure that he was going to die, and now he had survived this adventure without any injuries at all.

Turning to go down and tell Al all about it, Xanth tripped over Geordie's body and fell down the stairs.

Chapter Twenty-Two

"Al! Al!" Xanth stood shook his human friend, hoping to wake him up. Al sat up so suddenly that Xanth fell over backwards and hit his head for the third time in two minutes. The first two had been as he rolled down the stairs to the basement.

"Ow ow!" Xanth said.

"Is it morning already?" Al asked. "Can't be, I don't have a hangover yet."

"You won't believe what happened!" Xanth said as he stood up. "I was in my first Earth shootout, and the old lady didn't do any back flips but she did shoot Geordie, and the bad guys made a horrible mess upstairs and then they told me how to dial the telephone and some policemen came but they didn't sing their song."

Al stared at the alien. "Did you have another dream?" he asked.

"No! No! It all happened! The policemen are still upstairs. Did you know Earth doesn't have a Central Computer?"

"Slow down. First off, where am I?" Al looked around. "How did I get here?"

"Lenny helped me. I didn't know he was a bad guy then. I thought he was nice. Boy, I thought the old woman from even further upstairs was going to be like Kung Fu and kick everyone and then remember when she was a child and the old man called her Grasshopper and asked her to snatch a pebble out of his hand. Though I never knew what he was supposed to do with the pebble after he got it."

"Did you say, 'old lady from even further upstairs'?"

"Yes, she's from that place where they talk the language that was on the bottom of the screen when we saw '*E.T.*'"

"Mrs. Chang? You met Mrs. Chang?"

"Oh, you did say her name was Mrs. Chang. Wait a minute. If she's from the same place as Kung Fu, how come Kung Fu always spoke English? Were you just making up that stuff about other languages on Earth?"

136

"It was an American show, and David Carradine wasn't even Chinese...oh, never mind. We have to get out of here." Al stood up and put his hand to his head. "There's the beginning of that hangover."

"Yeah, you must have made up that language thing. It doesn't make any sense," Xanth said. "Though all the boxes upstairs do have the strange letters on them..."

"Xanth, it's not important right now! We have to get out of here! Help me get everyone up!"

Al and Xanth moved to around the room and roused the sleeping homeless people. When they got to Robert it took some shaking to wake him up, and he came to saying, "Don't let Medved write any more movie reviews, for the love of God!"

"Where'd you get that shiner, Robert?" Al asked.

"Lenny punched him," Xanth said. "That's when I figured out he was a bad guy."

"All right. Tell me the whole story later. Right now we have to get everyone out."

Al helped Ginny and Robert out the window. As Ginny staggered down the alley, they could hear her singing "Heat Wave!" under her breath.

Pretty soon everyone was out except Xanth, Al, and Puddintame. The old man wouldn't climb out the window, or even stand up. "Nope," he said, "I been to that place, and I didn't like it."

"What place?" Al asked.

"Ha. If I tell you, you'll take me there."

"I'm not going to take you anyplace."

"That's right, you're not."

"But you gotta get out of here. The cops are coming."

"Will they take me to that place?"

"I don't know what place you're talking about!"

"And I ain't gonna tell you, neither."

Al threw up his hands. "We can't force him. We'd better go." He and Xanth crawled through the window up to the alley just before the sound of clumping feet came down the basement stairs. Looking back, they could see Mrs. Chang, followed by two policemen.

"The little one tell me, he say people sleeping in basement. MY basement!"

As Xanth and Al walked away, they heard one of the policemen gruffly ask, "What's your name?" They barely heard the response, but they knew the old man was saying, "My name is Puddintame. Ask me again and I'll tell you the same."

After putting a few blocks behind them, with Al hugging his coat around himself in the chill night air, and Xanth trying to keep warm with no coat at all, Al said, "Now what?"

Xanth didn't know how to answer that. Since he had met Al, he had followed the human's lead.

"That basement was the best place I've ever found to sleep in," Al said. "Now I guess it's back to doorways and park benches."

"There must be someplace," Xanth said. "I don't really understand Earth, but I don't believe they let people just die outside with no shelter or food."

Al glanced sideways at the alien. "You're right, you don't understand Earth," he said.

A few more blocks, and Al decided to try the park. The cops didn't like anyone to sleep there, he said, but the park was huge and the cops couldn't check everywhere. They went east, towards the lake.

After crossing Michigan Avenue, they found themselves under trees. Al chose one that was completely in darkness, with no streetlight nearby. He sat down and put his back to the tree. Xanth sat on the ground nearby.

"All right," Al said. "Now you can tell me what happened back there."

"Back at the basement?"

"Yeah."

"The story really starts before we got back to the basement."

"OK, start before the basement."

"How much before?"

"Whenever the story starts."

"I always wanted to come to Earth and be a Movie star..."

"Fast forward."

"What?"

"Fast forward."

"I don't know what that means."

"You remember the movie machine when we saw *E.T.*?"

"Yes."

"It has a button that makes the tape move faster, so you can skip forward in the story."

"Oh. Okay. Um, in the shootout, Mrs. Chang had a big shotgun..."

"Rewind."

"What?"

"There's another button that makes the tape go backwards. It's called 'Rewind'."

"Oh. Let's see. I got on the cruise ship that was going near Earth..."

"Fast forward."

"I went up the stairs to see what the bad guys were doing..."

"Rewind."

"I got into my personal ship, and..."

"Fast forward!"

"Jerome started to smoke a cigarette..."

"Rewind!"

"When I landed on Earth I met a small human with a thing that I thought was an agrav device..."

"Fast forward!"

"Lenny called his friends on the telephone..."

"This is harder than finding the one nude scene in a whole movie."

"What?"

"Never mind. Where were we?"

"I met a small human."

"Right. Fast forward."

"Lenny and me got you back to the basement..."

"Rewind, but just a little."

"You bought a bottle at a store..."

"Fast forward just a tiny bit."

"We left the store..."

139

"It would be funny if you moved fast like the people on a speeded up tape."

"Huh?"

"Fast forward just a little bit more."

"You fell asleep in the alley."

"Great! Now, play."

"What?"

"That means start telling the story from there."

"Oh. Okay..." Xanth told everything that had happened that evening, from Al falling asleep to Xanth falling down the stairs.

"Whew," Al said.

"I don't know why Mrs. Chang didn't come down sooner. The bad guys made an awful lot of noise."

"She's a little hard of hearing. That's why we got away with sleeping there for so long. There were nights when Ginny sang "Heat Wave" for hours on end."

"She also seemed to be a little hard of seeing," Xanth said. "She could hardly tell where to point the shotgun."

"I'm glad you helped her out."

"I'm sorry we can't sleep there any more. I didn't mean to get us kicked out of there."

"Ah, it's all right. I managed for years before I found that place." Al winced. "That hangover is really coming on strong. So just speak softly, okay?"

Xanth said something Al couldn't hear.

"What was that?"

Xanth spoke a little louder, but the words weren't clear.

"Speak a little louder."

"I'm trying to speak softly." Xanth spoke so softly that Al could barely make out what he said.

"A little louder than that, please."

"I'M TRYING TO SPEAK SOFTLY!"

Al clutched his head. "More softly than that! Please!"

"Is this okay?"

"Yes, yes, that's just right. Geez, first I have to fast forward and rewind you, and now I have to adjust your volume. I wonder what would happen if I said 'Pause'."

Xanth stayed still, waiting for Al to explain what he meant.

"My God, it works."

"What works?"

"It's not important."

They sat companionably in the dark for a while. Xanth hugged himself for warmth. Just when Xanth thought Al had gone to sleep, he spoke instead.

"I've been thinking about what you should do," Al said.

"What I should do?"

"Yeah. You want to go to Hollywood, right?"

"Of course."

"Well, you're not going to get there hanging around me."

"You could help me get there."

"What you should do is, get a job and get some money, then find a way to get to Hollywood. Hell, a bus will get you there for not too much. You need to follow your dream."

"Come with me."

"No. I belong here. I've been in this city for thirty years."

"You're my only friend on Earth."

"So write me a post card. I belong here, you belong out in La-La Land, becoming the latest alien sensation."

"Please come with me."

"I can't. And you shouldn't hang around me, even before you go. Being homeless becomes a way of life pretty quickly, and after that there's no going back. In fact, you should leave right now. Find someplace else to sleep, and in the morning don't look for me. Look for your destiny."

"What? Go right now?"

"That's right."

"I don't want to."

"If you don't, you'll get stuck here. I don't want to be responsible for that."

"Please don't make me go."

"Go. Now. I don't want you here."

"Al..."

"I mean it. Get out of here."

Xanth stood up. He could barely see his human friend in the dark, so he couldn't see if his expression matched his harsh words.

"Please..." he said.

"I can't have some freak hanging around. It'll cramp my style."

Xanth turned and walked away. He fought back tears as he walked. He had gone a fair distance before his sensitive hearing picked up Al's voice. He was sure that Al didn't know Xanth could hear when he whispered, "See you in the movies."

Xanth moved in the direction they had been going earlier. As he went, he started to hear the sound of waves splashing on rocks. He walked until grass under his feet gave way to pavement. He jumped down from one level to another, and the water was very near. It was less dark here because there was a light high up on a pole. He walked onto some rough-cut square boulders, and the water splashed up between them and wetted his feet.

Xanth sat on the very edge of the water. It splashed up on his legs now. He couldn't see far out into the ocean, but all his senses told him that it went on forever. He had only seen large bodies of water when he visited Qaaxle, the tourist planet. He had been there once as a child, and again on the cruise. He still wore the t-shirt he got there. He had only seen the water from a distance, though. He had been thinking about Earth so much, he hadn't bothered to see the sights on the cruise.

He knew that his own species was semi-aquatic, meaning that they lived mostly in water on their home planet, but came up to breathe air. That home planet was long lost, and none of the few members of that species who lived in Galactic Central had any idea where it had been. No records in the Central Computer gave any clues.

Xanth gave way to his tears, tears for his lost home planet, for his lost comfortable room in Galactic Central, and for his lost friend Al. Then he slept.

Light woke Xanth up. He blinked and opened his eyes. The world was light again. Wind blew over him. Water splashed his legs. He sat up.

It was amazing. He had sensed in the dark that the lake was enormous, but now that he could see he could hardly believe it. The rolling water went on endlessly, over the horizon. It was more water than he had ever dreamed of. Water that came in towards Xanth in waves, crashed on the rocks and sent sprays of water into the air.

Then Xanth turned and gasped. The city of Chicago, where he had never meant to land, where he gotten lost and starved and kicked and almost shot, was beautiful. Graceful tall buildings curved around the shore of that vast ocean, reflecting sunlight in the early morning, and looking like they had been built for the visual effect alone. The park stretched along the lake as far as the eye could see, leaving open space with trees and grass between the buildings and the ocean.

Xanth stood and stretched. If this planet, despite its dangers, could be this beautiful, maybe it was worth coming here.

Turning again to the ocean, Xanth had a thought. Semi-aquatic? He'd always been told that he was. Here was his chance to find out. He pulled off his Qaaxle t-shirt and slipped out of his shorts and shoes. He stood on the edge of the rocks. Then he dived into the water.

"Oh my God!" a voice shouted. A middle aged woman in a jogging suit ran up to where Xanth had gone into the lake. Her dog followed and looked into the water.

Frantically, the woman turned and shouted, "Help! Help! A little boy just committed suicide!"

Chapter Twenty-Three

The water was wonderful. Xanth had never been immersed in water before. His quarters in Galactic Central had a small shower, and sometimes he had stood in its spray and imagined he was swimming the oceans of his ancestral planet, but he had never had a chance to really swim.

He spread his hands and feet and the webbing between the fingers and toes, always useless before, helped push him through the water. The water was murky, but he could see pretty well. He felt like he was gliding through a lost paradise, a place where all his troubles were washed away. He felt that way until he hit his head on a refrigerator.

The refrigerator wasn't the only human artifact lying on the bottom of the lake. Xanth caught a glimpse of a shopping cart, a large machine with the words "Mountain Dew" on it, and a riding lawn mower. It was the refrigerator, though, that intersected with Xanth's cranium and caused a jolt of pain to shoot through his head and down his spine. He also expelled all the air in his lungs and discovered what he had previously known only in theory. His species was built for swimming, but they were not water breathers. Xanth needed to find the surface and breathe air, and he needed to do it very soon.

The next problem was that Xanth no longer had any idea in which direction the surface was. He kicked out with all his newfound swimming skill and found himself reading the slogan "Do the Dew" on the sunken vending machine. Thus, it stood to reason that the surface was in the opposite direction.

Xanth swam with all his might. His lungs burned, his muscles screamed in protest, and his head hurt where he had hit it. Just when he was sure that he had come to Earth only to drown, he burst through the surface and was able to take a huge, life-saving breath.

At first all he could see was water. He was bobbing up and down in the waves, and no matter which way he turned, waves were

144

blocking his view of anything else. In a moment, one wave dipped low enough that Xanth saw some kind of human construction, an odd-shaped building on a pile of rocks. He started to swim towards it, then realized the pile of rocks was pretty far out in the ocean. Turning around some more, he spied the shore, with the park, the trees, and all those tall buildings in the background.

Starting to enjoy the swimming again, but this time staying on the surface, Xanth moved towards the shore and the rocky area where he had jumped in. Something was different there. Instead of a lonely stretch of rocky shore, it was alive with humans. One female with a dog by her side was pointing out at the lake and talking to a man in a jogging costume. About half a dozen other people also peered out in the direction she was pointing.

They were all standing next to Xanth's clothing. His shorts, sneakers, and Qaaxle T-shirt weren't worth much, but they were the only clothing he had. He had to get them back, but if he climbed out of the water now, he would be naked in front of a bunch of humans.

One thing Xanth had always wondered about *E.T.* was, why was he naked throughout the movie? Except for few scenes where the kids dressed him up, he went around naked most of the time. Probably the Earth filmmakers, and of course King of Earth Spielberg, made him do it. It hardly seemed to Xanth that the nudity was integral to the plot, but humans did seem to believe that aliens never wore clothing, which was proof enough that they hadn't had any major contact with the rest of the galaxy. Mr. Blackwell's annual best- and worst-dressed lists were major news in Galactic Central.

Xanth, after he got old enough to dress and bathe himself, had never been naked in front of another sentient being. He didn't plan to start now. But how could he get his clothes back?

Vehicles had begun to arrive at the shore. Police cars, a fire truck, and several different kinds of official cars with blinking lights were parked nearby. Official-looking people in various uniforms were talking to the woman with the dog.

What could have happened right there at the spot where Xanth had dived into the water that would draw all these humans? It was just the kind of luck he'd been having since he came to Earth.

Xanth swam along the shore, away from the frenzied activity. He tried to think of something. The only idea that came to mind was that he had to find Al, the only human who had ever helped him. The last time he saw Al, the old drunk was pushing him away, telling him not to come back. Still, maybe he would help in this emergency.

If Al wouldn't help, no one would. Xanth had learned enough about humans to know that. He reached a point far enough down the shore that he was sure that the humans couldn't see him. He swam close to the cement wall, using all his strength to keep from being battered against it by the waves.

Putting his hands on top of the wall, Xanth pulled himself up to see if the coast, literally, was clear. "Beep!" Xanth cursed. There was a male human with another dog. Xanth lowered himself down, keeping his hands on the wall. He looked up and saw the dog staring down at him.

The orange creature didn't bark or snarl, as they usually did in Movies, it just stared. Xanth knew that dogs weren't all the same. In some Movies they were killers, in some they were just friendly companions to humans. Small, fluffy ones tended to have terrible things happen to them in comedies. This one was pretty big.

"Come on, Agamemnon," the human called. Agamemnon continued to stare at Xanth. "Come on, Aggie," the human voice said. This time it was a lot closer. "Whatcha looking at, boy?"

If the human looked down where the dog was staring, he would see Xanth. Xanth was about to let go and slide down into the water, when Agamemnon gave out a "Whuf!" and turned away.

"Good boy, Aggie. Come on, let's run." The sounds of the human and dog faded away. Xanth let out a breath he hadn't realized he was holding.

Then it was up out of the water, across the broad expanse of cement, over a low wall, and into the park. Quickly Xanth hid behind a tree. It wasn't long before he realized that the term "behind a tree" was relative. He was in a city full of humans, and if he hid from the humans on the lakeshore, he was completely exposed to the humans in the rest of the park. If he hid on the other side of the tree, the humans walking along the lake would see his nakedness. It was a no-win situation. So before any humans came along from any direction, Xanth took off across the grass, running as fast as he could, crouching and trying to be less naked.

He threw himself into a bush when he heard voices. He watched three young men walk by, bouncing a basketball. The bush was a little better in the way of cover, because it worked equally well from all directions, but he couldn't stay there forever. When no one seemed to be nearby, Xanth bolted, heading in the direction that he thought vaguely was where he had last seen Al.

A short way further on, Xanth heard more voices. This time there was no cover at all, so he dived to the ground and lay there as still as he could. His hero *E.T.* had performed a similar trick, and it might work in this situation, Xanth thought, though he wasn't in a closet and he wasn't surrounded by toys.

The voices came closer, but no one yelled, "Hey! There's a naked alien lying still on the ground here!" Xanth pressed his face into the grass and smelled the dirt as he hoped with all his might that the humans would pass by without seeing him.

One of the human voices said, "I just have to finish my investigation into the crash, then I have to get back to NORAD."

Another voice said, "Investigation indeed. You know it was the commies that caused it." That voice sounded like an older female human.

"Yap!" a small dog barked, as if in agreement.

"MacArthur thinks so too." the older woman said.

"I'll pass your theory on to the brass, Mother," the first voice said, "but they will still want me to do an investigation."

"Your superiors are probably all fellow travelers and fifth columnists, boy. You should call that nice Senator McCarthy and report them. He'll have them up in front of the Unamerican Activities Committee in a jiffy!"

"Yes, Mother. My superiors are fifth columnist communists. Or fifth communist columnists, whichever. I'll give the senator a call as just as soon as I get back to my office."

With that, the voices faded away. Xanth lifted his face from the ground. They actually didn't see him. *E.T.*'s trick had worked, with no closet or toys in sight. Now Xanth really had to find Al. He walked and ran around the park, hoping to catch a glimpse of his friend. Al was nowhere to be found. Xanth hid from a few more groups of people, began to despair. He had come all the way to Earth just to die of embarrassment. Standing in an open area, looking around and feeling very unhappy, Xanth smelled a horrible stench, an eye watering, gut-wrenching odor. He whirled and shouted "Al!"

"Hey there, kid. I thought you would be in Hollywood by now." Al said.

"Oh, Al, I'm so glad to smell you, er, see you. You have to help me."

"What happened to your clothes?"

"I went for a swim in the lake, which was the first time I ever really swam in a body of water, and it was really nice except that I hit my head on a refrigerator, and when I came to the surface a bunch of people were standing around near my clothes and staring out at the ocean."

"Lake. It's a lake. So why didn't you just ask them for your clothes back?"

"I can't be naked in front of all those humans!"

"Until I met you, I thought aliens were always naked."

"You and the rest of humanity. Can you help me?"

"I guess," Al said. "Say, what are those?"

"What are what?" Xanth said, nervously trying to hide the parts of himself that he was most anxious that humans never see.

"Those things coming our of your sides?" Al asked.

"Nothing. Can we get my clothes?"

"Boy, that's completely different than human anatomy. What are they for?"

"I don't want to talk about it!" Xanth said.

"They're for sex, aren't they? How does your species have sex? Do you have orgasms?"

"I don't know! I've never even seen another member of my species except for my parents! Will you quit asking about this?"

"Let's see, you told me there are three sexes in your species...let me guess, you have one on each side, and you're all hooked together in a circle, right?"

"I DON'T KNOW!" Xanth screamed. Then he looked around to see if any people had heard him screaming.

"Didn't your parents tell you?"

"Al, one more word about this, and I'll run away and never talk to you again."

"You'll run away while you're still naked?" Al asked.

"Yes! No...I don't know...just stop asking about that."

"All right. Here." Al said. He took his jacket off and gave it to Xanth. Wrapping it around himself, Xanth was surrounded by Al's stench, but it came down to his knees and he pulled the front together and he felt much less naked.

"So where did you leave your clothes?" Al asked.

"I'll show you."

In addition to the police cars, fire trucks, ambulances, and gawkers that Xanth had seen from the lake, the news vans had now arrived at the spot where Xanth had left his clothing. Reporters were standing in front of cameras and gesturing out at the lake.

Al and Xanth hid behind a tree near the scene. This time, "behind a tree" was a more practical place to hide, since the people they were hiding from were in only one direction. They saw two men wearing black rubber suits and tanks on their backs walk towards the lake. They conferred with a policeman for a moment, then jumped off the rocky shore into the water.

"What did you do that caused all this?" Al asked.

"I didn't do anything." Xanth said. "It all started when I was swimming."

"Wait here," Al said, and walked towards all the people. Adopting a stagger that suggested he was a lot more drunk than he really was at the moment, Al moved closer to the assortment of police and fire fighters.

"What's going on here?" Al asked loudly. Several people turned to look, then a burly policemen moved up to stop Al. "Move along," the policeman said.

"What's going on? You gotta tell me."

"Nothing that concerns you. Move along."

Suddenly, Al and the policemen were flooded with light, as a news cameraman pointed his camera, and the bright light mounted on top of it, right at them. A well-dressed young woman with a microphone pushed her way in front of the camera also. "Did you witness the boy jump in the lake?" She asked.

"Jump in the lake?" Al drunkenly asked. "Was it little Timmy? I can't find little Timmy anywhere."

The reporter turned to face the camera, "We now know the boy's name was Timmy." Pushing the mike in Al's face, she asked, "Are you little Timmy's father?"

"You betcha," Al said. "Have you seen him? I can't find him anywhere."

"That's right," a man standing nearby holding the leash of his golden retriever said. "I saw them panhandling near the Art Institute yesterday. The boy's kinda funny-looking." Then the man walked away, saying to his dog, "Come on, Aggie, we have to get home."

Other reporters were converging on the spot, eager to find someone new to interview. More cameras and bright lights were shining on Al. Al made a break for it through their ranks and ran towards the lake.

A plain-clothes cop in a rumpled suit was kneeling where Xanth had left his clothing. He picked up the Qaaxle t-shirt with a gloved hand. He looked at it for a moment, then put it into a plastic bag he held in the other hand. The shorts and shoes were already in the bag.

"That's little Timmy's little shirt!" Al shouted as he ran. The pack of reporters ran on his heels. Al stopped near the cop and grabbed the bag away from him. "Oh, little Timmy, where are you?" Al sobbed.

"Hey, give that back," the cop said. He stood up and grabbed the bag, trying to pull it away from Al. The reporters caught up and shined their camera lights on the two men struggling over the bag of clothing.

Several uniformed policemen approached, shouting for Al to let go of the bag. Then they grabbed Al and reached for their handcuffs. Reporters were shoving their microphones at anyone who might be able to say something, and cameramen got in close to get good shots. All of these people struggled with each other on the rocks right next to the surging waters of the lake.

Who tripped first was unclear, but the mass of people started to topple over as one person's weight knocked over another, then more and more lost their footing on the rocks. Al pushed his way through, trying to get away from the falling group and still hold onto the bag. He managed to worm his way out just as he felt them fall.

Three reporters, two cameramen with cameras, the plain-clothes cop and two uniformed policemen, all fell off the rocks into the lake. Water splashed up and soaked two fire fighters and two eleven-year-old boys who had been riding bikes nearby and stopped to watch.

Al found himself standing on the shore, completely dry and holding the bag with Xanth's clothing in it. He looked out at the people in the water, and saw the police divers surface near them.

Al went back to the tree where Xanth was hiding and handed the alien his clothing.

"Did you find out why they're all here?" Xanth asked.

"They think a little boy fell in the lake."

"Really? Were they able to rescue him?"

"I don't think there was a boy. I think someone saw you jump in," Al said.

"Oh. You mean I caused all that?"

"Don't worry about it," Al said. He glanced at where all the reporters and policemen had fallen in. "At least now all that rescuing won't go to waste."

Xanth hurried to get his clothes out of the bag and put them on. When he was done he felt a lot better. "Come on," he said, "we don't want to be late."

Al looked at Xanth, turning away from the scene on the lakefront. "Huh? Be late to what?"

Xanth had already run away, shouting "I'm going to be in a Movie! I'm going to be in a Movie!"

Chapter Twenty-Four

"Is that everything?" Rita asked.

"Yeah," Tony said, putting a heavy silver case down.

The small group of film students stood in front of 600 S. Michigan Avenue, the main building of Columbia College. Several cases of equipment that they had just checked out of the film department sat on the sidewalk nearby. Loop office workers walked around the students and tried to pretend they didn't see them.

"Think they'll show?" Jeremy asked. He was holding a blindingly white piece of foam-core board. The morning sunlight reflected off of it, and Jeremy moved the board around, shining the light in the eyes of the others.

"Quit it," Rita said. "We'll give them five more minutes. Did you bring the mask?"

Jeremy whipped the alien mask out of his backpack and put it on. "Anal probe, anyone?" he asked.

Frank was reading a copy of *The Chicago Tribune*. "They still haven't found out what caused those two military jets to crash over the lake," he said.

"We abducted the pilots and anal probed them," Jeremy said in his best alien voice.

"Their bodies have been recovered from the lake," Frank said. "And the body of a civilian was found under some of the wreckage. Some poor guy just walking along the lake, and smoosh!"

"Speaking of aliens," Frank said, turning the pages of the paper, "an alien saved a store in Chinatown from getting robbed."

"We anal probe lots of Chinese people," Jeremy said.

"Stop with the anal probes," Rita said.

Jeremy took the mask off. "Does it really say that?"

"Yup. One of the robbers says it was an alien."

"Cool," Jeremy said.

"I don't think that kid is coming," Tony said, looking at his watch.

Rita looked at her watch too. "Another couple minutes." Tony said, "I heard on the radio this morning that a little boy jumped in the lake and drowned." No one responded.

Rita looked at her watch again. "All right, let's move out. Jeremy, looks like you're our alien."

"Yes!" Jeremy shouted. All four picked up the equipment and started walking towards the street. They waited for the walk signal to cross the broad, busy street, and headed into the park.

The film students hadn't gone very far into the park before they heard a small voice chanting something. The voice got closer, and after a short time they could make it out. "I'm going to be in a Movie! I'm going to be in a Movie!"

A deeper voice told the chanting voice to shut the hell up, but the chant went on. In a moment, a tall figure in a shabby coat and a funny-looking child appeared ahead.

"Jeremy," Rita said, "I guess you're on boom."

Jeremy put down the case he was carrying, whipped out the alien mask and put it on. "You mean I don't get to anal probe anyone?" he asked.

Xanth stopped chanting and pointed. "There they are!" he shouted, and ran towards the film students. Al hurried to catch up, just glad that Xanth was no longer shouting that he was going to be in a movie.

"Here I am!" Xanth said to the students. "Ready for you to make me a star!"

"Hi," Rita said. "What was your name again?"

"Xanthan Gumm. You can call me Xanth."

"Well, Xanth, are you ready to be an alien today?"

"I'm always an alien."

"Oh, so you're staying in character during the whole shoot."

"I'll agree to whatever you just said as long as it means I'll be in your Movie."

"You say movie as if it's capitalized."

Al walked up to the group. "You're Xanth's dad?" Rita asked.

"Yes. Poor little guy has always felt so different because of the way he looks. If playing an alien will help him, then let's do it."

Xanth bounced up to Al and Rita. "I'm not playing an alien. I AM an alien," he said.

"Of course you are," Al said, winking at Rita. "He likes it if you play along."

"Al," Xanth said, "You know I'm an alien. Tell her."

"Yes," Al said, winking alternately with both eyes. "Xanth is REALLY an ALIEN."

Rita leaned towards Xanth. "I understand," she said. "And such a scary alien too!" She raised her hands in mock horror. "Look, guys, a real, scary alien!"

The three other students all said, "A scary alien! Ooooh!"

"Move out," Rita said. "Let's get to our first location."

Rita, Tony, Frank, and Jeremy picked up the boxes they had put down and started walking. Xanth pulled on Al's coat and made him fall behind.

"What was all that?" Xanth asked.

"We don't really want them to think you're an alien," Al said.

"Why not?"

"Look, for all our fascination with the concept of aliens, most humans don't believe that aliens really exist. If they believed you were an honest to god, real live alien, no telling what they'd do."

"They'd put me in the Movies and make me a star!"

"They might call the government and you'd end up as the star of 'Alien Autopsy 2' on Fox."

General Les S. Moore brooded as he looked out over Lake Michigan. His mother sat on a nearby bench. "Get them, MacArthur!" she shouted, ordering the dog to attack some pigeons that had waddled towards her looking for a handout. MacArthur barked and ran at the birds, which sensibly took flight and got out of there. "Ha!" Mrs. Moore said, "No welfare here, birdies! None of that damn Roosevelt New Deal when I'm around! You'll work for your food or starve!"

Les sighed. His mother had told him the same thing at every meal when he was a child. He wondered for the millionth time what his childhood would have been like if his father had lived longer. Manny

Moore was an Army officer who died in Korea, and who was awarded several medals posthumously. Les grew up with all the military discipline, patriotism, and hatred of communism that his mother could possibly drill into his head. It was only when he was grown that he had talked to some other relatives and learned that his father had a sense of humor, and was always cheerful and smiling. In fact, Manny and his wife were kidders, jokers, people who burst into numbers from their favorite movie musicals at the drop of a top hat. They were very deeply in love.

Their love was so profound that Manny's death in Korea blew away his wife's smile forever. Before long she was the strident anti-communist that the young Les grew up with. Now she was still living in the red scare paranoia of the 1950's, her mind running in a loop that sometimes expanded to include the Kennedy administration, but usually stayed within the years when everyone liked Ike.

Les remembered those days pretty well himself. The days of "Duck and Cover", when an atomic bomb could explode at any moment and children were advised to duck under their school desks and cover their heads with their hands. Not much protection from the force that had turned the population of Hiroshima into ash in a few seconds.

As silly as some of that government advice had been, at least we knew in those days that we were right, Les thought. The United States of America was right and good and had saved the world from the Nazis and the Japs. Some bad people over in Russia were trying to destroy all that rightness, but we would prevail somehow. Because good always prevails.

Now, General Moore was determined to bring back the best part of those days. If the United States of America could find a new permanent enemy, a new outside force, someone better than unreliable terrorists, it could restore its own sense of rightness and goodness. It would once again be the good guy.

However, his plan involved finding some proof that it was an alien who caused the crash of the two fighter jets over Lake Michigan, and the death of the two heroic pilots, Smeg and Schneckman. Evidence that was sorely missing from the lakefront area where the UFO had landed. Les suspected that the mysterious agency that took the spaceship had been very thorough in eliminating any such evidence. But he was Les S. Moore, three star general, leader of men, patriot and (dare he think it?) future President. He would find the proof he needed, somehow.

"Les!" Mrs. Moore shouted, "I see some commies! Come here and get rid of them!"

Les walked back to where his mother was sitting and saw her pointing down at the ground. "Look at them, working together like that! Commies if I ever seen 'em! Get them!"

Les sighed and obligingly crushed the ant-hill under his shoe.

Nubarrion, Emperor of the Galaxy, wasn't actually Emperor of the Galaxy yet, but he was working on it. He was king of the Auflysmal people from the planet Miniskyool, but his ambitions were large. His species had only been in contact with Galactic Civilization for a few years. Before that, Nubarrion's title had been Emperor of Everything, because the Auflysmals' whole civilization existed inside their planet. They dug tunnels, farmed and worked, without ever seeing the stars or even the surface of their home world.

Being contacted by a vast galaxy of alien beings, most of who were much larger than the Auflysmals, was a blow to their belief in their own superiority. Before long, Nubarrion cut off all contact with the galaxy and tried to live and rule as if they had never been found by the larger civilization.

It didn't work. Nubarrion couldn't take the knowledge that he wasn't Emperor of Everything anymore. He decided that it was his rightful destiny to rule the galaxy as well as his own people.

The whole society worked to formulate a plan that would fulfill Nubarrion's destiny. Finally, when reviewing information about Galactic Civilization, the Emperor read about Earth, the forbidden planet, which had so much influence on Galactic culture. He started to learn as much as he could about this Earth. Before long he learned that Earth had its own population of small burrowing creatures, creatures who outnumbered humans by millions to one.

The Auflysmal civilization bent its entire productive output toward developing two things. The first was space flight capability. The second was the weapon that would allow Nubarrion to control Earth and then the galaxy. The Emperor drove his people until their economy was in ruin. No one was allowed to work on anything but The Plan.

When the ships were ready, Nubarrion flew to Earth. His armada landed on a likely spot in an Earth population center, and found the burrowers, creatures called ants. Nubarrion seized control of one of these ant colonies, using the mind control weapon developed under The Plan. The ants didn't need much controlling, for they had almost no minds. They were about the same size as the Auflysmals, but were not sentient. So much the better for the Emperor's plan.

The entire productive output of the ant colony was put to work building a bigger version of the mind control machine. For months of Earth time, the ants labored, along with the Auflysmal scientists and soldiers.

When the machine was activated, it would control the actions of every ant on Earth. The ants would attack the humans. When the human civilization was reduced to chaos, Nubarrion would control the broadcast facilities that had so influenced the galaxy. He would declare himself Emperor of the Galaxy. He would declare the Auflysmal language as the only legal language, replacing the horrible sounds that the humans emitted.

Two days before the machine was to be turned on, the scientists reported that the colony was under observation from orbit by a small craft (small by Galactic, not auflysmal standards). A red alert was sounded, but the craft withdrew its Viewscope and did nothing to foil Nubarrion's plan.

Now, the plan was about to come to fruition. The mind control machine was within moments of being activated. Two humans and a four-legged creature of some sort were nearby, but that did not matter. The genius of Nubarrion's plan was that ants were beneath the notice of humans. At least they were until hundreds of millions of them turned on the humans and started biting. The plan was perfect.

"Nz!" the chief auflysmal scientist said, which in his language meant, "Sire, one of the humans is pointing at us!"

Nubarrion looked at the monitor the scientist indicated. "Rp," he said, which in his language meant, "No matter, in a moment my destiny will begin."

"Aq!" The chief scientist said, meaning "The other human is moving its foot right over us!"

The last thing that Nubarrion, Emperor of the Galaxy, ever said was, "Xg!" which in his language meant "Noooooooooooooooooooooooooooo!"

Chapter Twenty-Five

Xanth raised his arms and said "Growl!"

Tony, sitting on a stone wall with his back to the lake, kept looking straight ahead.

"Cut!" Rita shouted.

"You said 'Cut!' Xanth said happily. "Just like in all the Movies about people making Movies!"

"Tony, why didn't you react?"

Tony looked around. "Did he growl? I didn't even hear it," he said.

"Exactly." Rita came out from behind the camera and walked towards Xanth.

"Can I put the boom down between takes?" Jeremy asked. "It's heavy." He was holding a long pole with a microphone on it over Tony's head. A cord ran from the pole to a DAT recorder on the ground.

"Just keep the mike off the ground," Rita said, and stopped in front of Xanth.

"Xanth, you're an alien."

"I knew you believed me!"

"In the MOVIE you're an alien."

"Oh. Right."

"You're sneaking up on Tony."

"That's what you told me to do."

"You look as scary as you can."

"Yeah."

"When you get close to him you growl."

"I did. I said, Growl!"

"You don't SAY growl, you growl!"

"Okay."

"Do you know what to do?"

"I sneak up on Tony."

"Right."

"I look as scary as I can."

"Good."

"And then I say Growl!"

Rita shook her head. Directing was harder than she had thought it would be.

Jeremy put the pole down, propping the mike on one of the aluminum equipment cases.

Frank was operating the DAT recorder. He was on his knees fussing with the settings. Jeremy stood beside him.

"This kid is no actor," Jeremy said.

"Not my department," Frank said. "As long as the sound is good, I've done my job."

"That's the whole reason you're going to film school? To be a sound man?"

"It's good job. I talked to a Hollywood sound guy once who said you can make a ton of money. You just buy your own rig and when the word gets around that you're good, the calls start pouring in."

"What about the artistic expression of telling a good story?"

"Not my department. The Hollywood guy said that on commercials you usually just show up for half a day and they shoot the rest without sound. You still make a bundle."

"Commercials," Jeremy said with disgust. "Can I read your newspaper?"

"Sure." Frank had it tucked under his arm. He handed it to Jeremy.

Jeremy walked away and sat down near his backpack. Nearby he had placed the piece of foam core board under another case. A stiff lake breeze was trying to make it fly away. The foam core was hard to hold onto in when it was windy, but they might need it at some point to reflect light onto an actor's face.

"Grrr," Rita said.

"Grrr," Xanth repeated.

"Grrrrrrrrrr."

"Grrrrrrrrrr."

"Good, now make a face. You're a big scary alien and you're going to eat Tony!"

"I don't want to eat Tony."

"You're an actor! Pretend you want to eat Tony!"

"Grrrrrraaaaoooooowl!" Xanth bared his teeth and widened his eyes and did his best to look hungry enough to consume an entire human.

"Great!" Rita said. "Let's take it!"

"He may be scary," Jeremy said, looking up from the newspaper.

"But he's not very big. Maybe he should be up on something high."

"Good idea." Rita looked around. "And I think I'll shoot at a low angle." She busied herself with the tripod that the camera was mounted on.

Tony stood up. "Give me that camera case," he said.

Jeremy took the case over and gave it to Tony.

"Stand on this," Tony told Xanth. He put the case behind the wall. Equipment cases were essential equipment themselves on film shoots.

Xanth carefully stepped up on the metal case. Tony sat back down at his place on the wall. "How's that?" he asked.

Rita had taken the camera off the tripod and was lying on the ground looking up through the lens.

"A little to your left, Tony."

Tony shifted.

"Xanth, come up behind him."

Xanth loomed over Tony's shoulder.

"Growl!" Rita said.

"Grrraaaaaooooowl!" Teeth bared, eyes widened, his hungriest look.

Rita put down the camera and burst into laughter.

"What?" Xanth asked.

"I'm sorry, you're still not scary."

Rita rehearsed Xanth over and over again. Jeremy was pretending to read the newspaper, but he was really watching Rita and the kid. He knew he would have been better in the rubber mask.

The big white foam-core board almost blew away in the increasing breeze, knocking over the case that was supposed to hold it down. Jeremy put the newspaper down and looked for another weight. He picked up his backpack, which had two textbooks in it, and put that on the board. Along with the case, this seemed to be enough weight. The board no longer threatened to blow away.

161

Jeremy sat down again. He reached for the newspaper. It wasn't there.

Looking up, Jeremy could see the pages of the newspaper rolling over and over on the ground, and a few flying though the air. He would never catch all of them, even if he ran after them. Oh well, he thought. The news is always the same anyway.

Jeremy started watching the acting lesson again. "What's with the t-shirt, anyway?" he said loudly. "I thought aliens didn't wear clothing."

Les Moore stood looking over the lake, with MacArthur running around his feet. His head was full of the future he saw for himself as Defender of the Earth. First, President of the United States, then maybe even President of United Earth. Why not? It was the late great Ronald Reagan who once said that the threat of alien invasion would unite the people of Earth against a common foe. A united Earth would need a leader.

First he had to find evidence of the damnable ship that had landed just two days before. Despite what the Mysterious Source had said, he had found no remaining evidence here at the landing site. Even the quarter-mile-long scrape in the ground that the ship had caused had been repaired and new sod planted on it.

Les turned to tell his mother, who was nodding off on her bench, that he needed to take her home and then get himself back to his mountain in Colorado. He had been away from his duties for too long.

A newspaper page slapped him in the face and stuck there, held by the brisk lake breeze. Les pulled it off. He was about to crumple it up and throw it away when a headline caught his eye.

1 KILLED AS "ALIEN" THWARTS ROBBERY

Alien? What's this? The article went on:

One man was shot and killed, and three others arrested, in a robbery in a video store near Chinatown last night. According to one of the

162

suspects who was arrested, an alien from outer
space helped the store's owner foil the crime.
"He was a little guy with yellow skin and pointy ears,"
said Jerome Tilby, one of three men who are in
custody this morning.

Les clutched the paper in his hand and raised his chin towards the
sky. This was his clue. And it was brought to him by the wind, as if it
was meant to happen. The alien was still in the city, and still up to its
murderous ways. He turned smartly, energized by this development.
"Mother, we're leaving," he said.

Rita said that Xanth could tie his shirt around his waist,
because only his head and shoulders would be in the shot. Xanth had
done his best to assure the young humans that aliens do wear clothing,
but Rita had decided that the man-eating alien in her script would not
wear a t-shirt that read "Qaaxle."
"What does that mean? Qaaxle?" Jeremy had asked. Xanth
explained all about the popular resort planet. "Like a ride at Disney
World or something?" Jeremy said.
Xanth gave up. They just didn't want to believe him.
Rita was losing faith in Xanth as her alien. She kept telling Xanth
how to act, but she didn't like how he did it.
"I'm trying!" Xanth said. Rita just shook her head and picked up
the camera again.
"Roll sound!" Rita said. Frank started the tape recorder. "Rolling."
he said.
Tony reached down behind the wall he was sitting on and
pulled up the slate with the scene number and take number written on
it in chalk. He held up the top of it, ready to clap it down at the right
time.
Jeremy hoisted the boom over Tony's head again. He looked
exhausted.
"Roll camera!" Rita said, even though she herself was operating
the camera.

163

Tony said, "Scene four, take five." He clapped the clapper, and hastily put the slate away behind the wall so it wouldn't be seen in the shot. Then he composed himself to act.

"Action!"

For the fifth time, Xanth raised his arms, stepped forward on the metal equipment case, put on his fiercest face and let out a "Graaaaaooooooowl!" Tony did his best to act scared at the sound, but couldn't help himself. He burst into giggles.

"Cut!" Rita shouted.

"Sorry! Sorry!" Tony laughed.

"We might have been able to use that one, Tony." Rita said. "We don't have much film left. We have to get this shot today."

"All right," Tony said. "Next one will be good, I promise."

Rita turned to Jeremy. "Let's get one of you in the mask," she said. "Just in case we can't use the others."

"A star is born!" Jeremy said and lowered the boom pole.

"Frank, you'll have to hold the boom," Rita said. Jeremy grinned and handed it to Frank.

Xanth stood in his place on the metal case and looked crestfallen. His first Movie and they were taking him out of it? They didn't like him? Had he come all the way to Earth only to be fired?

Jeremy came over with his ggnorphodor mask in his hand. "Move aside, Earthling," he said. "The real alien has arrived!"

Tears in his eyes, Xanth stepped down and ran away. He had failed! All the things he had been through and he was washed up as an actor!

"Alllllll!" Xanth said, finding his homeless friend sleeping under a nearby tree. He sat down next to the smelly human.

"What? What?" Al asked, partly opening his eyes. "Are they finished?"

"No, they don't want me. I'm not scary enough."

"So are they going to take us to lunch now?"

"Al, they might not use me in their Movie."

"It's just a student film, kid. They promised us lunch, they'd better come through whether they use you or not."

Xanth was barely listening. He was frantic for a way to be scary and make the humans put him in their Movie. He remembered something Al had said the first day they met.

"Don't worry, Al, I know what to do. You told me." Xanth jumped up with renewed enthusiasm.

"I told you? What did I tell you?" Al sat up.

When you were trying to convince me that you're an alien, why didn't you just do THAT? Al had asked. His wise words would guide Xanth now.

Xanth ran back to the group of humans, where Rita was focusing on the rubber face of the fake alien.

"Rita, can you give me one more chance?" he asked.

"I took five takes of you, Xanth," Rita said. "That's enough."

"I thought of something really really scary to do," Xanth pleaded. "Please. Please please please please please pleeeeeeeeese!"

"All right! All right!"

"Yes yes yes yes yes!"

Jeremy took off the mask and slowly went back to get the boom from Frank. "This better be good," He muttered.

Jeremy had moved the case aside because he was taller and didn't need it. Xanth pulled it back into place and stepped up on it. Tony dutifully sat on the wall facing the camera. Rita lay on the ground, pointed the camera up, and focused.

"Roll sound."

"Rolling."

"Roll camera," Rita told herself.

Tony slated the shot. "Scene Four, Take Six." He clapped the top of the slate and put it away.

"Action!"

Xanth came up behind Tony. He tried to think about eating something really big. He internally disconnected his lower jaw from his upper jaw, and inflated his neck with the special air bladders. His mouth opened wide, then wider, then a whole lot wider still. Xanth then separated the two halves of his upper palate, which made his head expand sideways.

165

Xanth extended his three-foot-long tongue and raised the knifelike barbs attached to it.

He added a really loud "Graaaaaoooooowl! " for good measure.

Tony turned in the middle of this and looked like he was going to laugh again. His expression quickly turned to one of very realistic terror. Tony is a good actor, Xanth thought.

Tony fell off the wall and crawled away. Rita kept the camera aimed at Xanth, though it was wobbling badly in her grasp.

There was a moment of silence. The camera was still rolling.

"Uh, cut," Rita finally said.

Xanth pulled his tongue in, reengaged his upper and lower jaws, and reconnected his upper palate, returning his head to its normal size.

"What do you think?" he asked.

Tony was still on the ground, staring at Xanth in horror. Jeremy and Frank were also staring, as if they had been directed to act along with Tony.

Rita carefully put the camera on the ground. "I think we just won this semester's student film festival," she said.

Chapter Twenty-Six

"It wasn't no alien," Lenny Brown said.

General Moore stared at the three reprobates who had been arrested at the video store. He couldn't believe that his noble quest to protect the Earth hinged on the memories of these three.

The leader of the group, Lenny, was a career criminal with a record as long as a defense appropriations bill.

The second man, Vernal D. Ackerlake, was a tattooed, long-haired, bearded stereotype of a Hell's Angel. The police had told him, though, that Ackerlake never rode a bike because he was allergic to chrome.

The third was the strangest of all. Jerome Watson was the tallest, fattest, most squeaky-voiced felon that Les Moore had ever had the misfortune to meet.

"Was too," Jerome said in his high voice.

The police hadn't been very happy with the idea of an Army general wandering into the First District and asking to speak to some suspects. Eventually his uniform, his bearing, and his chin, along with some double-talk about possible military charges, had persuaded them and they took him to an interview room. Then they brought the three men in.

They wanted a detective to remain in the room but General Moore started quoting sections of the Patriot Act about national security that he made up on the spot, and they left him alone with the suspects.

"Gentlemen," General Moore said. "I just want the facts. I..."

"It was just a mutant kid," Lenny said.

"Mutant? Like the X-Men?" Vernal asked.

"Naw, man..." Lenny started to say.

"Do you think he had powers? He was pretty messed up looking. What kind of powers do you think he had?" Ackerlake asked.

"I just meant he was a freak," Lenny said." I didn't say he had any powers."

Robin Reed

"Aliens got powers," Jerome said.

"He wasn't no alien!" Lenny shouted.

"Gentlemen, Gentlemen!" Les Moore tried to regain control. This was why everyone should be in the military, he thought. He was a lot better with people he could give orders to.

"Please describe the creature," Les said when the three crooks quieted down.

Lenny said, "He was this kid but he was yellow, or maybe green. And he had pointy ears."

"Maybe he was a shape-changer, like Nightcrawler," Vernal said.

"Nightcrawler is blue, you dumbass," Lenny said. "Besides, he's the teleporter. Mystique is the shape-changer."

"And she's blue too." Ackerlake offered.

"So?"

"So all shape changers must be blue."

"What the hell are you talking about?"

"Nightcrawler and Mystique are both blue, so all shape changers must be blue. The yellow guy can't be a shape changer."

"I told you Nightcrawler is a teleporter."

"Then I guess the yellow guy can't be a teleporter either."

Les was starting to get a headache. "I asked for a simple description!" he thundered.

"He was short and yellow and had pointy ears and he was an alien, not a X-Man," Jerome said.

"My favorite is Wolverine," Vernal said.

"You kidding? " Lenny asked. "That Mystique chick can look like anyone. I could have every supermodel I ever dreamed of with her. And she's damn hot all by herself."

"You know she's married to Uncle Jesse from Full House." Vernal said.

"Naw, they broke up."

"Really? If I had those knives in my hands like Wolverine I could break us out of here."

"You aren't going anywhere!" Les shouted, losing what patience he ever had for civilians. "Just describe the alien - the creature you saw."

168

"I kinda liked the red-haired chick." Vernal said.

"The one who can read your mind? Are you nuts? You really want a chick who can do that?"

Les knocked on the door of the interrogation room and asked the uniformed officer outside to remove Lenny and Vernal.

"The kid wasn't no alien!" Lenny shot over his shoulder as he left.

"What powers do you think the kid had?" Vernal asked Lenny as they were taken down the hallway.

"So," Les said to the massive Jerome Tilby when they were alone. "What makes you so sure that what you saw was an alien?"

"He looked like one." Jerome said.

"Ah. But couldn't he have been a deformed child, as your friend said?"

"No."

Les waited for more, but Jerome said nothing.

"Any other reason?"

"He had powers."

"Oh not this again."

"Not like Lenny said. Alien powers."

"What powers would those be?"

"He hated the smell of beer," Jerome said.

General Moore frowned. He enjoyed a cold beer on occasion. Only when he was off duty, of course, and he was rarely off duty. If this yellow-skinned creature hated beer it might not be proof that it was an alien from outer space, but it certainly had un-American tendencies.

"And he didn't know how to work a telephone."

"What's that?" Les asked.

"The alien was trying to call the cops on us, but he didn't know how to dial." Jerome said.

"What, it couldn't even push the buttons?"

"It was one of those old ones, with a dial."

"Oh. Well, a lot of young people aren't familiar with..."

"Not just that," Jerome insisted. "He kept talking about the Central Computer. He thought a computer would answer the phone."

"They often do. I always get lost in those damn voicemail systems. Tell me, did the creature kill your unfortunate colleague, Geordie Mason?"

"The old Chinese lady shot him."

Can't blame the alien directly for that death, Les thought. I'm sure it had a hand, or a tentacle or whatever, in it though.

"So the creature hated beer, couldn't dial a phone, and said something about a Central Computer. Is that why you're so sure it was an alien?"

"Sure. Cause of his powers."

Les' headache wasn't getting any better. "The things you have told me aren't really powers."

"Sure they are."

"What powers exactly?"

"The powers of being an alien."

Les stared at the man. This was useless. He wasn't going to get any useful information. He had yet to hear anything that would convince Admiral Sanderson and General Burns.

"Do you know why the creature was there?" Les asked. "Was it robbing the store too?"

Jerome shook his head. "He said they don't use money."

"What?"

"They use it, but for fun, like maybe Monopoly money. But they don't need it."

"Everyone needs money."

"Nope, he said they get anything they want. They just ask for what they need."

A chill ran down Les' spine. "Did this creature say anything about work? Do they work for a living?"

"He said everyone has a job, but they just do it because they're supposed to."

"He told you all this?" Les asked.

"He told Lenny, before we got there."

Could it be? Les thought. Could his crazy mother have been not so crazy all along?

170

"That's all," Les told Jerome. "Thank you for your help." He burst out of the interrogation room.

"Thank you, officer," Les said. "I'm finished." He walked out of the police station and onto the street, trembling inside.

The hated alien who had killed two fine American pilots in the air and a civilian on the ground, who had incited murder while vandalizing a video store, was after all the enemy he had learned about at his mother's knee.

Les looked up. The sky was still blue in the late afternoon, but the sun would soon set. Then the traitorous stars would come out, stars that hid swarms of enemy aliens, hordes that meant to come to Earth and defile all that was right and good and profit-motivated.

Les shook his fist at the sky. Aliens existed all right. He knew that now. They existed and, by God, they were commies.

Chapter Twenty-Seven

SPACE ALIEN TELLS DIET SECRETS!
YOU CAN BECOME WEIGHTLESS IN THIRTY DAYS!

Xanth stood transfixed. He hadn't even read the headline yet. He was looking at the picture - a picture of him! - on the cover of *The National Babbler*.

Al had physically dragged Xanth away from the film students after Rita filmed Xanth's expanding head. Rita shouted after them to come back, but Al's grip on Xanth's t-shirt, which was still tied around his waist, was merciless.

Al hurried Xanth down some steps and they found themselves in a vast underground parking garage. There had been no hint in the park above that such a subterranean complex existed.

"What are you doing!?" Xanth shouted as Al finally let go.

"I'm trying to protect you," Al said.

"But I was about to become a Movie Star!"

"Now that those kids know you're real, they're going to call the newspapers and the TV stations and they're going to get rich turning you in. YOU will end up in a government lab somewhere being anal probed by scientists!"

"That's ridiculous," Xanth said. He untied his t-shirt and put it back on properly. "That didn't happen to *E.T.*, or all those kosserads, or Alf!"

"I..." Al paused. "Alf is a puppet."

"A what?"

"A puppet, like the Muppets."

"He's not at all like the Muppets. They're from a completely different planet."

"They're...never mind. Look, let me tell you once and for all, most humans don't believe that aliens really exist. If they did believe, it would scare the bejesus out of them."

"But they're always making Movies about them," Xanth said. "Movies are all fiction, everyone in the galaxy knows that, but when real aliens keep landing here and you humans keep putting them in Movies, you have to know they are real."

"We believe that all aliens are made up. They're actors, or computer-animated, or something. They don't really exist."

Humans couldn't be that stupid, Xanth thought. Then he thought of some of the humans he had met, and realized he was wrong. He was trapped on The Planet of The Imbeciles.

"But real aliens really do appear in your Movies and there must be humans who know about them," Xanth said.

"Hollywood must have some way of keeping it secret," Al said. "Which is even more reason you need to go there as soon as possible."

"I want to go to Hollywood!" Xanth exclaimed.

"I think you told me that once or twice." Al started back up the steps. "So I need to figure out a way to get you there."

Just a few minutes later, Xanth and Al crossed back into the busy Loop. Many humans scurried about, unaware that an alien moved among them.

Al told Xanth to stay put while he tried to panhandle some money. He didn't think the sick child scenario would work as well here as it did for the suburban ladies at the Art Institute, so he was going to work alone.

"We didn't get lunch from those students, and I'm hungry. I'll get us some lunch money and you wait right here."

Right here was next to a wooden shack with a gaudy display of printed paper items. A man with a white beard and a reddish complexion stood inside the shack.

A busy businessman bumped past Xanth and handed the bearded man some coins. Then he grabbed a newspaper from a rack and took it with him.

A lot of the paper publications had pictures of human females on them. Some of these were wrapped in a plain brown band of paper, so Xanth could only see the heads of the women. What was that for? he wondered.

173

There were dozens of different publications with photos on them. One called *People* had a picture of a very thin young woman with a disproportionately large chest on the cover, another called *Motorcycle Weekly* had a picture of a very thin young woman with a disproportionately large chest sitting on a motorcycle, and a third, called *Derriere*, had a picture of a thin, nearly naked, young man doing something peculiar with a watermelon.

Before Xanth could look at that one more closely, the white-bearded man inside the shack leaned over and snatched it away.

"Oops," the man said, "that's supposed to be in my private collection. Say, son, are you going to buy anything?"

Xanth just backed off and shook his head.

"Then move along, this isn't a library."

Xanth turned away, but then he saw - himself! He was in the upper-right-hand corner of the cover of *The National Babbler*.

Xanth picked the magazine up. It was definitely him in the picture. Turning the publication around and looking at it from different angles didn't change a thing.

After standing frozen for a while staring, the man in the shack said, "If you want that, it's two sixty five. If you don't, put it back and get out of here."

"That's me!" Xanth told the man. "On there!"

"It's still two sixty five. Are you buying it or not?"

Afraid that it was an illusion and it would disappear if he looked away, Xanth continued to stare at the magazine.

"That's it." The bearded man disappeared and then came around the outside of the shack, stomping towards Xanth. He shouted, "Get outta here! Gawan!"

"What's going on?" Al's voice asked.

"Is this kid with you? " the bearded man asked.

"Look, Al! That's me! On there!" Xanth said.

Al looked. "How the hell did that happen?" he asked.

"Two sixty five!" the bearded man said.

"I don't have that much," Al said. He took the magazine away from Xanth and put it back on the rack. "Come on." He pulled Xanth away from the shack.

"But I'm on there!" Xanth wailed.

"Sorry, but if you can't buy it, you can't have it."

The disheveled human pulled the alien down the street. Xanth kept looking back.

"How the hell did you end up on a tabloid cover?" Al asked.

"I don't know," Xanth said. "A man did take my picture the first day I came, before I met you."

"Who was he?"

"I don't know." Then, "Oh yeah! He gave me a card with his name on it!"

The card was crumpled and dirty, but it was still in the pocket of Xanth's shorts. "Lucky I didn't lose my clothing at the lake," he said.

TED GRANGER
THE NATIONAL BABBLER

it said. There was also a phone number.

"This is just great," Al said. "Well, no one believes tabloid stories, so I hope no one will come looking for you."

What else was it that Granger had said? Xanth thought about the conversation he had had with the man. It was shortly after he arrived on Earth and was greeted by Granma's purse, so he wasn't sure he had understood everything that the reporter said.

"He said aliens are boring and he wasn't interested in helping me."

"No surprise," Al said. "Anyone who works at a rag like that must be a bad person."

"He liked it when I told him I was really hungry. That's when he took my picture."

Al and Xanth were still on the busy street, winding their way through hurrying humans.

"Only morons buy papers like that, Xanth. And only bad people work at a paper like that."

"There was something else he said."

"You're lucky you didn't get mixed up with him. He would have just exploited you and then turned you in to the government. He's a real nasty son of a bitch, I'm sure."

"He said if I called him he would get me some money." Xanth said.

"Well let's give the wonderful fellow a call!" Al said.

They found a pay phone on a street corner. Al said that pay phones weren't as common any more, now that so many people had cell phones.

"Cell phones?" Xanth asked. "Are those phones that people have in prison?"

"What?" Al asked. "No, they're portable..." He saw Xanth trying to control his laughter.

"Oh, very funny. I hope this reporter will take a collect call."

"If I dial the number wrong, is that an incollect call?" Xanth asked, and once again couldn't stop laughing.

"Stop it. Puns are against the law here."

"Really?" Xanth quieted down and looked around.

"Yeah, really. You want us to be pun-ished?" Al paused and looked for Xanth to laugh.

Xanth shook his head. "Really, Al. That one's so old it's inscribed on the ruins of the lost civilization of Ancientium. Now are we here to joke around or to make this phone call?"

"Okay, okay, show me the card again."

Xanth did.

"Great. It's an eight-hundred number. Go ahead and dial."

The phone was the kind with buttons. Xanth studied it carefully. "There's really no Central Computer on this planet?" he asked.

"A what?"

"I guess not. I just push the buttons with the same numbers as on the card?"

"Yeah. Dial the numbers."

"This isn't a dial. It's a keypad."

"What?"

"That other phone I used had a dial. This doesn't. How can I dial if there is no dial?"

"We still call it dialing, even though there's no dial."

"Humans are very weird," Xanth said.

"So dial."

"Okay." Xanth started to push the buttons that corresponded to the numbers on the card.

"You have to dial one first," Al said.

"You mean push the 'one' button."

"Yes, yes. Dial one."

"When do I 'dial' the number one?"

"Before all the other numbers."

"That's not on the card."

"Everyone knows it."

"I don't know it."

"Everyone but you knows it."

"So it's a secret code?"

"No...yes...I don't know. Just hang up and start over."

Xanth slammed the handset down and picked it up again. "Why is everything on Earth so confusing?" He pushed the number one.

"Okay?"

"Good. Now dial the rest of the numbers."

"Push the other buttons?"

"Yes!"

"I'm doing my best, Al." Xanth pushed all the numbers in order.

There was a hum and a click. "If there are any more buttons I have to push that no one told me about, I am done here! You understand?" Xanth was really sick of this stupid phone and its secret codes.

"Don't worry, there won't be," Al said.

The phone clicked again and a voice came on.

"Thank you for calling *The National Babbler*," it said. "To continue in English, press one. Para continuar en Español, oprima el numero dos."

Xanth dropped the handset and walked away.

Chapter Twenty-Eight

"Granger."

"Hey, Ted," the voice on the phone said. It was one of his sources. "I have something for you."

"Shoot."

"The real President of the United States is a bigfoot named Yekkitesaxis."

"This is *The National Babbler*, you idiot," Granger said. "Take it to someplace that prints the truth."

Granger shook his head as he hung up. Some of his sources just didn't understand what the *Babbler* was all about. He turned to his computer, where he had been surfing the Web, hoping to find a real story for next week's issue.

He hadn't been able to find much. There was a new web site that claimed that Willy Waldo, the fast food clown, was the savior. Some guy claimed he had witnessed a miracle in a Willy Waldo restaurant in Chicago. Granger decided to leave it for a while, though, and see if the guy gained any followers. The story would be a lot better if there was whole cult of clown worshippers.

Strangely enough, Granger had been in Chicago on the same day that the so-called miracle had occurred. He was there trying to track down the ghost of John Belushi. John was a pretty reliable source; he could get in and out of the hotel rooms of celebrities without being seen.

Granger hadn't been able to find Belushi on that trip, but he did meet a new alien who gave him an idea for a story. He hoped the little guy was doing all right. Granger hadn't been able to help him at the time, but he had gotten some shots of the military and the Men in Brown removing the ship the alien arrived in. He had the pictures in his files now, ready to use in one way or another.

Unlike many of his colleagues at the *Babbler*, Ted Granger had never subscribed to anything as useless as journalistic ethics. He didn't come from a news background. He had been a struggling screenwriter for years, selling mainly to the cheesier cable networks. Then he had started to sell celebrity stories to the tabloids, and found himself a whole lot richer than he had ever been as a screenwriter. *The Enquirer* wanted true stories that could be backed up with facts, and that quickly bored Granger. When he found the *Babbler*, he found his niche.

The unofficial motto of *The National Babbler* was "All the news that we make up." It was a rag dedicated to fiction of the wildest sort. They always based their stories on rumors, gossip, and lies, and then gave them an extra twist. Granger found his flair for the dramatic was well-rewarded.

What Granger loved the most about his job was that the more he faked his stories, the more the readers believed them.

Now he lived near the headquarters of the *Babbler* in Boca Raton, Florida. He pretty much lived IN the headquarters of the *Babbler*, only going to his small, spare apartment when he wasn't traveling or sleeping on a cot in his office.

The phone rang again. He picked it up.

"Granger."

"Hi, Mr. Granger?" It didn't sound like one of his regular sources.

"Yup. Shoot."

"Uh, my name is Al Henley. I'm calling for a friend, his name is Xanthan Gumm?"

"I'm a busy man. What's your tip?"

The man's voice became harder to understand, as if he was no longer talking into the phone. "Come back here," it said. "I'm talking to him."

Another voice even further away said something.

"Yes, it's important," the man said. "If he promised you money."

Granger almost hung up, but he thought what the hell, he didn't have a story to write anyway.

Then Henley came back on. "He's a, an alien. He says you met him in the park the other day."

Granger perked up. "Oh, yes. Can I talk to him?"

After a moment, the other, softer voice came on the line.

"Hello?" it said. "Have I pushed enough buttons this time?"

"This is Ted Granger. Are you the little yellow-skinned fellow I met the other day?

"Are you the human who gave me a card with his phone number on it?"

"Yes, glad you called, I..."

"How come it doesn't say to dial one first? Then after I dialed all the numbers I had to dial for English, then I had to start over again, then Al dialed this extension number that's on the card, whatever that is, and besides there's no dial on this phone anyway."

Granger was surprised. Usually new galactic visitors had taken the 'Earth 101' course before they set foot on the planet, but somehow this guy had bypassed the system. It was rare, but it happened.

At least the alien had found a human who was helping him. With that thought, something tickled the back of Granger's creative mind, something about aliens with friends, but he put it aside for the moment.

"Okay, I know this planet is confusing at first," Granger said. "I think I can help. Did you see your picture in the paper?"

"Yes," Gumm said. "That's why we called, 'cause you said something about money, and Al says that's important."

This one really was naive about Earth. "My editor wouldn't give me much, it was a pretty small story. But I think I can throw a grand your way."

"A grand what?"

Granger sighed. "Can I talk to your friend?"

"I guess." There were sounds like the phone was being passed from one hand to another.

"This is Al Henley, sir."

"Yeah, I got a small stipend for your friend Mr. Gumm, for helping me out on that story. I'll wire you the cash, since he doesn't have ID yet."

"You're going to send him money?"

"Yeah, I couldn't get much, just a thousand."

"A thousand."

"Right."

"Dollars?"

"Sure."

Granger wasn't sure what was going on for the next thirty seconds or so, it sounded like the fellow Al was shouting "Yahoo!" and the alien was asking him what was wrong with him.

Then Henley's voice came back on the line. His voice trembled. "You can't believe how much this is going to help, sir." he said.

"It's nothing. I'll just wire it to you and you can show ID at any Western Union location and pick it up."

"Oh." Henley sounded mournful. "I don't have any ID either, sir. I've been homeless a lot of years."

"Ah. Not to worry. Write down this address, and the cash will be waiting there for you."

Henley repeated the information, but it didn't sound like he was writing it down. Probably didn't have a pen. Granger hoped he had a good memory. "And let me talk to Mr. Gumm again please."

"Xanth. I call him Xanth."

The phone changed hands again.

"Hello?"

"Do you trust this human, Xanth? I don't want him to abscond with your money."

"Al's been my only friend since I got here," Xanth said.

Once again, aliens with friends, friends of aliens, seemed to Granger to have promise. He pushed the thought back. "Good," he said. "When you find a place to stay give me another call," Granger said. "Maybe you can help me with more stories."

"Um, okay," Xanth said. The phone went dead.

Granger made another quick phone call to make sure that the promised cash would indeed be waiting for Xanth and his friend.

Well, that was some business taken care of. It didn't help him write his next story, though. Granger stared at his computer, trying to come up with something.

Friends of aliens. Friendly aliens. What could he do with that? Aliens who had friends. Aliens who were more than friends.

Aliens. More than friends.

That was it! Granger pulled up Photoshop on his computer and opened a new file. He dropped in a picture of a ggnorphodor, the standard big-eyed alien that the public expected in such stories. Then he dropped in another copy of the same picture.

He had two ggnorphodors. He moved their heads closer together.

He wasn't an artist, but it didn't take much skill to make it look like one alien had its arm around the other one. The graphics department would clean it up, and put it through the filter that would make the photos look faked. *Babbler* stories always had an element of plausible falsity to them.

Was there anything else he could do? He quickly drew in a few hearts rising from the two aliens, who now looked like they were happily cuddling. Then he turned each of their tiny mouths into an enigmatic smile.

And the headline? Granger had to admit to himself that he was brilliant. His editor would love this.

He used Photoshop to type one large word over the picture. GAYLIENS.

Chapter Twenty-Nine

"You were right all along, Mother," General Les S. Moore said. He took a sip of tea.

"Of course I was, boy. Right about what?"

Les sat in his mother's living room, trying to hide in one of her armchairs. He was physically and mentally exhausted. His mind was a whirl of fear and disgust. The world he had built for himself, in which his mother was crazy and the communist threat was a matter for dusty history books, was falling apart. They were out there, waiting, ready to invade in their space ships when the world least expected it.

"Everything. The commies. They're everywhere. Everywhere!"

"I've been telling you your whole life, son," Mrs. Moore said. "Now you're paying attention?"

"I'm sorry. I listened to the disinformation. I really thought they were gone." Les raised his gaze from his teacup and looked into his mother's eyes. "Can you ever forgive me?"

"Don't ask me, boy. Ask General MacArthur. Ask Ike! Ask Senator McCarthy! They're the ones that have been fighting the good fight while you went off believing in this twaddle about the Russkies giving up!"

Les nodded. "Yes," he said. "Yes!"

"Not that you've come to your senses, march out of here and help the President fight them on the beaches! On the streets! On the golf courses! Help MacArthur push the Red Chinese back into the Pacific! Help McCarthy find the fifth columnists, who live among us and scheme to pollute our precious bodily fluids! Help the red-blooded Americans like Werner von Braun build the rockets that will send the bomb over to all those god-forsaken places where the commies hide in their hovels and their bread lines! Help the A-bomb that God himself gave us wipe out the eastern hemisphere before those dirty bastards can send the A-bomb that the devil himself gave them to wipe us out first!"

"YES!" Les stood up and saluted. "And when that is done we can face the big threat! The commies from outer space!" He pointed straight up. Les stood at attention, flushed and excited about the battles ahead of him.

Mrs. Moore had to sit down. She had always been afraid of this. Les was a delicate boy. She had thought he was coming to his senses, but now the poor boy had gone completely crazy.

Al was singing again. It sounded like a Beatles song, but if that was the case, something was choking the life out of Lennon and McCartney's melody.

Xanth had always been an Earth Movie fan, but sometimes he listened to Earth Music too. Many Galactic cultures were devoted to Earth Music. The Eltonians had changed the very name of their species and they all wore elaborate glasses and platform shoes. This made them look a bit odd, because their eyes were in their feet.

Along with Al's songicide, the sound of splashing water came out from behind the closed door of the bathroom.

"Ow!" Al said, interrupting his singing. "That was really crusted on there!"

Xanth lay on one of the two beds in the larger room. It was soft and very comfortable. Much more comfortable than the floor of the basement under the video store, or the ground in the park. It was also very cool in the room. Cold air was blowing out from a vent under the large window.

It was mid afternoon, and sunlight streamed in the window. Xanth had spent some time looking out at the vast city. There were so many humans here, in so many buildings. He had seen sights like this in the Movies, but of course had just considered them to be special effects. It was tiring to think about all those humans so he had gone to lie down on the bed that was away from the window.

"Al," Xanth called, "if there are rooms like this for humans to live in, why are you homeless?"

"What?" Al asked. "Whoa, it washed right off! My skin isn't green down there!"

Al was splashing happily in his bath, so Xanth decided not to bother him any more. He supposed the answer to his question was the same as the answer to many of his other questions. Money. Green pieces of paper really made a difference down here.

Money was one of the silliest concepts in Earth Movies. People fighting, killing, chasing, obsessing over green pieces of paper. Yet it was a theme in so many Movies that he should have realized that it was more than just another Earth fiction.

Mr. Granger had sent Xanth some money, and now he could stay in this hotel. Would the money help him get to Hollywood? He hoped so.

The bathroom door opened and a stranger wrapped in a towel walked into the big room. Xanth jumped off the bed and hid behind it.

"Who are you?" Xanth shouted.

"It's me, kid," Al said.

It was. Al was all pink, and the hair on his face was gone. The few hairs on his head were combed neatly.

Xanth stood up. "Wow, this bath thing really changed you."

"My first one in over a year, and the last one was just a shower at a shelter."

"Is there a shower here? I had a shower booth in my quarters at Galactic Central."

"Sure," Al said. "Oh, let me clean up in there before you go in. It's pretty nasty."

Al went back into the bathroom. There was silence for a couple of minutes before Al said, "Gotcha!" In a moment the toilet flushed.

Al came back out. "All clear," he said.

Xanth went into the bathroom. There was no shower booth like he had in his quarters back home, but he figured out that the tub thing could be operated as a shower.

He undressed, then stepped into the tub and waited for the shower to start. Nothing happened. Then he realized that it wasn't going to. That was another function of the Central Computer back home. He didn't want to ask Al how to do it, so he started twisting every knob and pulling every handle that was in there.

"Ooooooooow!" Xanth shouted as a spray of boiling hot water shot out of the nozzle. He jumped out of the tub. "OW!. OW OW!" he said. Soon the whole room was full of hot clouds of steam.

He almost went out and asked Al what to do, but he felt stupid not knowing how to work something as simple as a shower. He stuck his head in past the plastic curtain, where the water wouldn't hit him but he could look at the knobs.

One of them said H and had a red semicircle on it. It was turned almost all the way up. Xanth turned it back down. The water stopped. Feeling smarter, Xanth stepped back into the tub. Now he knew what to do. The other knob had the letter C on it and a blue semicircle. He turned that one all the way up.

"OW! OW OW!" Xanth said as he fled the tub again. Now a blast of water as cold as Blabscreet spit had hit him. Blabscreets lived in asteroids and their spit consisted mainly of liquid hydrogen.

Once again vowing to be brave, Xanth examined the knobs again. He set both of them halfway, and this time felt the spray before he got back in the tub.

When he was done, Xanth felt a lot better. He looked for the control for the drying feature, but there didn't seem to be one. How did humans dry off after washing?

He dripped on the floor as he got out of the tub. He looked around. There were stacks of towels on a high shelf. Xanth had to step up on the toilet to reach one. When he pulled it out, most of the others fell down all around him.

He used the one he had grabbed to rub himself dry. It was primitive, but it worked. Another thing in the Movies that humans actually do. So far he knew that humans really shoot each other, really care about money, and really use towels. He was learning a lot.

He put his Qaaxle shirt and shorts back on, though now that he was clean he realized they were a little stinky. He went out into the big room.

Al was sitting up on one of the beds, with his back against the headboard and his legs tucked under the covers, eating a sandwich. A table had appeared in the room, and it had food on it. "Hope you don't mind, I got some room service." Al said. He was still wearing just a towel. "Dig in."

There were several sandwiches on a plate, a large bottle of a dark liquid, some fancy glasses, and two smaller plates with pieces of pie on them.

Al was holding a small glass bottle. Al saw that Xanth was looking at it, and raised it in a toast. "To you, Xanth, for getting us the money to stay here," he said. Then he drank from the bottle.

"You went out and got all this?" Xanth asked.

"Room service. You just call on the phone and they bring it to your room."

"Really? Like when I call the Central Computer and a dinner tray comes to the meal slot in my quarters."

"That's cool. Sounds to me like you had a pretty sweet deal back in Galactic Central. What ever made you come here?"

"I wanted..."

"To be a movie star. Yeah, yeah. Some people just don't know when they got it good. Well, I got food for you too. Eat up."

"Oh no, my body is still not quite finished processing that pizza."

"That was two days ago," Al said.

"My species eats once every two to three days. Then after elimination, we are ready to eat again. When it is time for elimination..."

"You'll let me know. I'm aquiver with anticipation. At least have some Crike."

"Crike?"

"Crikey-Cola. Australian soda pop. It's my favorite."

Xanth picked up the large plastic bottle and looked at the label. It had a drawing of a man in a broad-brimmed hat. He had a word balloon next to him that read, "Guaranteed to spit in yer eye."

"You said you don't drink booze," Al said, "so I thought you might like that stuff. But be careful, it has enough caffeine to keep you awake for a year."

Xanth turned the bottle over and around, looking for a way to get the liquid out.

"Twist the cap off," Al said.

Xanth did, and there was a loud hiss of escaping gas, accompanied by an explosion of liquid that shot into Xanth's eyes.

"Oh! I'm sorry! I should have warned you," Al said, but he didn't sound all that sorry. In fact, he was laughing.

Xanth shook his head and wiped his eyes with his shirt. "What happened?" he asked. "Is this bottle defective?"

"Most soda does that only if the bottle has been shaken up. But Crikey Cola guarantees it or your money back." Al was still smiling. "Go ahead, take a swig."

"I can still drink it?"

"Sure. It's good."

Xanth tipped the small opening of the large bottle to his mouth. Soon a sweet but also bitter taste filled his senses. The cola snarled its way down, scratching the back of his throat on the way.

It was so good Xanth kept drinking. The bottle was half empty when he lowered it.

"Crikey!" Al said. With that much in you, you won't get any sleep tonight."

Xanth climbed up on the other bed and put his legs under the covers. He still clutched the bottle.

"This stuff is great!" he said. "Even if it does keep me awake, I..."

In the middle of that sentence, the world went away.

Chapter Thirty

A monster ran through Xanth's dreams, a monster with a clanging voice and tentacles that were everywhere. Tentacles that covered his eyes, so he couldn't see. Tentacles that tangled him in their grasp, so he couldn't move.

"Hello?" Al's voice said in the dream.

The clanging stopped. That was something, but Xanth was still captured by the tentacles and everything was dark.

"Sure," Al said. "Xanth? Are you awake?"

"Al!" Xanth said. "I'm being attacked! I can't see anything!"

Light exploded from a source on the wall, between the beds. Al had turned on a lamp. "Mr. Granger wants to talk to you." He held a black object out towards Xanth, across the space between the beds.

Under the light, Xanth could see that he was wrapped in blankets and sheets. He looked around quickly. There was no monster in the room unless it was now skulking under a bed. The window was dark. Night must have fallen while he was asleep.

"What was that noise?" Xanth asked.

"What noise?"

"The big ringing clanging noise!"

"You mean the phone ringing?"

"The phone? You mean like in the Movies? Earth phones really do that?"

"They do."

"Why would it do it when I'm asleep? It scared the beep out of me."

"Mr. Granger called, so it rang."

"Can't the Central Computer just notify me when I'm awake that I had a call? Oh, right."

"So talk to the man."

Xanth managed to get an arm loose from the bedcovers, then reached up and took the telephone handset from Al. "Yo, Adrian," he said into it.

"Show me the money!" Ted Granger said. It was the standard response in Galactic Civilization. Mr. Granger did seem to know a lot about aliens.

"Speaking of money, I take it you successfully acquired the cash I sent you." Granger continued.

"Yes we did. Then Al suggested we get a room in a hotel. Al took a bath then I took a shower and I had some Crikey Cola and Al said it would keep me awake but I fell right to sleep."

"Be careful here, things like caffeine can have different effects on aliens than they do on humans."

"Really?"

"Sure. I knew a terpidon once who swelled up like a balloon when he had some butter on his English muffin."

"That wasn't the butter. Terpidons do that when they're embarrassed. The phrase 'English muffin' is really embarrassing to terpidons."

"Oh. Why?"

Xanth shrugged. "They won't tell anyone, they're too embarrassed."

"Anyway, I..." Granger said.

"Hey, how did you know where I was to call me on the phone?" Xanth asked.

"Oh, Carl told me. I asked him to keep an eye on you."

"Carl? That person that gave us the money? He was very grumpy."

"Ha! Yes, that's Carl. Say, I..."

"Is Carl a human? Al says sometimes humans are very short and they're called Little People. But he seemed like he might be an alien."

"Let's just say that there are more kinds of people on this planet than humans. I..."

"He said you owe him big time for this."

"Okay, thanks for the message. Now listen, I..."

"He was really really upset about giving us money."

"Okay! Xanth! Listen! I called because I have a line on your spaceship."

"A what?"

"One of my sources told me where they took your ship. It's still in Chicago. You might be able to go get it."

"I could get my ship back?"

"Maybe, if you act fast. It's in a location on the south side. The Men in Brown keep secret facilities all over the place. But they're going to ship it out to one of their long-term storage bases in the morning."

"You mean Men In Black, like Will Smith and Tommy Lee Jones?"

"Yeah, but the real ones, not movie characters. A couple of years ago they started showing up in brown suits. No one knows why."

"There are real Men in Black, I mean, Brown, who are different than the ones in the Movies? But everything in the Movies is supposed to be fiction!"

"Take down this address."

"Take it down where?"

"WRITE it down." Granger said.

"Oh." Xanth looked up. "Al! Do you have any way to write something down?"

"Hmmm?" Al asked. He had almost gone back to sleep.

"Mr. Granger wants me to write down an address."

"Let me talk to him. I'll remember it like I did the other address where we met that little guy."

Al took the phone. "Mmm hmmm," he said. "Mmm hmmm. Seventy first? Mmm hmmm. Thanks." He hung up the phone.

"OK," Al said to Xanth. "He says if we act fast you can get your ship back."

"I know, he told me. But how can we get there fast enough? It sounds like it's really far away."

"You forget, we have money now. We can travel in style."

Al lifted the covers, but quickly put them back down. "Uh, ahem..." he said.

"What?" Xanth asked.

"I find myself to be naked. Could you bring me my clothes?"
Xanth saw that Al's ragged old clothing was draped over a chair.
He could smell it across the room.

"Do I have to? It stinks."

"I know, but we have to get going."

"Why didn't you put it in the cleaning slot?"

"The what?"

"The cleaning slot. You put your clothes in it when you go to bed
and they're all clean when you wake up."

Al's expression told him the answer to his question. There were no
cleaning slots on Earth. This planet was too primitive to believe.

Xanth stood up. He was still dressed in his own clothing, which
was a little whiffy too. He walked over to the chair, which was next to
a small table near the window.

The closer he got, the more his nose objected. Finally the stench
was too much. Then he had a brilliant idea.

"Can we buy clothing with the money?" he asked.

Al looked surprise. "You can buy anything with money on this
planet," he said. "But it's your money, really. Are you offering to buy
me some clothing?"

Xanth took another sniff.

"I insist," he said.

"Well, thank you," Al said. "I long ago learned not to look charity
in the horse's mouth. Or something like that."

"So do we just call on the phone and they bring it up, like the
food?"

"I doubt they would do that. But let me call the desk and see what
is available."

Al picked up the phone and talked briefly to someone. Then he
waited a moment, and talked to what seemed to be a different person.

"We're in luck. It's not as late as I thought, it's still evening.
There's a clothing store in the lobby. I just told them my size and
what I want. I just need you to go down and pick the stuff up."

"Me?" Xanth asked. "Go down there all by myself?"

"Unless you want me to don my old clothes and venture out in all
my olfactory glory."

"What?"

"Unless you want me to go down there in my stinky clothes."

Xanth looked anxiously at the door of the hotel room. Then he sniffed the air inside the room.

"I'm going," he said.

The hallway was empty of life. Lime green carpeting covered the floor. Glass shaded lamps on the wall threw circles of light on the ceiling.

Xanth felt the wad of money in his pocket. He had fetched it out of Al's coat, holding his breath as he did. Al said there was over seven hundred dollars left, and he should be very careful. Do not show anyone the whole wad, he said. Keep your hand on it so no one will pick pocket you.

"Pick pocket?" Xanth asked.

"Steal," Al said. "Take it from you without you knowing."

"Like the Artful Dodger! He's in a Movie!"

"Yeah."

The song about stealing from people's pockets ran through Xanth's head as he walked down the hall.

He stopped at the big doors of the elevator. He pushed the button with the Down arrow. He had seen Al push the Up button earlier, so he knew that the elevator didn't respond to voice commands.

After a short while, the doors slid open. A very old human couple was already in the elevator. The male human was leaning on a metal support with four rubber-footed legs. The female was standing without such a support, but looked like she would need one soon.

The humans looked away as the alien boarded. The doors closed and Xanth found himself alone with the couple.

Recorded music came from somewhere above, clashing with the pick-pocket song in Xanth's head. He looked at the old humans. He thought that maybe they could help.

"My friend is naked," he said. "I'll give you money to dress him up."

The old couple shuffled as far as they could into the corner and stared at him the rest of the way down.

Chapter Thirty-One

Les Moore was twelve years old. He was building an authentic model of a B-52 that would join the other models hanging from the ceiling of his bedroom. At the toy store he had asked his mother for a model of the Wolfman, standing there in all his lupine glory and growling at anyone who dared get near. "How is that going to help you fight the commies?" Mrs. Moore asked. "It isn't, that's how."

He tossed and turned, knees folded so his 6' 4" frame fit onto the bed his mother bought when he was seven.

He was fifteen and starry eyed about a girl at school named Amanda. His mother said, "A soldier is married to the army.".

He was fifty-five, a three-star general sleeping in the room he grew up in. Dreaming about commies chasing him through his childhood.

"Awaken, human," said a voice.

Les shook off his dream and opened his eyes halfway. Someone stood next to the bed.

"I have beamed down to warn you," the voice said.

"What?" Les said. "What the hell are you doing here? " He reached for the sidearm he kept next to his bed, then realized that he wasn't in his quarters. When he visited his Mother's house, she made him stow his pistol in her combination gun/china cabinet.

A bright light shined through the window, so the figure was in silhouette. The light source moved up and down, so the figure's shadow was in motion. An eerie whistle came from outside.

"You can prevent it if you are fast enough."

"Prevent what?"

"The ship you are looking for is about to be moved. If it is, you will never find it."

"Ship?"

"Yes, ship, you idiot. The one you've been looking for."

194

Les had to think. Oh yes, that ship. "Who are you?" he croaked.

"It doesn't matter who I am. Do you want to find the stupid ship or not?"

"I command you to identify yourself."

"You can't command ME."

The figure made a gesture and a light bloomed in its right hand. It held the light under its chin and the large-eyed, chinless face of an alien sprang into view.

Les gasped and pulled back. "You!" he exclaimed. "You killed those pilots!"

"That wasn't me, numbnuts. That was another alien." It swung the light down so its face was in shadow again.

"You all look alike to me," Les said.

"Listen, do you want to find the ship or not? I don't have all night +here."

"This is highly irregular. You should send your information through proper channels."

"I give up," the alien said. It stepped backwards towards the window. "This is what I get for trying to do a human a favor."

"No, wait," Les said. He swung his legs off the bed. "Please tell me."

"It's in a location on Seventy-First Street."

"Just a minute, let me get a pencil." Les yanked open a drawer in his childhood desk, which was painted red, white, and blue, but swirled in psychedelic loops and twirls, his one small rebellion when his mother wouldn't let him choose his own colors. He felt inside for a pencil.

"I'm waiting."

"Okay, okay." He found a nub of a pencil.

"The address is..."

"I need paper," Les said. He pulled open another drawer.

"Geez louise," the alien said. "This is the last time I try to help a human."

"I'll write on the desk," Les said. "Go ahead."

"There's nothing else? You don't need me to wait while you get a glass of water?"

"No, no, go ahead."

The strange whistling noise from outside the window faltered.

"I could use a glass of water," another voice said.

"I wasn't talking to *you*," The alien in Les' room said.

"I can't keep whistling like that. You said you'd be in there for a minute, tops."

"I didn't know that the Crimson Chin here was such a moron."

"Hey!" Les exploded. He leapt to his feet, and bumped his head on the very B52 model he had just been dreaming about. It caused the rest of the model squadron to swing back and forth.

"I am a Lieutenant General, and I demand the respect that my rank deserves!" He didn't feel as in command as usual while ducking the swinging model airplanes.

"All right, all right," the alien muttered. "Write down this address so we can get out of here."

Les poised the pencil above the desk. "Shine that light over here," he said.

When the light was moved to illuminate the section of the desk, Les was surprised to see that it wasn't coming out of the alien's finger. A bright red plastic flashlight was clutched in the three fingered hand.

The alien gave him the address, and Les wrote it down on a white swirl on the desk.

"I'm outta here," the alien said. It receded towards the window and was gone in a moment. The light cast by the UFO still came into the room.

"Turn it off," one alien voice whispered from outside the window.

"Oh, yeah," the other one said. The light went out.

Les barely noticed. His quest was on. He had a lead and he would find the filthy pilot-murdering alien's ship, and then the filthy pilot-murdering alien itself.

But first he had to get out of the house without waking his mother.

"Turn it off," Ralph said.

"Oh yeah," Ed said. He fumbled with the portable spotlight and flipped the switch. The pool of light around the window went out.

"Let's get out of here."

"Okay."

Ralph put his foot on Ed's head. "Hold still," he said.

"Ow," Ed said. Ralph's other foot swung, looking for a place to land, and was planted on Ed's shoulder.

"Ow! Ow!" Ed objected.

Ralph let go of the first floor window and jumped down, then he turned on his companion.

"Give me the sweatshirt."

Ed handed Ralph the sweatshirt that had been hanging on a bush. Ralph quickly slipped it over his head. It came down to his knees and he had to pull the sleeves up to free his hands.

"That's better," Ralph said. He pulled the hood up. In the light from a street lamp in the nearby alley the word DePaul could be seen on the front of the sweatshirt. "Why did we ever make humans think that we don't wear clothing?"

"What happened in there?" Ed asked. He was dressed in a similar sweatshirt, with no college logo.

"He was supposed to think there was a ship outside." Ralph said. "You weren't supposed to say anything."

"Why couldn't we have a real ship anyway?"

"They don't let us requisition ships for practical jokes," Ralph said.

Ralph moved away, through the small yard of the three-flat building.

The two ggnorphodors had some difficulty getting over the wooden fence, but after a lot of muttering and swearing they were in a litter-strewn alley.

"You think that Xanthan Gumm character will be there too?" Ed asked.

"I tipped off Ted Granger at the *Babbler*. I'm sure he called Gumm with the info."

"What do you think will happen when they all get there?"

"Something worth watching, that's for sure." The pair paused for a moment and indulged themselves in some nasal, high-pitched laughter.

"Now let's go, I don't want to miss it."

197

Ralph and Ed walked a short distance, their alien forms casting alien shadows on the fence. Ralph started looking around wildly.

"Damn. Where is it?"

"Where's what?"

"The car, idiot."

Ed looked around too. Ralph was right. The 1995 Chrysler New Yorker that they had parked in the alley was gone.

Chapter Thirty-Two

"It's true," Xanth said.

"What's true?" Al asked. He tugged the bottom of his new shirt down, trying to make it cover his belly. When he let go it rose to reveal about two inches of flesh.

"Water really falls out of the sky on planet surfaces."

"You've never seen rain before?" Al asked. He raised his hand as a taxi drove by without stopping. Then he had to tug the shirt down again.

Xanth held his head back and let the rain caress his face. "It's amazing," he said.

"We have a saying on this planet about people who don't have enough sense to come in out of the rain." Al said. He pulled his coat together to try and keep the rain out.

"What's the saying?" Xanth asked.

"That some people don't have the sense to come in out of the rain."

"Oh."

"Here comes another one." Al raised his hand and waved. The yellow car pulled up next to Al and stopped.

Al opened the rear door of the car. "Come on, get in."

Xanth peeked inside the vehicle. "So this is what a real Earth taxi is like."

"Yeah. Now let me in," Al said.

Xanth sat on the seat inside the car and slid across to make room for Al.

"Seventy-first Street," Al said after he slammed the door shut.

"Are you kidding?" a voice said from the front. "Get out."

"Give him a fifty," Al said to Xanth.

"What?"

"A fifty-dollar bill."

Xanth pulled the money from the pocket of his new shorts. He found one with the number fifty on it.

Al took it and passed it up to the front. "That's just your tip." The voice didn't speak again. The car started to move. Al tugged his shirt down again.

"I'm sorry I got the wrong clothes," Xanth said.

Al's t-shirt was black and featured a picture of a tall building on the front, with the words "John Hancock Center." He was wearing a pair of sweat pants with red and white stripes. The pants were little too small also.

"It's all right. Not what I ordered from the store, but they'll do."

"I went in the first store where I saw clothing."

"I didn't tell you which store to go to, it was my fault," Al said.

Xanth had on an identical John Hancock t-shirt, but his was too big. He also had red shorts with blue pockets.

"They had lots of other cool stuff too," Xanth said, "and the lady there was very nice."

"Souvenir shops are pretty cool," Al said. He smiled. "Still have your little building?

Xanth felt his other pocket. The little metal John Hancock building was there, digging into his leg through the cloth.

Coming out of the elevator, Xanth had looked very carefully for the clothing store. He walked by a store that had jewelry, one that had magazines and newspapers, and one that had headless sculptures of humans wearing suits. Why there was a headless statue store in the hotel Xanth had no idea.

Then he saw it. A shop with many different items, including T-shirts on hangers. He walked in and gawked at all the things on display.

It was a lot like the shop on Qaaxle where he got his current outfit. All the T-shirts had pictures of local sights or words like CUBS, SOX, BULLS, or BEARS. They seemed to be fond of animals in Chicago, though he had never heard of a SOX before. He would have to find out what kind of animal that was.

"I've never seen one of you guys here before," someone said. Xanth turned and saw a young female human standing behind a glass counter. Her hair was spiky and she had metal bits embedded in her eyebrows, ears, and nose.

"Uh...you've seen someone like me before?"

"Just in my mom's basement when I'm like, smoking."

"Okay," Xanth said. He didn't know what else to say.

"Gonna buy something or gonna float away through the ceiling?"

"I need clothing for my friend," Xanth said. "He called down and ordered what he wanted."

"Like, nobody called me," she said.

"Oh. Then I don't know what to get."

"What's your friend's size?"

"Uh. Lots bigger than me. He's a human."

"Sorry," the young woman said. "Humans are soooo boring. Sounds like he needs an XL." She bustled around the counter and searched through the shirts.

"I have a John Hancock and a Water Tower in XL." She held up two shirts.

"I like the big building."

"'K. Anything else?"

"He needs pants too."

"Pants. He needs ACTION LEGS!" The woman went back behind the counter, taking the John Hancock shirt with her. She leaned down and picked up a cardboard box.

"These are so cool but they weren't selling so my boss--" She made a gesture of putting her finger down her throat and a gagging sound, "--made me pack them up." She pulled a pair of red and white striped sweatpants out of the box. Let's see if we have any that would fit an XL."

After looking at several pairs, she decided she did. She laid the sweatpants on top of the T-shirt.

"You want something?" she asked.

"Me?" Xanth asked. "I already have clothing."

"You can have like, more than one outfit. Gotta look good when you're floating through the ceiling."

Xanth stood there, transfixed. The idea of owning more than one shirt and pair of shorts had never occurred to him. He only got new clothing when the old stuff was worn out.

He had gotten the Qaaxle shirt because he fell down on a tour of the Caves of Squinth, famous for the hibernating Gleaves which lined the ceilings and drooled pure non-clumping mascara, and torn his other shirt, which had a picture of The Galaxy's Biggest Ball of Twine on it.

"I can?" he asked.

"Like, yeah," the woman said.

"Do you have a smaller shirt with the big building on it? And some pants like that in a small size but they're shorts?"

"Oog. Problem. ACTION LEGS! don't come in shorts."

Xanth was crestfallen. The wild carefree life of owning multiple items of clothing that he had seen spreading before him was gone.

"Like they, like, say," the woman said, grinning, "let's make lemonade."

She didn't make any lemonade, but she did produce a pair of scissors from behind the counter. Then she pulled out the smallest pair of ACTION LEGS! that she could find, red with blue pockets, and cut each leg short.

"Like, cool or what?"

Xanth smiled. "Cool." he said.

Once the clothes were bundled in a large plastic bag, the woman pushed some keys on a machine that beeped a lot.

"Is that a cash register?" Xanth asked.

"Yeah. Now we gotta deal with the bring-me-down money part."

"Oh! Money! I have some money!" Xanth pulled the wad out of his pocket. He spread the bills out and put them on the counter.

"I don't know which one of these to give you," he said.

She took two of the bills that had the number one hundred on them. "This is exactly the amount you owe," she said.

Xanth took the bag and walked towards the door. Then he saw a shelf at exactly his eye height. It had little metal reproductions of the same building that was on the new shirt. He picked one up and turned back.

"Can I get this too, for that amount of money?"

"Normally it would be, like, more, but I like you so you can have it."

"Th - like, thanks." Xanth said. He left the store.

"What a rip," the woman said. "He didn't even float through the ceiling."

"I am commandeering this car in the name of the United States Army!" Les shouted through the closed window of the Volkswagen Beetle.

He was sure it would work. Policemen in the movies did it all the time. They had badges to show, but he was in full uniform with three stars on each shoulder. Any patriotic American citizen would surely be happy to lend his or her car to the Army.

The driver, a blonde woman in a pink suit, flashed her middle finger at the general, hit the gas and sped down the street. Les's left foot was almost run over by the rear tire.

What was wrong with people today? Les wondered. Aren't they raised to respect the symbols and institutions of this country?

Getting tipped off by the alien was a lucky break, but it was certainly badly timed. He didn't have a car standing by. He was expecting one at eight a.m., but that would be way too late. He couldn't call for one, because the only phone in the apartment was in his mother's bedroom. She would take a trenching tool to his backside for waking her up, just as she had done for so many other reasons when he was younger.

For the same reason, he couldn't call for a taxi. All he could do was get dressed and follow the alien out the window. He had trouble getting over the wooden fence, and his uniform was definitely not in shape for an inspection when he put his feet down in the alley. He had to pause for a moment to tuck his shirt in.

The address he had been given wasn't terribly far, but far enough that hoofing it would no doubt mean the ship would be gone when he got there. Besides, it had started to rain and he hated getting his uniform wet.

He had reached Stony Island, a major street that ran north and south, when he decided to commandeer a car, an idea that he decided to forget a minute later when the back of the Volkswagen disappeared into the rain.

He could find a pay phone and call for a military vehicle, but it would take too long to get there. He could call for a taxi, but it would also take a while at night and in the rain and in this neighborhood.

Then he spotted his salvation. He started to run down the block. He had to make it or wait another half hour at least before the next one came.

The bus passed Les and stopped at the corner bus stop. Les was right behind it, though, and managed to huff and puff his way up to the door just before it closed.

"Hold it!" he tried to say authoritatively, but it came out as a squeak.

"I don't have all night," the bus driver said.

Les climbed the three steps to the floor of the bus. He wiped rain off his face and turned to find a seat.

"Hey," the driver said. He gestured to the fare box.

"This is important army business," Les said. "A matter of national security." There. He had his order-giving voice back.

"My ass. Pay the fare or get off."

Les cursed under his breath. All right, he thought, I'll just pay and be done with it. He put his hand in the pants pocket of his uniform.

General Les. S. Moore usually kept a careful control on his emotions, but a look of panic swept over his face at that moment. He checked his other pocket.

"I'm on a schedule, Colonel," the bus driver said.

"I am a Lieutenant General!" Les shouted. "And I...don't have my wallet."

"Out," the olive skinned man said.

"This is really really important," Les said, not liking the whine in his voice.

"No fare, no ride."

"Look, I'll send it to you. Just tell me where to send it."

"I'll tell you where to put it..." the driver said angrily.

"I have it, driver," a third voice chimed in. The sound of coins clanking down the chute of the fare box could be heard.

Les looked back at the already retreating figure of the person who had paid his fare. It was a short fellow wearing a hooded sweatshirt. The hood was up, so Les couldn't tell a thing about his benefactor.

"Thank you...sir," Les said, not even sure if it was a man.

The bus driver gave Les one last look, then said, "Stand behind the line."

Les moved, finding a seat on the nearly empty bus. He felt strange about accepting the stranger's gift. He had never accepted charity in his life. This was important Army business, though. Maybe the stranger was a patriot. That must be it. A real red-blooded American, born in this country, unlike the foreign-looking driver.

He looked towards the back of the bus. The stranger had joined another similarly-clad person in the very last seat. They both had their heads down so he couldn't see their faces.

Just in case they could see him, Les snapped a salute towards the back of the bus.

He assumed they didn't see it, and the fact that they both burst into high-pitched, nasal laughter had nothing to do with him.

Chapter Thirty-Three

"What are you looking at?"

"The water coming down the window," Xanth said. He watched one drop of water join another, and together they continued faster than before. "It's fascinating."

The taxi zipped down a highway that Al had called Lake Shore Drive. Many other cars drove alongside. None of the cars seemed to be chasing any others, though, and no one was jumping from one car to another. It was disappointing, but it did prove that most of what he had seen in The Movies was indeed fiction.

"Don't forget me when you get to Hollywood," Al said. He took a drink from the bottle that he had ordered from room service. Xanth could smell it from across the seat.

Xanth sat up. It hadn't really sunk in. He was going to get his ship back, and when he got it, he could go to Hollywood. Tonight. Soon.

"I'll send you lots of money when I become a star," Xanth said.

"You do that. I hope you have learned that things on Earth aren't as easy as you thought when you first got here."

"Oh yes, I have learned a lot. I was so naive when I first got here! Now I know that life on Earth is not what I expected."

"Good."

"I thought Stephen Spielberg would be waiting for me at Hollywood and Vine," Xanth said.

"I'm glad you know better." Al said.

"I'll have to go to his office," Xanth said. "I'm sure anyone in Hollywood will be willing to tell me where it is."

"Well..."

"Then after I sign a contract and become a star in his next Movie, I'll send you lots of money."

Al shook his head. "I hope it does happen like that. I really do." He took another drink.

"I will live in a big mansion with a pool, and make lots of Movies, and people all over the galaxy will see the Movies and wish they were me."

Al drank some more. He was starting to look unhappy. "I hope you find someone you can trust out there," he said.

"You could come there!" Xanth said. "I mean, you wouldn't fit in my ship, but you could come later. Then you wouldn't be homeless because you could live in my mansion."

"I'll drink to that," Al said, and he did.

"Everything will be all right from now on," Xanth said. "Nothing can stop me now!"

At that moment, as if by cosmic coincidence, the taxi lurched to the right and a horrible flapping noise came from the right rear wheel. The taxi swerved and almost hit a mini-van, then screeched to a halt on the shoulder of the highway.

"Why did you do that?" asked the night manager at Cosmic Coincidence Control. Remclen, a cosmic being of pure energy who had been monitoring the taxi said, "Do what?"

The night manager, Marglak, another cosmic being of pure energy but who glowed blue in contrast to Remclen's pinkish light, said, "That. He said 'Nothing can stop me now,' and then he was stopped."

Cosmic Coincidence Control was an infinite space containing an infinite number of cosmic beings of pure energy, sitting in an infinite number of office chairs (Galactic Catalog #T-138-HB) and watching an infinite number of monitors that each showed one of the infinite number of beings who lived in the universe. Each monitor was surrounded by a finite number of buttons that could be used to effect the life of the particular resident of the cosmos who was being viewed.

Remclen looked at his monitor. He saw the Earth taxi stopped with a flat tire next to the Earth highway. "Oops," he said. "I must have leaned on the 'Irony' button when I dozed off."

Xanth and Al were a little shaken up, but unhurt. They could hear the driver swearing from the front seat. "What happened?" Xanth asked.

"Must be a flat tire." Al said.

"But I have to go get my ship."

"We may not make it. Sorry."

"We have to make it! I have to go to Hollywood!"

"Things don't always work out," Al said. "We'll try, but this world has a way of ruining your plans."

Xanth considered the possibility that his ship would be sent somewhere where he would never see it again, and he would be stuck in Chicago. "No." he said. "No no no no no..."

"So it really was a coincidence?" Marglak asked.

"We don't have to log it that way, do we?" Remclen asked anxiously. "It wouldn't look good on my record."

"Good thing for you that our motto is 'There are no coincidences.' I'll put it down as a planned action."

"Thanks," Remclen said.

"Now, did you say you couldn't caddy for me on Saturday?"

"Uh, of course not. I'll just change my plans. My daughter can get married next weekend."

"Good," Marglak said and moved off.

Remclen clenched a pure energy fist and slammed it on the console next to the monitor. Then he watched in amazement as a little truck stopped behind the taxi on the shoulder of the highway and the driver got out.

A small pickup truck stopped behind the taxi, on the shoulder of Lake Shore Drive. A human male with long hair got out and walked to the passenger window of the cab. He tapped on the glass. "Need a ride, dudes?" he asked.

"We're saved!" Xanth shouted. He scrabbled at the door of the taxi. His fingers found a lever that opened the door when he pulled it. "Yes!" he told the long-haired human. "Thank you!"

Al opened his own door. This was suspiciously convenient, but he felt he had to go along and make sure Xanth got to where his ship was.

"Hey!" The taxi driver said. "The fare?"

"Flat tire discount," he said, and got out.

Remclen watched the alien and the older human get into the long-haired human's car. How had that happened so fast, he wondered. He looked at where he had hit the console. Damn, he thought. I'm in trouble now.

He had accidentally hit the 'Deus Ex Machina' button.

"You landed on Venus!" Mrs. Blunt exclaimed. "That's two hundred dollars!"

"Venus can't possibly be worth two hundred bucks," Mr. Blunt said.

"It is with two enviro-domes on it. Pay up! And stop fiddling with that thing."

Gil Blunt took two hundred-dollar bills from a pile that he had tucked under the Monopoly board and offered them to his wife. She snatched them greedily. Then he went back to fiddling with the memory modulator, a camera-sized device that was supposed to alter the memory of people that they talked to in the field.

"Do we have to play Monopoly®?" Gil asked.

"You want to quit when I'm winning?" Carmen Blunt asked. "Not a chance." She picked up the dice and shook them. "Don't worry about the modulator. It worked on that general, didn't it?"

"Not well enough. I heard he is still looking for the ship."

"Well, put it away. We're playing here."

"We used to have a lot of fun on these long waits," Gil said. He reluctantly put the memory modulator on the floor. "When we were waiting for the Bunradians to land for the first time, we really steamed up the inside of that surveillance van."

"We still have fun like that," Carmen said.

"Twice a week, like clockwork," Gil muttered. " And then only when we're at home. On this job how often are we at home?"

"You know how much trouble we could get in if they saw us doing that on the job?" Mrs. Blunt asked.

Gil stood up and walked away from the table. "I doubt they're really watching us," he said. He walked towards the tarp-draped ship that sat nearby. "The way they've cut the budget, they probably can't afford to."

Carmen stood up and smoothed down the fabric of her brown suit. Then she walked over to her husband.

"Come on, at least they let us work together now. Remember how much they resisted having a woman in the corps?" She imitated Mr. Vaughn, the boss they had worked under ten years before. "We're the MEN in Black, Mrs. Blunt. Not the GIRLS in Black."

Gil laughed. "Mr. Vaughn always was a traditionalist. He would have had a heart attack when we switched to brown suits. He was lucky that he was eaten by that parbitenritenditter."

"The parbitenritenditter wasn't so lucky. The poor thing had indigestion for days," Carmen said.

"A single-celled organism should think more carefully before devouring an adult human being," Gil said.

"I remember those days well," Carmen said. "The corps has certainly changed since then."

"Just look at this place," Gil said. "We used to have underground headquarters in every city, with facilities for every kind of alien known in the galaxy." He waved his hand around at the cement walls. "Now all they can fit into the budget is an abandoned body shop."

"As long as we're together," Carmen said, hugging Gil. She straightened his brown tie. "Now let's get back to the game."

Gil let himself be towed back to the wobbly plastic table. He sat in a wobbly plastic chair. "Whose turn is it?"

"Mine." Carmen shook the dice and threw them. "Community Chest! Yes!" She pulled a card off the top of the pile.

At least we're playing with a special version of Monopoly, Gil thought, made just for the Men in Brown. It made it a little more interesting.

"You have been declared Empress of Mondolium," Carmen read. "You may have any player of your choice beheaded."

"Does it really say that?" Gil asked.

"I'm the empress," Carmen said. "It says whatever I say it says."

Gil Grinned. "Empress and Slave Boy," was one of their favorite games, and it had very little resemblance to Monopoly®.

Chapter Thirty-Four

The bus air-braked to a stop at Seventy-First Street. Les would have missed the stop and traveled on in the bus to who knows where if one of the sweatshirt-clad little men hadn't stood on a seat and pulled the stop cord.

Les hadn't been on a bus since he was a teenager. He used to ride all over Chicago, not wanting to go home to his mother's inspections and gas attack drills. Finally he had joined the army, escaping his mother by doing exactly what she wanted him to do.

Now he was used to barking orders to someone who would drive him wherever he wanted to go. He had forgotten that buses don't stop unless there is someone waiting at the stop or someone inside pulls the cord running above the windows.

The two small men in sweatshirts and sneakers pushed their way out the rear door of the bus. Les stood and made his way out of the front door. He may have been riding a conveyance of the common man, but he at least exited it in the more dignified fashion.

He stepped onto the sidewalk, and the door closed behind him. The bus pulled away. There was no sign of the small men near the stop. The rain had settled down into a drizzle.

Train tracks ran down Seventy-First, a commuter line that was called the Illinois Central when he was young. Whether it still was he did not know.

The address was six blocks west, and he didn't have a transfer or cash for another bus. He didn't want to sit and wait for one to come anyway. The accursed alien's ship could be moved at any time.

It looked like he was in for some walking. He could still do five miles in the mud with fifty pounds of gear, so it wouldn't be a problem.

He turned the corner onto Seventy-First and set out briskly for the secret location where the ship was being held.

Ralph and Ed huddled in the doorway of an abandoned store. The human army general passed them without a glance in their direction. When he was out of earshot Ed said, "We were supposed to get there before he does."

"I didn't plan for the car to be stolen," Ralph said. "So we'll just have to try to keep up with the big lug."

"My feet hurt already," Ed complained.

Ralph slipped out of the darkness of the shop doorway. "You're acting like you're still a tadpole," he said.

"Why not?" Ed asked, following Ralph. "I was happy when I was a tadpole."

"Dudes!" Dweezil Johanssen said.

Xanth and Al glanced at each other. They were crowded together in the seat of the little truck. They didn't know why their new friend Dweezil had exclaimed "Dudes!" but he did it every minute or two, so they had become used to it.

"Thanks for picking us up," Xanth said.

"No prob, dudes," Dweezil said. "I was just like cruising along and I had a sudden urge to help someone. And there you were? It was like some kind of cosmic coincidence."

A plastic figure on a surfboard hung from the rearview mirror, swinging as the truck moved. Posters of surfers were plastered over every interior surface of the truck's cab. This, combined with Dweezil's liberal use of the word "dude," made Al say, "So you're a surfer?"

"Northern Illinois Champion three years running!" Dweezil said proudly. He changed gears suddenly and zoomed into the left-hand lane.

"Really?" Xanth asked. "I've seen Movies about surfing. Humans really do that?"

Dweezil didn't answer because his truck went airborne for just a second, after going over a bump on a small bridge. Al grimaced, and even Xanth was surprised, though he had experienced zero gee a number of times in the popular Weightless Café in Galactic Central.

"I always come down the Drive so I can hit that bump like that," Dweezil said. "Even though trucks aren't supposed to go on the Drive. Cool, huh?"

"Cool, yeah," Al said, with his hand on his stomach. "A little warning would have been nice."

"Sorry, dude."

"So you really stand on a little board on the water like in the Movies?" Xanth asked.

Dweezil made a face. "Naw, I can't swim. Besides I've never been out of Illinois. The lake is big, but it doesn't have waves like that."

There was silence for a while as Al and Xanth processed this statement. The truck barreled down Lake Shore Drive, narrowly missing a Mini Cooper.

Al took a sip from his bottle. "So if you don't actually surf, why are you Northern Illinois Champion?"

"Surf City Four!" Dweezil said.

"What?" Xanth asked.

"Surf City Four!" Dweezil said. "On Playstation 2, dude!"

"You're a surf champion on a video game." Al said.

"Not just any video game, dude. Surf City Four! It's the best!"

This explained a lot, Al thought. For all Dweezil's "Dude this" and "Dude that," he didn't look like a surfer. He was plump and wore thick glasses with black frames. Only his longish hair gave him any resemblance to a California surfer, and it lost points for being more than a little sparse in the forehead area.

"Sounds like fun," Xanth said. "I've never played a video game."

"Dude!" Dweezil exclaimed in shock. He swerved across two lanes, making several drivers honk in anger. When he had the truck under control he turned wide eyes on Xanth.

"You are one seriously deprived little dude, dude."

Al drank a big gulp from his bottle. He hoped that they would survive the three-time Northern Illinois Surf City Four Champion's driving long enough to get to Sixty-First Street.

Or was it Seventy-Ninth?

Al thought desperately. His brain was nicely warm and fuzzy from the booze, and it didn't want to actually think, but he forced it to. What was the street they were going to? What was the address?

Dweezil's truck hurtled down the highway toward a destination that Al could no longer remember.

Chapter Thirty-Five

"Hooooray for Hoooollywood," Xanth sang to himself. "Ba rup bup bup bup Hollywood!" He didn't know any more words for that song. It didn't matter. He would be there tonight!

Maybe it wouldn't be exactly as he had always dreamed, maybe it would be a little harder to become a Movie star than he had expected. His experience in Chicago had taught him that everything on Earth was harder than he had expected.

So it might take a week to become a Movie star, instead of being instant. He could manage. The tough times in his first few days on Earth would be a great story to tell on the mini-Movie called The Tonight Show.

"You know, Jay," he would say, "I first came to Earth in a place called Chicago."

"You don't say," Jay would say.

"I do. Back then, I thought everyone on Earth made Movies and they would instantly make me a star."

"Just a little naive, were you?" Jay would ask.

"Just a little," Xanth would say with a hearty laugh. The audience would laugh along, loving him for his vulnerability.

"Then I made it to Hollywood, where everyone was making Movies and they instantly made me a star!"

The audience would cheer. Jay would invite him back. Yes, that's how it would go, about a week from now.

A jolt as the truck hit a pothole brought Xanth back to reality. He looked out the window. They were driving down a street that was a lot different than the highway. How long had he been daydreaming? He kind of remembered passing a huge building with columns and a sign that said something about Science and Industry. Other than that he had obviously missed a lot.

Hey! There was a Willy Waldo sign! Was there more than one restaurant with that name?

Al said something, and Dweezil turned the car at a corner. A train track ran down the center of this new street. Xanth had seen lots of Movies with trains in them. He didn't see any gangs on horses waiting to rob the train, though.

Al and Dweezil were talking, but Xanth didn't listen. His head was full of images of Hollywood and his soon-to-be career. Maybe after his first success in traditional alien roles, he should branch out. He would do serious drama. Why not a remake of "Terms of Endearment"? Jack Nicholson had played an astronaut, so why not recast the role as an alien? Xanth was sure it would work.

There were two figures walking down the sidewalk. They were wearing sweatshirts with the hoods pulled up and sneakers. There was something about them that was familiar.

They were short for humans, for one thing. Human children? But even children wore pants, and these two had bare legs between the bottoms of their sweatshirts and their shoes. Bare legs that were very thin and had stringy muscles and were a peculiar color.

The truck was passing them, and Xanth was about to look away, when the one closest to the street glanced quickly in his direction. He saw a noseless face and one great big black eye.

Al wasn't feeling very good. He had eaten too much, with the bounty of room service available to him. He had also had too much scotch. The bottle just had an inch of liquid sloshing at the bottom. Al's stomach was beginning to complain, and he belched, tasting stomach acid.

He had truly forgotten where they were going. Sixty-Eighth Street? Seventy-Fourth Street? The problem was confounded by Chicago's system of streets and places with the same number. If you wanted to go to Eighty-Ninth Street, you could turn on it, park, and get out of your car before you realized you were on Eighty-Ninth Place, the wrong street entirely.

Dweezil was getting impatient. "I gotta get to my friend Eddie's house, dude," he said. "He just got 'Shoot Lots of Innocent People 3' for his Xbox."

"Doesn't sound like there's any surfing in that," Al said as his stomach rumbled.

"I do other stuff than surf, man," Dweezil said. "I have a life, dude, I'm a well-rounded individual. I play lots of different games."

"Ok," Al said. "Turn here."

Dweezil turned onto Seventy-First Street. Was that it? It sounded like maybe it was right. Xanth was making happy noises to himself. Probably dreaming of Hollywood.

The street didn't look very promising. The train track down the middle was the most civilized feature. A lot of the lots were empty and abandoned, and there were groups of some seedy looking stores. Dweezil's truck passed under a major overpass, then another.

Al felt really bad that soon he would have to disappoint his alien friend and tell him that their destination was lost in an alcoholic haze. He didn't want to do it, so he let Dweezil drive on for a few more blocks.

When his stomach gave a lurch that told him that he would have to get to a bathroom soon, Al decided he had to tell Xanth the truth. He opened his mouth and was about to say it, when Xanth started shouting excitedly.

"There are two ggnorphodors walking down the street!"

Xanth pointed excitedly at the two figures on the sidewalk. Dweezil's truck passed them and Al twisted to look back. "Are you sure?" he asked.

"Two what?" Dweezil said.

"Ggnorphodors!" Xanth exclaimed.

"Gunyawho?" Dweezil peered at the sidewalk, but they were past the two pedestrians.

"Aliens," Xanth said. "They're a type of aliens."

"Ixnay on the alienhays," Al tried to tell Xanth.

Ignoring Al, Xanth said, "Go around the block, I want to see them again."

Muttering about needing to meet Eddie, Dweezil turned right at the next street. This took them onto a much narrower street, lined with three-flat apartment buildings.

"Maybe it was another kid in a mask," Al said.

"It was real ones, I'm sure," Xanth said.

"What would they be doing here?" Al asked.

"I don't get it," Dweezil said, turning right again.

Both Al and Xanth looked at Dweezil. "Get what?" Al asked.

"Two aliens are walking down the street? That's not funny. They should walk into a bar."

"What?" Xanth said.

"A horse walked into a bar. A priest, a minister, and a rabbi walked into a bar. Say 'Two aliens walked into a bar' and you have a joke. They're just walking down the street, you got nothing."

"A...joke." Al said. "Yeah, a joke! My little friend here was telling a joke."

"I was not..." Xanth started to say, but Al glared at him and he stopped.

Dweezil turned right the third time, facing the truck back towards Seventy-First Street. "So what's the rest of it?" he asked.

"The rest of it?" Al said.

"Two aliens walked into a bar. What happens?" Dweezil made a rolling stop at a stop sign, turning right onto Seventy-First.

"We're still working on that," Al said. "Right, Xanth?"

Xanth was looking out the window again. He wasn't sure what Al and the guy who was driving were talking about, so he had stopped listening.

"You don't know the end?" Dweezil asked.

"We're writing it. We're, ah, joke writers."

Xanth saw the two figures in the sweatshirts, about to walk across the small side street where the truck had started its journey around the block.

"There they are," Xanth said.

"Maybe you're right, Xanth," Al said. "There is something funny about them."

"I haven't heard anything funny yet," Dweezil said. "You guys must be pretty bad joke writers."

"Slow down," Al said.

Dweezil brought the truck to a slow roll.

219

"See?" Xanth asked. "Those aren't humans."

"Maybe they're gray-skinned children with knobby knees," Al said.

"I know ggnorphodors when I see them," Xanth replied. "And now I see a soldier!"

"A soldier?" Al asked, but Xanth was right, a tall man in a military uniform was striding down the street a little further ahead.

"OK, so two aliens and a soldier walk into a bar." Dweezil said.

"Then the bartender says to them, what'll you have?"

"That's good," Al said. "Maybe you should become a joke writer too."

"Really? Well, I suppose that could be a backup if my video surfing career ends. Video surfing is a young man's game, it can't last forever."

The soldier stopped under a sign, looked at the address of the building, and knocked on the door.

"Stop here," Al told Dweezil. The truck came to a halt.

Soon the ggnorphodors walked past the truck.

"They're going in there," Xanth said, pointing. It was the door of the building just before where the soldier was knocking. The ggnorphodors disappeared inside.

"Let us out here," Al said.

"You want to hear the rest of the joke?"

"Write it down and send it to us." Al reached over Xanth and pulled the door handle.

"Uh, OK."

Xanth and Al stepped onto the street, walked between two parked cars and onto the sidewalk.

"What's your email address?" Dweezil asked.

His passengers had gone into the building. Dweezil looked up. There was a sign saying "Rose Tavern" over the door where they entered. The soldier man, who could be straight out of one of the Tom Clancy games, was trying to get in the next door, under a sign that said, "Sammy's Body Shop."

Dweezil pulled a tiny cell phone out of a pocket and dialed a number.

al tags where they

Xanthan Gumm

"Dude, it's me," he said into the phone.

"You coming or not, dude?" Eddie replied. "I want to start shooting lots of innocent people."

"Dude, listen, I'm writing a joke. Two aliens, and old guy, and a mutant kid walk into a bar," Dweezil said. "While a soldier tries to get into a body shop. What do you think should happen next?"

"Whaddya mean, writing a joke? Nobody writes jokes, they get them off the net."

"Oh yeah. Sorry, dude. See ya in a little bit."

221

Chapter Thirty-Six

Les concentrated on the addresses as he walked. He felt a little exposed without his sidearm, and he had to keep reminding himself that this wasn't Beirut or Baghdad, though the empty lots did make it look a little menacing. The main danger to his hope and happiness in this city was asleep back in her apartment. He hoped she was sleeping and hadn't noticed that he had sneaked out.

He passed stores that were closed and shuttered, either for the night or forever. The address was getting closer.

On the street, a small pickup truck was rolling very slowly, not far behind Les. Clearly the driver was also looking for an address. He didn't know what the driver could be looking for. Nothing was open.

He came to a side street. His destination, his destiny, was in the next block. He would find the alien ship and the murderous alien scum who flew it. He would expose the evil alien communist plot to the world, and a grateful public would make him their next President. America would enter a glorious century or two of leading the battle against the hideous invaders.

General Les S. Moore, future leader of the free world, walked across the side street.

He noticed peripherally that the little truck was still behind him. He considered but then dismissed the possibility that he was being followed. No one from the CIA, NSA, Military Intelligence, or FBI would drive a crappy little Japanese pickup truck.

He passed a bar, the Rose Tavern. He hadn't been in a seedy dive like that since his college years. He might be tempted to go in and have a snort, but he was on a mission.

Then the address appeared before him. It was a body shop. There was a large garage door. It was firmly shut. There was also a smaller door into the office of the place and that too was tightly locked.

The little truck stopped in front of the bar. Someone got out of it. Les wished they would just go away. He didn't want to be observed.

He rapped firmly on the door to the body shop office. If anyone was in there he was going to get some answers.

A knock resounded throughout the echoing space of the body shop. Carmen sat up. "Who could that be?" she asked.

"Ignore it, they'll go away," Gil said.

Carmen slapped his hand away from her thigh. "We are on duty," she said.

"Damn it, we never get to do anything fun," Gil muttered.

Carmen stood up and started to straighten her clothing. She and Gil had been lying on a greasy mat that was the best thing they could find to protect them from the greasy floor.

Gill stood also, and zipped his fly. The loud knock on the door came again.

Another noise, this time a scraping accompanied by footsteps, was heard.

Gil and Carmen looked towards the second sound. The two ggnorphodors who called themselves Ralph and Ed were coming through the secret entrance from the bar.

"Where have you two been?" Gil shouted at them, walking in their direction. "You were supposed to be repairing the ship. And you left us without a car. You better not have damaged that car."

Ed let the wooden door swing back into place, where it looked like part of the wall of the body shop office. "The car was kind of sto--"

Ralph broke in, "We'll get it back, but that's not important right now. We brought you some fun."

"What do you mean?" Carmen asked, walking up behind her husband.

"You know the little twerp, Gumm, who came in that ship?" He gestured at the tarp-covered form in the middle of the floor.

"And the general too!" Ed interjected.

"General?" Gil asked.

The ggnorphodors started to laugh their nasal laugh.

"Coming here!"

"Who's coming here?" Carmen said.

"Both of them! All of them!"

"Do you know what they're talking about?" Gil asked his wife.
"Sounds like one of their practical jokes."
"Great. Just what we needed."
The knocking on the front door of the body shop continued with even greater force.

By the time Al and Xanth got into the bar, the two aliens were nowhere to be seen. There were a few customers sitting at tables contemplating their mortality while staring into their drinks. A bartender sat on a stool near the cash register reading the Daily Racing Form.
Al approached the bartender. "Excuse me," he said. "Did you see two short fellows come in here?"
The bartender jerked his head towards the back of the establishment. He was an enormously fat black man wearing a felt hat.
"Uh, thanks."
"Come on, Al," Xanth said.
Al paused and then said, "I can't help but notice that you're reading yesterday's racing form."
The bartender didn't look up.
"All those races have been run already," Al said.
The bartender put a finger to his lips. "Shh," he said. "Don't ruin the ending for me."
Al followed Xanth towards the back. There were two doors back there. One had a small sign that said, "Guys" and the other one said, "Dolls."
Al's stomach rolled. He hurriedly pushed the "Guys" door open. Xanth followed him into the tiny, smelly room.
"You don't know how much I need this," Al said. There were two stalls. Al pulled open the door of the one closest to the wall.
The sound of nasal laughter could be heard through the wall.
"That's them," Xanth said. "I would know that laughter anywhere."
"There must be some door or something in here," Al said. "Just let me use the toilet, and I'll help you find it."

Xanth pulled on Al's arm. "We don't have time, we might lose them," he said.

"I really have to use the crapper, Xanth," Al said.

"My ship is there, I know it."

"There's probably some sophisticated hidden mechanism that opens the door. It'll take time to find it. I'll help you in a minute." Xanth pushed past Al into the stall. Then he placed one hand on the back wall behind the toilet. A section of wall opened.

"Come on," Xanth said.

Al sighed. He couldn't let the little guy go in there alone. He bent low and went through the secret door. His intestines let him know how much he would regret passing up this opportunity to take a dump.

Xanth charged through the door thinking about getting his ship and getting to Hollywood. He supposed he would find the two ggnorphodors there also, but they were harmless, if annoying. It hadn't occurred to him that there would be two humans as well.

The humans, a male and a female, both wearing brown suits, the female's with a nice pleated skirt instead of pants, stared at Xanth. He paused. "Uh," he said. "Hi?"

"Who are you?" the man asked.

"You weren't supposed to come through there," one of the ggnorphodors said. He had pushed the hood of his sweatshirt down, which revealed his bulbous head and big black eyes.

"Who is this?" the female human asked the ggnorphodors.

Then both humans looked even more surprised, as Al entered through the secret door.

"Who are you?" Al asked.

"Who are you?" the two humans asked Al.

A loud knocking came from the front door.

"What is that?" Al asked.

"Who are they?" the male human asked the ggnorphodors.

"We thought they'd come to the front door, like the General," the ggnorphodor with his hood down said.

"Where's my ship?" Xanth asked.

"WHAT IS GOING ON HERE!" the male human said.

225

"We thought it would be funny." the bare-headed ggnorphodor said.

"Yeah, funny," the other ggnorphodor, with his hood still up, said.

"Thought WHAT would be funny?" the male human asked.

"Is that it?" Xanth darted past the two brown-clad humans towards the only thing in the large bare room that could be his ship. It was covered in a cloth, but it seemed the right size.

"Get him!" the female human shouted. The male human chased after Xanth.

Xanth ran to the ship and pulled on the cloth. It slid off and there stood his Glexo Nebula with an overhead fusion injection engine, 53,000 light years on the meter and a pair of fuzzy dice hanging from the rearview monitor.

The male human grabbed Xanth from behind and lifted him up. Xanth struggled and kicked, but he couldn't get free. The man turned around and faced the female human, the two ggnorphodors, and Al, who were all running in his direction.

"You let him go!" Al said as he arrived, holding his side and breathing hard.

"I don't know who you are," the man holding Xanth said. "But you're dealing with the Men in Brown. Consider yourself under arrest."

Al bent over and his body started to shake. When he straightened up, his face was convulsed with laughter. "Men in...BROWN!?"

Another, louder knock on the front door echoed through the room, along with Al's uncontrollable laughter.

Chapter Thirty-Seven

"WHAT?" the man holding Xanth said.

"Come on," Al said, still sputtering. "Everyone knows it's Men in Black. I saw the movies. Who are you trying to kid?"

The two secret government agents exchanged a glance. "We had to change..." the woman said.

"Ever since that damn movie came out, then the sequel..." the man said.

"People always asked us, whenever we were out on a mission..." the woman said.

"Where's Will Smith? Where's Tommy Lee Jones?"

"We couldn't get any work done."

"The black suits were supposed to make us anonymous."

"It just wasn't working any more. We had to change," the woman concluded.

Al shook his head. "But, brown?"

"I voted for a nice pin stripe, actually," the male agent said.

"Honey," the woman said, "you know that wouldn't be anonymous-looking enough."

"Excuse me," Xanth said. "I came to get my ship back." As he said it, Xanth started to get a familiar feeling, one he hadn't felt since before he came to Earth.

"Sorry," the man holding him said. "We have to ship it to Area Sixty-Eight."

"Al..." Xanth said.

"You mean Area Fifty-One?" Al asked.

"This isn't as funny as I thought it would be," one of the ggnorphodors said to the other.

"It's pretty funny," the second ggnorphodor said.

"Sure, but it could be funnier."

"QUIET!" The male Man in Brown said. "I have to think. And no, it's Area Sixty-Eight. Pretty much the same deal as the suits. We had to move operations to a different area because Fifty-One became too well known."

"How many areas are there?" Al asked

"Al," Xanth said. "Remember when I said I would tell you when I was ready to excrete the pizza I ate?"

"Now? Why didn't you let me stop in the bathroom if you needed to go too?"

"I don't use a toilet. I excrete through my pores."

"Eeeyuch."

"I need to get to a shower, or I will soon be all messy and..."

The Man in Brown gave a start and made a disgusted face as goo poured out of Xanth's pores and stained all his clothing. Xanth fell through his arms and hit the floor with a squishing noise.

"...slippery," Xanth finished.

"Now that's funny," one of the ggnorphodors said. The other nodded.

"Get to your ship!" Al shouted. "I'll open the door!"

"I can't get in my ship now," Xanth said. "I'm all icky."

Al ran towards the roll up door. "Do it now or they'll catch you!"

Xanth realized Al was right, although cleaning out the Nebula was going to be no fun later. He stood, slipping once then regaining his footing. He ran towards his ship.

"He's going to take the ship, Gil," Carmen said.

"Look at my suit."

"We can't let him take the ship."

"I'll never get it clean," Gil said.

"You had to pay extra for the Italian custom job," Carmen said. "You weren't happy with the government issue."

"It made my hips look too big."

"HE'S GOING TO TAKE THE SHIP, GIL!"

Xanth jumped up on the running board of the ship, and hit the canopy button. The top popped open with a hiss. He climbed in and settled into the seat. The canopy came down and sealed itself.

Looking around the dingy room, Xanth saw the two ggnorphodors standing back and giggling, and the two agents arguing about something. Where was Al? Oh yes, he said he would open the door.

Xanth hit the start button. The ship's engine roared to life, then settled into a purr. The agrav array was on line, and the votulator fluid level was adequate, if a little low.

The ship turned as Xanth turned the steering wheel. Soon he was facing the big door, floating two feet off of the floor.

Xanth keyed the microphone so he could be heard outside. He could also hear the sounds from out there.

"I'm ready, Al."

Al gave a thumbs up. "When you're a star, I'll be your biggest fan!"

Xanth couldn't resist this opening. "Be sure to get out of the way," he said, grinning. "Or the ship will hit the fan."

Al put his hand on his stomach and looked ill. Xanth was pleased. Al knew a good pun when he heard it.

Chapter Thirty-Eight

Les fumed as he pounded on the door of the body shop. There was something going on in there, he was sure of it. There were voices, and nasal laughter.

How dare they? Whoever they were, they were not properly acknowledging his authority. He stopped knocking on the door to the office of the place, and began to pound on the garage door.

Shortly after that, the door raised up an inch, then settled down again. Yes! They were finally going to let him in. He would assess the situation, find the ship, and get to the bottom of the whole scenario.

The door started up again. A rectangle of light from the interior spilled out. Soon Les could see a figure pulling on the chain that opened the door.

When the door opened fully, Les saw the alien. It was utterly fantastic, a parody of the human form. It was hideous, totally alien, an affront to his humanity.

The thing was disguised as a middle-aged, balding human, but Les knew it to be the extraterrestrial. What gave it away was its atrocious taste in clothing. A middle-aged human male did not wear gaily-striped sweatpants and a souvenir T-shirt from a famous skyscraper. Only a creature that was unused to wearing clothing would choose such an outfit.

The monster from the depths of space confirmed its identity even more by opening its atrocious maw and spewing forth a torrent of alien slime.

Chapter Thirty-Nine

Al turned to the garage door. It opened by pulling on a chain. Al reached up, ignoring his roiling stomach, and pulled. It was harder than it looked. The door went up an inch, then settled back. Al gave it all his strength. Pulling the chain hurt his hands, but he had to do it. The door went up again, then more. The pulling started to get easier. Xanth was hovering in his little ship, ready to fly.

The door went up all the way and stopped. Al turned to look at the ship and waved. For some reason Xanth didn't accelerate out and fly away.

Al turned back to look out the door. Standing on the sidewalk and looking very angry was the tall military man, in a uniform that Al now recognized, seeing it close up, as belonging to a three-star general.

Al had spent an unpleasant two years as a supply clerk in Germany. He had never seen an officer of this rank so closely before, but he instantly had the gut reaction he had learned in those two years. Officers are to be feared, and avoided if possible. He had spent his military stint trying to be invisible to the brass.

When he found himself staring at a general in this unexpected moment, his gut reaction was to open his mouth wide and empty that gut all over the immaculate uniform.

Then he passed out.

Chapter Forty

When Al opened the door the soldier was standing there in the way. Xanth couldn't go through the door without hurting the tall man with the impressive chin.

Then Al brilliantly improvised by vomiting on the man. Xanth hadn't known that humans could vomit on cue. Well, he still had a lot of things to learn about humans.

Al also fell against the soldier, knocking him down. Now Xanth was free to take the ship out through the big door. He went forward slowly, until he was passing over Al and the soldier. Al was doing a good job of holding the man down.

Xanth thought of something. He popped the canopy of the Glexo. He reached in his pocket and found the Earth money.

"Here, Al," Xanth said. "I won't need this in Hollywood. They'll give me lots more." He threw the green bills over the side.

"I'll contact you when I can," Xanth said, then closed the canopy. He accelerated outside to where he had nothing above him but the sky and nothing to keep him from his future in The Movies.

"He took the ship, Gil," Carmen said.

"My tailor will not be happy about this," Gil said.

"How are we going to explain this to the agency?"

Gil looked around. The ship was gone, and two people lay in the open garage door, smelling of vomit.

"We tell the truth," Gil said. "We blame THEM!" He turned and pointed at the two giggling ggnorphodors.

"It was worth it," Ralph said. Ed nodded in agreement. "It was funny as hell."

Gil moved towards the two aliens with a murderous glint in his eye, and Ralph and Ed decided that running away, though not funny, was a pretty good idea.

Chapter Forty-One

While running, Ralph said, "Did you actually fix that ship?"

Ed, also running, said, "Nah, I just put some votulator fluid in. It'll fly for a few minutes is all."

"Remember when I said it would be funny to reverse the directions in that jerk's navigation computer?"

"Yeah."

"Did you do it?" Ralph asked.

"No. I mean, yeah. I think I did."

Ralph looked back and saw that Gil was gaining on them. He and Ed ran faster.

Chapter Forty-Two

The Glexo Nebula shot straight up, as if it meant to flee the Earth and its solar system as well. Xanth cut back on the throttle, and hovered just under a large cloud.

It was night, so even though he could see the foggy cloud and the water that ran down the windshield, he couldn't see anything else. He would have to rely on his navigation computer.

Xanth turned on the navigation computer. Al had told him that Hollywood was west of Chicago. All he had to do was set the computer for west. When the ship's sensors sensed an ocean underneath the ship, he would be near his destination.

West. Go west, young man. Someone said that in some Movie. West he would go.

The navigation computer locked onto the westerly direction, and the ship turned and flew towards Hollywood. Before he could say, "There's no business like show business," he would be there.

Soon he would be lounging around a pool with the other Movie stars, talking to his agent on a cell phone, and being rude to screenwriters.

A pleasant tone sounded. It meant that the navigation computer had confirmed that the ship was above the western ocean. Xanth put out the Viewscope.

There it was, the vast watery sea, the waves pounding the shore. Hollywood would be just a little bit inland. Xanth stowed the Viewscope and took manual control of his craft. He flew it over a rocky beach. He didn't see a big city, but he would find it soon.

He did see a major highway, with many Earth cars, driven by many humans, going both north and south along the many-laned road.

Then the left front votulator flange gave out again and the ship fell straight down. Hadn't the humans fixed that? He assumed they had, since the ship flew so well at first.

He had no bottle of votulator fluid this time. Fortunately he was a lot closer to the ground when he started to fall. The ship hit hard, and when it came to a halt, Xanth had a headache that wouldn't go away. Plus, the smell of his own excretory function, unwashed and now smeared all over the inside of the ship, was not very pleasant.

When he could, Xanth popped the canopy. The sound of rushing Earth vehicles filled his ears. He looked and saw many, many cars, most visible only as pairs of headlights, speeding along the highway.

The Glexo was on an embankment. It was hard to get out of the ship because of the angle at which it was tilted. Xanth was determined to make a good impression on any humans who might be nearby, so he declaimed loudly as soon as he had decent footing, "I am Xanthan Gumm from Galactic Central. I have come to Earth be a Movie Star!"

No humans could hear him. There were plenty in their cars, each spotlighting Xanth with its headlights for a moment, bt they went by too fast to notice him.

There was a large sign, just a little further down. Xanth walked a short way. The sign was alternately lit and darkened as cars went by. A very large vehicle, a semi-truck, Xanth thought it was called, lit up the sign with powerful lights.

The sign would tell him where he was. It would tell him how to get to Hollywood. Everything would be all right as soon as he read the sign.

The truck's lights illuminated the large words on the sign, which said:

WELCOME TO CONNECTICUT

Xanth will return in

**Xanthan Gumm
Working Class Clown**

if anyone buys this book.

Printed in the United States
45185LVS00004B/28-123

9 781591 138990